nobody
nothing
never

nobody nothing never

juan josé saer

translated by helen lane

SERPENT'S TAIL

Library of Congress Catalog Card Number: 93–84556

A CIP record for this book can be obtained from the
British Library on request

The right of Juan José Saer to be identified as author of
this work has been asserted by him in accordance with
the Copyright, Designs and Patents Act 1988

First published in 1980 as *nadie nada nunca* by Edicions Destino SA,
Barcelona
Copyright © 1980 by Juan José Saer
Translation copyright © 1993 by Helen Lane

This edition first published in 1993 by
Serpent's Tail, 4 Blackstock Mews, London N4, and
401 West Broadway #1, New York, NY 10012

Set in 11pt Bembo by Servis Filmsetting Ltd, Manchester
Printed in France by Firmin-Didot, Groupe Hérissey

to noe jitrik

They had given day the name *torture*;
and, conversely, torture was *day*.

... ever was, and is, and shall be,
ever-living Fire, in measure being kindled
and in measure going out.

Heraclitus, 30

In the beginning, there is nothing. Nothing. The smooth, golden river, without a single ripple, and behind, low-lying, dusty, in full sunlight, its bank sloping gently downward, half worn away by the water, the island. Cat withdraws from the window, leaving it empty, and looks around, on the red floor tiles, for the cigarettes and matches. Squatting down, he lights a cigarette, and, without shaking the match to put it out, amid the cloud of smoke from the first drag, lets it fall to the floor where, on hitting the tiles, it suddenly goes out. He goes back over to the window and props his elbow on it; he now spies Tilty, mounted precariously on the yellow-white horse, with his legs crossed on top of its back so as not to get his trousers wet. The water swirls around the horse's chest. It emerges, little by little, from the water, as though with very slight, discontinuous jerks, till finally its delicate legs touch the riverbank.

He is now cutting, on the tabletop, unhurriedly, slices of salami. When he has covered nearly the entire surface of the white plate with reddish slices, he places it in the middle of the table alongside the bread and the glasses. He takes out of the refrigerator a bottle of red wine still half full and sets it down between the two glasses. Without the slightest movement, without even blinking, Tilty watches him intently as he sits down. To encourage him, Cat serves himself a slice of salami. Tilty finally decides to give it a go, and with two fingers on which a faint shine from the fat will appear, helps himself to his first slice. He peels it, slowly and carefully, and raises it to his mouth.

The yellow-white horse seeks out the shade, instinctively, without the least sign of nervousness. It crops, from among the old battery casings and the old tires half rotted away, the tall grass. The two rusted, corrugated tin oil drums, struck by the afternoon sun, grow hotter, one standing up vertically, the other lying on its side, flattening the weeds, drying them out altogether. Chewing the last cut slices of salami, each of them with his glass in his hand, Cat and Tilty watch the yellow-white horse from the warm and muggy shade of the porch.

"Stop worrying. Nobody's going to lay a hand on it here," Cat says.

"All right, Don Gato," Tilty says.

The hard, cold red-tiled floor makes him shiver when he lies down on it bare-backed. He puts the cigarettes and matches on his chest. He looks at the ceiling. He is thinking of nothing at all. His skin warms the tiles almost immediately. He closes his eyes and breathes slowly, motionlessly, making the cellophane of the package of cigarettes placed on his chest rustle lightly. There reaches his ears, without shrillness, the sound of February, the unreal month, coagulated, as though clotted in the afternoon heat. He sits up, leaning on his forearm, and the cigarettes and matches suddenly slide off his chest, onto either side of his body, hitting the red-tiled floor. He sits up a little straighter and remains seated, looking all around. There are the table and chairs, the white walls, the rectangle of the window through which the afternoon light, indirect and blazing, fills the room with a somewhat less violent luminosity. Against the wall is the ashtray of fired clay, and between his body and the wall, in an untidy heap, his espadrilles. And on the ashtray, black, immobile, stuck to the smoke-fired clay, all of a sudden, the spider.

Although the tip of the espadrille is almost touching it, it remains motionless, as if it were a black design, a Rorschach blot imprinted on the outer surface of the ashtray. But it is too thick to create that illusion. And it emits, because it is alive, something, a fluid, a current, that lets one know, even without having seen it, that it is there. When the espadrille touches it, it draws back for a moment—it seems as though it is going to draw back but all it does is to begin to move its hind legs— and then it leaps to one side, detaching itself from the ashtray. It has barely reached the floor when the sole of the espadrille, which Cat is brandishing, crushes it against the red floor tile. The center of the black body has been turned into a viscous mass, but the legs continue to move, swiftly. Cat, with the espadrille held aloft, all ready to let it fall for a second time, remains motionless: from the viscous mass there has begun to come out, after a moment of confusion, a handful of identical little spiders, smaller replicas of the one that is dying, which scatter, in terror, all over the room. Cat's face breaks into a perplexed, amazed smile, and after a second's hesitation, the espadrille strikes the tile once again, resoundingly. Now the blob is lying there, motionless for good, stuck to the red tile. Cat looks around him: of the newborn ones, the product of the lightning-quick multiplication that has just taken place, not a trace.

The yellow-white horse grazes peacefully, amid the eucalyptus trees at the far end of the backyard. When Cat comes out onto the porch, it raises its head and contemplates him, still chewing. Its yellowish hide is marked with the imprint of patches of sunlight, of a lighter color, filtering through the foliage. Its gaze appears to pass through Cat's body and focus itself farther away, on an indeterminate point, but it is really Cat that it is gazing at. They now pretend to ignore each other's presence and as the horse goes on grazing, Cat walks over closer to the edge of the porch, marked with the imprint of a strip of sunlight, and looks at the open space on the near side of the trees in the background, the space strewn with scattered, half-buried batteries, and with rotting tires, stained with dried mud. The two oil drums, one vertical, the other lying on its side, flattening the weeds, are corroding out in the open. In the background, the yellow-white horse tranquilly stretches out its long neck toward the grass. Everything else is motionless.

He gradually leaves the house, the trees, behind, and is now walking over the warm sand. On the little beach are a number of crumpled pieces of paper, empty, crushed, cigarette packages, trash. At a distance of some thirty yards in the direction of the little wooded slope, the beach attendant is conversing with a ma. wearing a white shirt, a pair of dark-colored trousers and a straw sombrero. They have taken refuge underneath a tree. Cat watches them, with a fleeting look out of the corner of his eye, without turning his head, so as to avoid having to say hello to them. Driven away by the afternoon heat, the bathers will be back when dusk begins to fall. A wet and muddy strip of beach, on which the hoofprints of the yellow-white horse are still visible, separates the dry strand from the water. Standing on this wet strip, Cat raises his head and contemplates the island; low-lying, compact, its dusty vegetation and its reddish, irregular bank that descends to the water. Nearly fifty yards separate the two banks of the river.

The water encircles Cat's ankles.

The warm water flows over his body. He vigorously soaps his head, his armpits, his anus, his genitals, his feet. Then he allows the warm rain to wash away the lather, helping it along with his hands. For a moment he is blind, motionless, perceiving the sound of the water splashing against his head and running down his body in heavy streams. He is thinking of nothing at all. Dense, opaque, solid, for a minute, until he stretches out his hand and turns off the faucet. He continues to stand there motionless, with his eyes closed, for a few seconds

more. Drops fall from his body at intervals farther and farther
apart, resounding against the bottom of the bathtub.

Night falls reluctantly. In the stationary, electric-blue
semi-darkness, a monotonous buzzing of mosquitoes is heard.
In the background, under the tall trees with flat black crowns
whose foliage is full of blue spots that sparkle, the yellowish-
white horse moves, vaguely: a huge beige body changing
position every once in a while. Its tail lifts up and shakes,
spreading out and then falling back down. Closer by is the
space without trees, strewn with half-buried batteries and
rotting tires, and the rusted, corrugated tin oil drums, one
vertical and the other lying on its side. Cat takes a long swig of
white wine, making the ice inside the glass tinkle, and then
sets the glass back down on the straw seat of the straight-
backed chair. When he stretches out again in the deck chair,
his bare back, drenched with sweat, sticks to the rough
orange-colored canvas. The stationary blue air does not seem
to want to change; smooth, transparent, as though made of
glass. Cat reaches his hand out toward the glass of white wine
and empties it in one swallow. He fills it again from the bottle
on the floor, between the straight-backed chair and the deck
chair. He sweats and sweats.

The moment he stretches out in bed, in the darkness, bare
naked, the sheet is soaking wet. The lighted end of the
mosquito coil, on the night table, next to the fan that hums
monotonously, gleams dimly but steadily. He can see a little
better in the dark now. The white glow of the walls, of the
sheet, the silhouette of the chair, the rectangle of the window
full of the gnawed darkness of the trees. Cat turns over
ponderously, in a daze, in the bed, making it creak. Besides
being soaked, the sheet is warm, and with every movement of
his body, thick, flattened creases form in it, leaving deep
imprints on his skin. Turning in semi-circles, the fan sends
his way, periodically and regularly, feeble drafts of fresh air

that are nonetheless unable to efface his anxiety, his feeling of suffocation.

He is standing, when he wakes up, or when, rather, he begins to wake up, alongside the bed. The sheet, the white walls, gleam in the dark, and the fan is still humming monotonously. The coil has burned entirely away. He is emerging, as he awakens, from a dense, diffuse horror, and when he realizes that he is now almost awake, naked, standing alongside the bed, the horror sends his way, still, like the fan, intermittent gusts. He goes back to bed again, lying face downward. His face flattened against the damp pillow gazes, in an oblique line, at the window: the same black patches of the trees being gnawed away by the spent darkness. The same ones: the same ones as what or as when? He closes his eye, hearing the fan, and suddenly, not so far away, rending not so much the silence as the darkness, a cock crowing.

The pump motor labors in the sun. The sun is rising. Cat turns on the faucet and places beneath the gushing stream the red plastic pail, whose outer surface allows the luminous reflections, like veining, of the water that is filling it to show through. When the pail is nearly full, Cat turns the faucet off and leaves the motor running so that it will search, deep underground, in furious combat with the sun, more coolness.

Holding the red pail by the curved handle in his right hand, Cat turns his back on the motor humming in complex rhythms in the sunlight; his right hand thrust slightly forward, his left hand backward, so that his arms are separated from his body, in an oblique line, his legs apart, the entire length of the sole of his right foot resting on the ground in front of him, his left foot resting on its tip, his toes pinched together and bent back, his shadow projected on the packed earth in which not a single blade of grass is growing.

His left foot rises in the air, his hand holding the pail slightly behind, his left one forward, his left foot lifting up slightly so that it tends to arch and to remain resting on its tip, his entire body leaning to the right from the weight of the red pail.

The two taps on the street door are soft, almost inaudible ones, at the moment when Cat straightens up after having set down the plastic pail, full of fresh water, in front of the yellow-white horse whose muscles, moving in a complex and multiple rhythm along its entire body betray, to a greater degree than its head, which remains in the same spot pretending not to have heard the taps, a slight excitement.

Tilty spreads forage out in front of the beige equine, which changes from grass to forage without a sign of rebellion, chewing slowly. Cat picks up the empty pail and heads for the humming motor. When he turns the faucet on, a white stream gushes into the pail, which overflows immediately: a whitish plume, sheets of transparent water which spill over the sides and drops that take off in all directions with an evanescent sparkle in the noonday light. Tilty watches the beige horse eat. Cat sets the red pail down amid the forage scattered about on the ground, reduced now by the compact and almost continuous mouthfuls taken by the animal.

II In the beginning, there is nothing. Nothing. The smooth, golden river, without a single ripple, and behind, low-lying, dusty, in full sunlight, its bank descending, half worn away by the water, the island. And on leaning out the window, smoking, I see, in the middle of the river, coming toward the house, Tilty, his head sunk down between his crooked shoulders, mounted on the beige horse.

The stream of smoke that I allow to escape dissolves slowly, interposing, between the sunlit river and me, between the horseman who moves forward leaving the middle of the river behind and the window shaded from the sun, a grayish, very fine mist, which never completely disperses. The yellow-gray mount comes out of the water, crosses the deserted beach, its delicate legs entangled in their own shadow, and after walking a fair distance across the stretch of sparse yellowish grass that separates the house from the beach, halts three or four yards from the window. Tilty looks at me for a moment without speaking as the yellow horse slowly shakes its head. Then he says hello. Your uncle Layo, he says, has asked me to keep the yellow horse at the back of the house for him for a few days.

I motion with my head for him to go around the house and come in through the back.

I slowly make my way through the cool rooms with red-tiled floors, between the white walls, crossing through the open doors painted black, and when I reach the back porch, on which the sun is beating down, I throw what remains of the cigarette into the middle of the backyard. Mounted on the beige horse, Tilty is patiently waiting on the other side of the heavy wooden entry door.

Now he dismounts, well in the background, underneath the eucalyptus trees, and laboriously frees the horse of its reins and saddle. The perforations of light that filter through the foliage leave spots on man and horse that move when they move. The whole ground is strewn with circles of light.

I take the salami out of the refrigerator, the bread out of the sack. Tilty follows my movements as he talks.

"Night before last they killed another one in Santa Rosa," he says. "That makes nine."

"Ten," I say. "Last night they killed one here in Rincón."
"It's downright wickedness," Tilty says.
On the cutting board on top of the kitchen stove, I cut, slowly and carefully, the first slice of salami.

He'll come back, he says, before leaving each day to bring it food. His eyes, set close together, his frowning eyebrows meeting, his gloomy air, and, above all, his entire head buried between his crooked shoulders, turned away from the porch toward the horse that is peacefully grazing, are evidence of his apprehension: would that the hand with the pistol not appear, suddenly, silently and gently press the barrel to the horse's head. That the detonation not ring out.

When the sole of the espadrille swiftly hit the spider, I saw a dozen terrified baby spiders come out in all directions and then disappear. Now the espadrille swats again. A viscous, blackish blob remains on the red tile. The baby spiders have undoubtedly found refuge underneath the furniture, or in the fissures between the colored tiles and the white wall. The viscous, blackish blob is still there: it is no longer a spider or anything at all. It is a blob, viscous, flattened, blackish, that may mean anything to a person who doesn't know: in and of itself, it is practically nothing at all now.

In the silence of the blazing-hot afternoon, from beneath the trees pierced, at this hour, by light, from its own silence, having left off grazing for a moment, in distraction, withdrawn, grave, circumspect, the beige horse contemplates me.

The water, lukewarm, caramel-colored, encircles my ankles.

Now the water, motionless, lukewarm, encircles my knees.

The island, opposite, with its gently sloping ravine, dwarf vegetation and laughable flowers, everything deserted, dusty and burned to a crisp, and the lukewarm, dark water, that now encircles my chest.

The blurred, warm mass is yellowish, full of luminous veinings; there is, one may presume, an exterior from which that light comes. It lets a profound, muted, multiple murmur escape, on all sides, which, because of its constant presence, affords an idea of its size. Little semi-solid convulsions rise, from one moment to the next, from the bottom, and remain in suspension for a long time, as though the particles composing it were subject to new and rigorous laws. Everything seems to be, continuously, in movement and expansion, but in an intermittent fashion, unhurried and without agitation. The mass is seemingly elastic, under pressure; I make headway, so to speak, with difficulty. And when I burst out with a loud, liquid explosion, on the surface, I see, underneath the trees, a few yards from the house, beyond the yellow strip of beach, the attendant and the man in a white shirt and a straw sombrero who are talking together, although at this distance I am unable to hear their voices. They move, in the silent heat of the afternoon, their arms, their heads.

Some thirty bathers or so, scattered over the beach and in the water, fill the calcined air with shouts and cries. They remain motionless, or move about restlessly, or walk, in the dying light. Those who are in the river make the water reverberate with their strokes and their kicks, forming white vortexes on the surface. The bodies streak, with their goings and comings, the space that opens up between the house and the island. The river, with a slight violet tinge, flows between the yellowish sand and the now-discolored green of the island. All the bathers stay close to this shore. One of them, however, who has ventured toward the other bank and has been moving underwater, suddenly surfaces near the island. His tanned body emerges from the water, and bending forward, treading cautiously, begins to climb the slope. He stands, ramrod-straight, at the top, his hands resting on his hips, and looks toward the beach. He raises his arms, making sweeping, incomprehensible signals now. He raises his hands to his mouth, now, so as to use them as a megaphone and shouts, now, in the direction of the beach.

As I close the door, I can still hear his shouts and those of a woman, on this side of the river, in answer. The white room is there, the red tile floor, and behind me, and in front of me, on the other side of the room, the black doors. The murmur that the beach sends forth, above which, from one moment to another, shrill shouts are forthcoming, is continuous. I cross the room, slowly: the left foot, the right, the left, the right, the left now, the right now, I open the black door now, and enter the second room. The first room is now in back of me. I now close the black door after me.

Behind me is the black door, and to my right, on the side wall, another black door. There is also a black door opposite me, in the white wall, beyond the empty space and the floor covered with red tiles. Turning to the side door, the left, the right, the left now, the right now, I open the black door that I leave ajar behind me, after going through the doorway. The noise from the beach continues, more muffled now: not a single shout modifies its intensity.

I am naked. The pair of white shorts is lying in a damp heap on the floor: for a few seconds I do nothing.

Now the warm rain runs, with a monotonous murmur, down my body, gradually washing away the soap. I am standing with my eyes closed, thinking of nothing, remembering nothing, in the warm rain, simply helping, with my hands, to wash the soap away with the water: thinking of

nothing and remembering nothing, in a darkness filled only
with the sound of the water.

Two oil drums, one vertical, the other lying on its side, and
in front and behind, half-buried in the grass, scattered about
the backyard, old battery casings and rotted tires, and in the
background the beige horse gleaming in the first blue semi-
darkness traversed by the continuous buzzing of the mosquitoes and the chirring of a million cicadas. And that is all.
Beneath the trees, the horse shakes its tail or its head every so
often, trying, unsuccessfully, to chase away the mosquitoes
that must be swarming all around it. I believe I see, from amid
the semi-darkness, being directed toward me, the horse's
gaze, more concentrated, though less visible than the blue air.
It comes from its eyes, from out of that warm body, of hair
and blood, that shakes itself and that palpitates, a material
object. It traverses, gently, the blue air, without leaving a
single trace in it, and reaches me. We are now looking at each
other, motionless, the animal with its head raised slightly,
turned slightly to one side, I sitting slightly erect, in the deck
chair of orange-colored canvas, my hand holding the glass of
wine with ice raised halfway toward my mouth, the blue air
now slightly black. I lean my naked back against the rough
canvas of the deck chair and drink white wine from the glass
until I have emptied it. I fill it once more and set down, on the
straw seat of the straight-backed chair, alongside the glass and
the bowl full of ice cubes, the nearly empty bottle, which
maintains a precarious balance on the irregular surface of the
seat. We look at each other: the animal with its head raised
slightly, turned slightly to one side, its body slightly tensed, I
leaning slightly back against the rough fabric of the deck
chair, the fingers of my hands slightly separated and my hands
slightly raised, elbows resting on the wood of the deck chair,
in the air traversed, or rather, full of the buzzing of a million
mosquitoes and the monotonous chirring of a million cicadas.
The whole house is in semi-darkness. A few voices, tired out,

tarry on the beach. I lift the glass of white wine off the straw
seat and put it back down again, after having taken a brief
swallow. I take a piece of ice out of the white bowl and drop
it, with a tinkling sound, into the glass. I stand up. Now we
are looking straight at each other, the horse's beige body
horizontal to the gallery, beyond the oil drums, the blackish
stains of the tires full of mud, beyond the batteries half-buried
in the dried-out grass, underneath the trees, its head turned
toward me, walking over from the deck chair to the edge of
the porch, standing on the strip of cement that separates the
red tiles of the floor from the ground. Warmer, or softer,
rather, than the blackened air, the ground keeps us, matter in
space, motionless. Its head raised slightly, it shakes itself
slightly now, its warm body full of pulsations, of palpitations,
of blood, moves a little now, slightly, the body that had been
slightly motionless, shakes itself again, now, in the black air. I
go off, leaving behind the strip of cement, the oil drums the
batteries and the tires stained with dried mud half-buried in
the grass and, farther in the distance, the yellow canvas deck
chair, the bowl full of ice cubes, the glass of wine. I am inside a
circle that is given off, hot, constant, by the beige horse. For
half a minute, or more, we do not move: and now I hesitate,
coming closer, with my arms open, flexed, my fingers apart,
seeking the way, the method, as the equine begins to shake
itself anxiously, until finally I now take a leap and hang from
its neck, pulling downward, feeling the horse's body shaking,
its hoofs resounding as its legs kick the ground, two or three
feeble whinnies that rise above the buzzing of the mosquitoes
and the strident sound of the cicadas. We struggle for a
moment, our strength equal, my entire body, hanging suspended from its neck, pulling downward, the horse's muscles,
tensed to the utmost, pushing upward, its anxious stamping
and its confused brain still not understanding, its brain that
receives a murmur of orders or of rapid, incompleted plans
leading nowhere. Its damp, warm hair clings to my cheek and
I can feel not only its breathing but also its breath. We do not

give in: in tense embrace, the sweat-soaked neck pushing upward, my arms crossed around it pulling downward, its free hoofs resounding on the ground, my firm legs half bent. Now, panting, coughing, abandoning the big yellowish body that is still moving, anxious, uncomprehending, I give a leap backwards.

The whole house is in darkness. I see, above the trees in the background, under which the yellowish bulk keeps chewing without a pause, veiled by the warm vapor that the heat of the night sets moving, the reddish stars. Neither in the patio nor in the immediate surroundings is there, for the moment, a single sound, but from all around, from every point on the horizon, comes a sparse chorus of frogs, the ones that the drought has left and that have doubtless been crowded together in the last puddles of stagnant water. It is discontinuous, intermittent, as though the little voices were obliged, now and again, to try to emit, from deep inside, just one more croak. And the illusion of continuity that the circular chorus gives, every so often, would appear to stem from nothing save a misapprehension, or from the unexamined acceptance brought on by distance. There is not a breath of air. The trees, grayish, languishing, are motionless. The yellowish shape produces, as it rips out the grass with its teeth, hard, drawn-out, sharp, indescribable sounds. I get up out of the deck chair and as I go through the door frame I turn on the light of the room next to the porch. A yellow trapezoid is projected from the room to the porch, onto the red tiles, onto the straw-bottomed chair whose lengthened shadow is imprinted, amid the light, as far as the cement border and the ground of the backyard. My own shadow now bends over the straight-backed chair: the glass, the bottle, are empty. The white bowl contains nothing but water, still cool. I return to the adjoining room and turn out the light. Blinded for a few seconds by the brightness that has been extinguished I do not see, in all of the pitch-black darkness outside, anything but the orange canvas of the deck chair and the white bowl, on the chair with the straw seat: they phosphoresce or, rather, emit a nimbus, or a splendor that contaminates the darkness around them.

Tomatis tells me, laughing, about a clandestine spot where people can play roulette. He has come to the house on horseback: he is dressed in riding clothes—boots, breeches, and even has a little riding crop in his hand and a riding derby on his head. I find his get-up a bit ridiculous and tell him so: he answers by saying that in the gaming room it is necessary to show that one is a man of *quality*. He says *cualidad* and not *calidad*, and the thought crosses my mind that he has used this unusual term as though he were employing ultra-refined language in front of the employees of the gambling house so as to impress them. Even though, he says, they doubtless already know who we are. I reply that he has need of so much *vestimientiary* ostentation (when I utter the word Tomatis bursts out laughing at the "mistake" I've made) because his social background is dubious, whereas everybody knows me: our family, as is a well-known fact, is descended from the founder of the city. "Come off it, everybody knows that your granddaddy was a butcher," Tomatis says. At that moment the hilarity reaches a climax. Then we wonder how we're going to get to the gaming house. Tomatis claims the two of us should go together on his horse: the idea strikes me as absurd and a bit malicious: it seems quite clear that, in one way or another, he wants to humiliate me or make me look ridiculous, since it's obvious that he'll be the one who'll be holding the reins. So I turn down his proposal. We finally decide that he'll ride his horse and I'll take the beige one. When we go out into the yard—it is still daylight—we discover that the latter is in rut and so it's not a good idea to use it as a mount. The horse's enormous rod, red and wet, in full erection, is pissing out a yellow, foaming stream, that bounces on the ground. Tomatis says in a grave voice that horses can't stand having a rider when they're rutting, that they go wild and that he knows two or three cases of riders who've been killed by rutting horses and then he adds, with feeling and making rather theatrical gestures, that horses in rut ought not to be mounted not only out of fear but also out of respect, that horses in rut symbolize life. He says that in the religion of the ancient Dromites a horse in rut was the principal object of worsh:p and that San Enrico Imperatore tells how he saw, in Dromidia, a whole herd of horses kneeling, near a lagoon, at dusk, worshiping two or three rutting horses. Then we decide that we'll go separately: I'll mention his name in order to get in. Since the game room won't be open till much later, I tell him that I'll go to the city first to do a series of errands and drop in to see my mother. In the end, I cross the river in a boat. The trip is filled with anxiety, and I have a strong sensation of insecurity the whole time, because the boat is too small, first of all, and secondly because I have to go slowly since I have only one oar that I hardly know how to use, and thirdly, because, either on account of my clumsiness or else owing to the fact that the water, although I don't notice it, is very rough, the boat rolls and pitches continually and rather violently. In the city I do two or three stupid things; first of all, when I go to the butcher shop, I note that I've gone into one that sells only horse meat: I realize this (the butcher happens not to be there) because the enormous ribs hung up on hooks are yellowish and transparent. As I go out again, I conclude that I have made the mistake more or less because of the conversation I had a while before with Tomatis. Then I wander about the city. Everyone is commenting on the death of the horses along the shore. An article in the daily *La Región* states that the victims have been eleven in number. The thought then occurs to me that another one must have been exterminated the night before without my knowing. Along with the article there is a blurred photograph that I can't manage to make out very well. Underneath the photograph is a caption: San Enrico Imperatore. I realize that Tomatis has come by all of his supposed erudition concerning horse worship from the article in *La Región*. Or maybe he himself was the one who wrote it. In the city it is noticeable that a large-scale deployment of police is taking place in order to catch the horse-killer: contingents continually head off for the road that goes to the shore. I wonder, as I pass one of those contingents, if they'll be coming by the house. In any case, they'll find it closed. As a precaution, in order to demonstrate my innocence—my second mistake—I tell an officer whom I meet in the bar of the arcade to try to pass the word along that there's no use coming to my place if they're thinking of dropping by to question me, as I assume they must be interrogating everybody who lives in the area, because I'm going to be spending two or three days in the city and the Rincón house will be empty. I've dared to have a word with the officer because he's an acquaintance of Mama's. To judge by the expression on his face, the police officer thinks I've committed I don't know what violation of the law. "That's enough of all this childishness, my friend," he says to me. The word "childishness" in particular utterly bewilders me. Does the officer consider the fact that I've abandoned the house in Rincón—on account of the beige horse—to be *childishness*, or is it the fact that I spoke to him so as to inform him of it? He then begins a conversation with two or three men who are drinking beer out of tall transparent glasses: the yellow beer is topped by a layer of white foam. Since every so often they turn, more or less discreetly, and take a look at me, I have the not very pleasant impression that they're talking about me. I feel the urge, two or three times, to have a word with the officer, to remind him of the respect he owes my mother, but in the end I tell myself that it isn't worth the trouble because my mother doesn't hold him in very high esteem anyway, since he's only a minor police official. When I get back home, I note that Mama is in bed; another of her manias: she's sold the television set and had an old radio put in working order—a set that must be at least thirty years old— and has decided to spend her time in bed, listening to the radio. It emits terrible static, so that anybody listening can hardly make out what the man who's speaking is saying. On her night table Mama has a letter from Pigeon: "Your brother is worried by the news about the horses that has reached him in France," Mama says. She picks up the letter and holds it out to me: when I take it, I realize that because the room is in semi-darkness she must have made a mistake and given me the electric bill instead of Pigeon's letter: she owes twenty-one hundred pesos. With her usual pride, Mama falls into a rage when I tell her—my third mistake—that if she likes, I can give her the money to pay the electric bill. Later on I go wandering about in the downtown district of the city again. Now that darkness has fallen, there are many fewer people in the streets. In the bar in the arcade I try several times, without success, to light a half-smoked cigarette that I must have put in my pocket a while before. It's no use: almost the moment the flame touches the end of the cigarette, it goes out. Since it's already late at night, a bar employee begins to wash down the place. He throws a pail of soapy water onto the floor, which wets the tip of my shoes. I am about to protest, but then I realize that I'm the only customer left in the bar, and therefore I prefer to keep my mouth shut so that they'll let me finish my beer in peace: *as long as they don't say anything to me*, I think, *I'm not moving from here.* But the beer is warm, of a viscous consistency, cloudy, a little bit salty. It is nothing but foam. I set the glass down without finishing it. In the doorway of the gambling house—which is quite dark—I run into Elisa. Tomatis has given her the address. Elisa tries to keep me from going in because she has a hunch that I'm going to lose. She advises me above all not to take a gamble on number three. I point out to her that her advice is ambiguous: is she trying to tell me not to play *the* number three, as if I had a number three to lose, something designated by the number three, or is she telling me not to place any bet on that number? I object to her suggestion laughingly, in a pretentious way, but she goes on, solemn and concerned. "Are you afraid I won't have a number three left?" I ask her, full of guile, not even hinting that I am thinking of how Freud uses the number three to designate the genitals, and then, putting my hand on her pubis above the silky dress she's wearing, I say to her, laughingly: "The number three stands for a person's little bush." But Elisa's face retains its expression of sadness and concern. As I fear that the attitude I've assumed is too brazen, even though Elisa apparently hasn't even heard me, I say to her, putting my hand this time, with ostentatious tenderness, on her head: "No, silly, I said it only for a joke." The word *only* placed before the noun phrase makes me feel a little ridiculous: it sounds affectedly Spanish-American. We finally go inside the gambling house together, which, as is immediately evident, is also a brothel. Among the women peeking out of the doors of the rooms as we go by, I see two or three I know. Some of the rooms have a red light showing; others, a green one. The women's attire indicates, without the shadow of a doubt, their profession. A man who is reading the paper—open to the page with the blurred photograph of San Enrico Imperatore—points out a spiral staircase that goes up to the gambling room. I have Elisa go ahead and walk in front of me, so as to see the way her buttocks move in the tight white silk dress, as she goes up the staircase. To conceal what I'm doing, I comment: "These winding staircases are lamentable." I don't know why I've used the word *lamentable*. As I say it, it sounds out of place to me. In the game room there is almost no one: the gambling hasn't started yet. I have the impression that I'm in the one lighted room of a huge pitch-black building. I sit down at the head of the table and wait. There's a croupier at the other end, alongside the roulette wheel. I don't know if we're alone or if there's somebody else in the room. The ceiling is very low. On the side wall, in place of a window there's a porthole. "A nautical decoration," I think, but I'm beginning to feel uneasy. The croupier gives a sort of military salute, with the little roulette ball in his hand, and says: "Start." I don't know whether to interpret this to mean that a game is going to be played, that this is the beginning (the start) of it, or that the gambling is starting and we're on the point of taking off for the evening. Instead of chips, I have in my hands in front of me a bunch of little pieces of raw meat. I can feel the softish meat, cold and sticky, in my hands. Just as the roulette wheel begins to turn, the entire room pitches and I see, through the thick glass disk, the black line of the horizon in the moonlight beginning to move violently up and down. I realize that I'm on a boat, in the middle of the night, on the high seas, and that a storm is making it shudder, and will doubtless capsize it and sink it at any moment. And that's when I become aware that it's a dream: I've dreamed that the gambling room suddenly turned into an ocean liner. I am lying in bed, face up, in the darkness, stretched out on the damp sheet hearing, in a vague way, the hum of the fan. I go over the dream in my mind: I've had a visit from Tomatis, who was dressed in a riding habit, I've wandered about the city, I've seen Elisa and my mother, I've ended up in the gambling den which was also a brothel. Instead of chips, bets were made by using little pieces of raw meat. All of a sudden, the entire room began to pitch and roll and I realized that I was on a boat, in the middle of the night and in the middle of a storm. I think I also went into a butcher's: yes, a butcher's, where the only thing they sold was horse meat. I am lying in bed now, stretched out on the damp sheet, listening to the hum of the fan. I am thinking of the article that I read in *La Región* a few days ago, on San Enrico Imperatore, in which it is mentioned that San Enrico Imperatore also saw, in Dromidia, a horse couple with a spider, whereupon a bunch of baby spiders came out of the spider's body. The way in which the horse copulated with the spider, the article in *La Región* said, was as follows: the spider clung to the horse's penis with its legs and sucked out its sperm with her mouth: the same system used by bedbugs to suck the blood of mammals. After the ejaculation, the spider dropped off, fat and full, and if at that moment someone crushed her, a whole bunch of little spiders would come out of her body. If I didn't know that I was awake, the spider's copulation with the horse would strike me as absurd: but I am wide awake. I am wide awake, lying face up, on the wet sheet, vaguely hearing the hum of the fan. The article in *La Región*: what day did it come out? Where did I read it? And when? No: I'm in bed just finishing waking up, thinking of the blurred picture of San Enrico Imperatore, lying on my back on the damp sheet, vaguely hearing the hum of the fan and *dreaming*. Dreaming that I'm in bed just waking up, thinking of the blurred picture of San Enrico Imperatore, lying on my back on the damp sheet and vaguely hearing the hum of the fan. I leap out of bed, as if to wrench myself out of the dream.

III He is standing, when he wakes up, or when, rather, he begins to wake up, alongside the bed. The sheet, the white walls, gleam in the dark, and the fan is still humming monotonously. He is emerging, awakening, from a vague, dense, unknown horror, and when he realizes that he is now nearly awake, naked, standing alongside the bed, the horror, like the fan, sends his way, still, intermittent gusts. He goes back to bed again, lying face downward. His face flattened against the damp pillow gazes, in an oblique line, at the window: the same black patches of trees, gnawed by the semi-darkness. The same ones? the same ones as when or as what? He closes his eye, hearing the fan, and suddenly, not so far away, rending not so much the silence as the darkness, a cock crowing.

The morning light enters the room with a sort of slight shrillness. And there, vague, intermittent, the shouts of the bathers come up from the beach. Cat opens his eyes: the foliage of the tree that blocks the window is riddled with sunlight. And amid the leaves, in the spaces that open up from time to time between one branch and another, there is also, apart from the yellow patches projected on the leaves and the branches, a vague white brightness, of which it could be said that it is an ultimate state of light, being dispersed amid the most intense incandescence, before disintegrating completely.

The yellow canvas deck chair, the straw-bottomed chair with the glass, the empty bottle, the white bowl full of lukewarm water, are heating up in the sun once again. In the water in the bowl a dark-colored moth floats, drowned. And in the backyard, beyond the rusted oil drums, one vertical, the other lying horizontal on the ground, beyond the space strewn with batteries and old half-rotted tires, partly buried amid the weeds, stained with dried mud, the beige horse, motionless underneath the trees, alerted by the sudden appearance of Cat, whose shadow is projected against the white wall of the porch, between the bedroom door and the kitchen door covered by the blue canvas curtain, leaves off chewing for a few seconds.

Cat approaches, at a slow pace, Tilty's twisted body. With his back turned, he is looking over his shoulder and watching the beige horse eat. He is carrying the red pail full of water in his right hand, and the motion of his walking jostles the water in the pail, so that the luminous reflections that show through the outer surface of the red plastic move tirelessly, changing form and even place on the red surface, allowing them to be seen as though projected on a screen, and, over the edge of the pail, two or three times, between Tilty and the horse, the water leaps out and spatters the ground and the grass. The beige horse attacks the second pail of water as avidly as the first one. Contemplating the animal, Tilty breathes loudly.

This afternoon or tomorrow, he tells him, he's going to take him out for a training session. He'll be back Monday morning. His eyes, set close together on either side of his nose, his wandering gaze, his wrinkled forehead, contracted in a frown, his twisted shadow intermingled with the strips of shadow projected on the ground of the backyard by the entry door, a single thought seems to be flitting about in his mind: that the hand with the pistol not appear, suddenly, silently, and slowly lean the barrel of it against the innocent temple. That the detonation not ring out.

The beach attendant strolls, in his bathing trunks and with his white helmet on his head, among the bathers lying face up or face down on bright-colored towels spread out on the sand. The bulky, tanned body of the beach attendant makes its way around the bodies stretched out, the baskets, the bags, the mounds of clothes carefully piled up on the ground. The beach attendant also watches the bodies splashing in the water, near the riverbank. Farther away, in the middle of the river, Tilty's green boat moves on downstream. At each stroke of the oars the boat, which appears to be motionless, emerges for a moment from its immobility, only to fall, almost instantaneously, back into it once more. For no known reason, that intermittent series of movements gives, moment by moment, an illusion of continuity. Cat's gaze follows, from the window, the abrupt halts of the boat, each one followed by an abrupt resumption of its motion.

The beach attendant also watches the bodies splashing in the water, near the riverbank: two bathers enter the river at a run, and a young woman, blonde, tanned, in a sky-blue bikini emerges from the opposite direction, dripping water, and walks toward the beach. A little farther in the distance, horizontal to the beach, someone moves along, churning up a liquid, whitish tumult, with his kicking and his arm strokes. Three little kids sit playing in the water, very close to shore, as

two other youngsters, both boys of about twelve, chase each
other, going in and out of the water, running and prancing:
the one who is ahead of the other has, in his hands, a multi-
colored rubber ball.

Moving farther downstream, in abrupt jerks, the green
boat, in the middle of which Tilty bends, back and forth, with
a regular rhythm, leaves on the caramel-colored surface a
wake whose edges, which are moving farther apart, are
visible even from the window. At each stroke of the oars the
green, elongated form proceeds, imperceptibly, and in an
almost instantaneous way, from movement to immobility,
affording a glimpse, every so often, over and above its illusory
continuity, of the abrupt halts, not only of the boat, but also of
the body and of the oars that touch the water at the sides of the
stern, move forward from below the surface, reappear, creat-
ing two off-white vortexes at either side of the bow, and
return through the air to the stern to fall once again into the
water and begin all over again.

The one who is ahead has the multi-colored rubber ball in
his hands: the one chasing him, on leaping into the water,
raises a whitish vortex. The distance separating him from the
one carrying the ball is, at every moment, constant. The one
who is ahead has given up the tactic of suddenly swerving, of
feinting, of pretending to change direction and is running,
like the other boy, straight forward, two or three yards ahead,
through the water, horizontal to the beach. The one behind is
not gaining on him by a single inch, so to speak: in the course
of the chase, the same distance, immutable, separates them,
the same stretch of empty air, beyond which, because they
have withdrawn a short distance away from the space meant
for the bathers, is the smooth river, golden or caramel,
without one ripple, and behind, low-lying, dusty, in full
sunlight, its bank sloping gently downward, half worn away,
the island.

The woman in the sky-blue bikini comes out of the water and when her feet touch the edge of the beach she stops and begins to shake herself and wring out her wet hair. Isolated drops of water running down her tanned skin gleam in the sun. Behind her back, several yards from the shoreline, there passes by, horizontal to the riverbank, the man who is moving upstream, in the opposite direction from the one being followed, in the center of the river, by the boat. The two boys who are running toward deeper water, with the water already up to their thighs, are beginning to move forward with increasing difficulty, because of the resistance of the water, becoming deeper and deeper, until finally the two of them let themselves fall into it: the sunlit air all about is filled with drops that rise up and sparkle for a fraction of a second, before falling back, and the loud echo of their bodies hitting the water resounds from one end of the beach to the other.

The low-lying, dusty island, in full sunlight, its reddish bank sloping down gently, half worn away by the water, is motionless, with no birds, no butterflies flying up from amid the stunted trees stirred by not a single breath of air, from amid the red, yellow, white flowers, being burned to cinders in the branches and in the underbrush, being charred to a crisp in the light of February, that unreal month, without there being perceived, at any time, on the irregular shoreline, the gentle quivers of the wake that the green boat is leaving behind as it moves upriver, in abrupt jerks, in the middle of the stream, leaving behind the visible edges of the wake that imperceptibly move apart and that streak the caramel water on which the scorching light sparkles, in multiple and arbitrary directions.

The one who is farther ahead takes a sudden leap sideways, in such a way that his pursuer, impelled by the inertia of his running, goes on in a straight line for several yards before reacting. But the one who is carrying the ball has doubled,

thanks to his surprise move, the lead he had. He runs swiftly
out of the water and keeps running, threading his way amid
the bodies stretched out on the big bright-colored beach
towels, the bags and the baskets and the mounds of clothes
meticulously piled up, in the opposite direction from the
river. His pursuer imitates him, but with less skill and agility,
so that the distance that separates them increases still more.
The pursuer is even blocked, involuntarily, by the beach
attendant who is moving about amid the bathers watching
the beach, the water, the bathers, the boat, the island. Every so
often he even takes a quick look in the direction of the
window from which Cat is standing watching the scene.
Cat's gaze follows the youngster coming at a run from the
beach toward the empty space, covered with sparse gray grass
burned to a crisp, that separates the white house from the
beach. His pursuer, far behind, goes on chasing him. He'll
never catch up with him now. When he reaches the empty
space on the side of the beach closest to the house, the one
farther ahead suddenly stops, throws the ball in the air in front
of him, and before it touches the ground again kicks it back
up in the air, with the end of his foot, a kick so energetic that
the effort causes him to fall in a sitting position on the ground.
The ball kicked upward soars like a shot, in a straight line.

The multi-colored sphere is in the air, motionless, suspended against the blue sky, having attained the upper limit
of its trajectory, its extreme of tension, against the immense,
empty blue vault, and Cat's head, leaning slightly backward,
since it has followed the vertical motion from the window, is
likewise fixed, inert, his eyes half-closed from the effort, his
mouth open, his elbows leaning on the window frame and his
forearms dangling outside, his hands as though they were
dead, with his contracted, separated fingers hanging down.
The multi-colored sphere is in the air, motionless, suspended
against the blue sky. In the air. Motionless. Suspended.
Against the blue sky.

From the scintillations that whirl around the sun's disk, and that force one's gaze to be lowered, so that the observer's eyes intuit, rather than actually see, that area of incandescence, there is emitted a sort of whitish dust, or a dusty, very fine, free-floating light that slowly disperses through the air and the sky: the unreal hour of the month of mad delirium, and the drops of sweat, as thick as beads of glass, little by little leave tortuous, thick trails down the face and the torso of Cat, whose shadow, in the backyard, is nothing more than a shapeless bulk beneath his feet shod in straw sandals that tread underfoot the red mosaic tiles of the porch: he is motionless, his eyes closed, his head thrown backward and his arms outstretched, exposing himself to the sun. By the position of his body he appears to be submissive to, or defiant of, that burning-hot light bearing down so powerfully. To one side of him are the deck chairs of orange-colored canvas, the chair on which there rests the empty bottle, the empty glass, the white bowl half full of almost lukewarm water in which there floats a drowned moth. And beyond the space strewn with old batteries and half-rotted tires to be seen amid the dry weeds burned to cinders by the sun, beyond the rusted oil drums, beyond even the red pail and the fodder scattered on the ground, beneath the eucalyptus trees, protecting itself as best it can from the heat beneath the shadow riddled with luminous holes, the yellow-white horse calmly grazes: its huge mouth moves ceaselessly, so that its black and white muzzle shows its pink inner side and the big white teeth that slowly grind its food to bits. Cat stands up straight, raising his head, hugging his arms against his ribs and opening his eyes. There is a profound silence that envelops the house and the entire region. If a voice were to be raised amid the boiling-hot silence in which there are not even murmurs or creaks, not even the harsh sound of the heat or the squeak of the slow wheel of midday would reach this far, as though muffled by padding, as though lifeless. Cat's eyes close halfway again, and his entire body becomes motionless, trying yet again, to no avail, to listen: there is not a sound to be heard, not one chirring: the wheel, whose load is at this moment, or rather this very instant, in a state of passivity that is not even a pause, because the bridge whereby it could be reached is cut off, is not moving for any reason, in any way, in any direction. It is inert, as wide as it is long, and full of lifeless things that are being reduced to ashes in the coagulated light, or that are like remains, without a temperature of their own, of things already burned and turned to ashes. Firmly in place, constant, suspended, the things that make up the wheel just lie where they are, in a spectral dimension now

and now, approaching, disencumbering itself little by little of the strata of distance that muffle it less and less, that free it as it comes closer, expanding, and becoming more complex and louder, the sound of a car engine that gradually brings Cat out of his dream-like state.

Beyond the vertical stripes of the wooden door, and beyond the deserted sidewalk, still enveloped in the cloud of whitish dust that it has raised as it arrived, the black car, of which only the rear end is visible since it has stopped a little beyond the door, tilted at an angle because of the slight convexity of the dirt street, continues to give off vibrations of the body that appears to come to a stop a second after the engine. In back of it, the long horizontal cloud of whitish dust, scattered about in the sun-drenched air, floats, semi-opaque and slow, blocking the view of the trees that are imperceptibly withering beyond the dirt street. The thin whitish smudge slowly rotates as it disperses, expanding, without falling.

"So it's Saturday today?" Cat asks.

"Yes, Saturday. As a matter of fact."

The one-piece dress of white linen reaches halfway down her thighs and also leaves her shoulders bare; all her visible flesh is tanned. Elisa holds her straw bag against her lower belly with both hands, covering her pubis with it. Her left foot, moving slightly forward, rests its weight on its tip, thus freeing the heel. Two leather straps, leading from a bronze ring located at the level of her instep, hold the sandal down, after winding two or three times around her ankle, just below her calf. Cat stares at the bronze ring.

"Saturday, already," he says.

"Yes, Saturday," Elisa says.

Cat slowly shakes his head.

"Saturday," he says.

The city is deserted: in the late afternoon, there is not a soul to be seen in the downtown area, when usually it is crowded. In the morning, around noon, even on a Saturday, the few shops that haven't closed are empty, despite the relative coolness that their doorways give off. The dark blue asphalt of the streets is melting in the sun. The tables in the bars are unoccupied. If by chance the afternoon heat surprises someone walking down a neighborhood street without trees, in full sunlight, far from the river and with no mini-bus stop close by, the feeling of unreality is so great that the light, on the white sidewalks, begins to flow swiftly, to fall to pieces and emit sparks. The sound of the light can even be heard. A slight odor of putrefaction spreads from the central market. When two strangers meet on an empty street, their eyes, that meet for a moment in a confused and dejected interchange, begin immediately to wander off once more or stare at the gray mosaic tiles and are not raised again. They are unable to keep looking straight into each other's eyes. At times, as night comes on, there can be perceived, from some window, the veiled eyes of a mature woman who, a gourdful of mate already cold in her hand, a soft, ample body, gray hair, contemplates the deserted street from the semi-darkness. Her eyes above all: the rest looks as though it were blended into the shadow. Only at night do people come out onto the sidewalk: because the insides of the houses have turned so hot during the

day that there is no way, or time, during the night, for them to
cool off again; before the night air takes effect, the rising sun
will begin heating them up again. They move the television
set into the front entryway and all sit on the sidewalk, facing
the inside of the house. A pitcher of lemonade or a quart bottle
of beer pass from hand to hand. Along entire blocks, the same
steely light of television sets twinkles from every entryway
and the same voices and the same sounds, artificial and full of
echoes, fill the air. The viewers' stony silhouettes are encircled
with a blue halo every so often in the light of the television
sets. The movie theaters are empty too. At some of them, on
two or three occasions, the performance had to be canceled
for lack of an audience. At certain hours—those close to
midday—only reasons of *force majeure*, sickness or work,
induce people to go out of doors. Many people wonder,
jokingly (but everybody knows what meaning jokes may
come to have), whether it is not purely and simply the end of
the world. Here Elisa raises her eyes, smiling and leaving
suspended in the air, halfway to her mouth, the fork with the
slice of tomato from which a drop of oil falls onto the plate.
Cat watches the drop of oil fall without leaving off chewing,
leaning against the back of his chair. Their table settings are
resting on the edge of the white plate in which the slices of
tomato lie drenched in yellowish oil. Several bright gold
circles form around the seeds that have fallen out of the slices.
Cat bends over toward his glass of white wine; drops of ice-
cold water trickle down the sides of the glass. With her
eyebrows raised slightly, her smile fading, her fork halfway
between the plate and her mouth, Elisa watches him pick up
the glass and raise it to his mouth. Tomatis, Elisa continues, is
of that opinion. Tomatis and his life-long business partner,
Horacio Barco, were arguing two or three nights ago in the
bar in the arcade, that skepticism in the face of the possibility
of the end of the world is based entirely on the concept of
experience; because there hasn't been an end of the world
yesterday, or this morning, there won't be one right now, or

tomorrow morning. The streets are scorching hot in the heat of the afternoon; and the houses, abandoned, are going bone-dry in the sun. The water, the trees are still there; the last source, to all appearances, of life. But the trees can hardly withstand the heat either, they are already turning yellow or drooping over, and the water is growing clouded, becoming dense, sluggish, pungent. In the great white sphere of the day, ablaze, the city is being consumed, is drying up, creaking but nonetheless not crackling. Will fall come at last, as always? That question can be read, uncertainly, in the eyes of the people one meets on the street. Fleetingly: for it is difficult, in the city, when one's path crosses a stranger's, not to avert one's eyes. The eyes that seek out others', however, in order to find relief in the common uncertainty, quickly glide away and glance downward, staring at the sidewalk once again. It is neither out of shyness nor bashfulness, but out of simple modesty, so as not to expose the old fear, like a naked body, to the gaze of others. Late yesterday afternoon, for instance, as she was accompanying Héctor and the children to the bus station, she had seen, for the first time in several days, a large number of people gathered together, as though all of them had rushed to take a trip somewhere, seeking safety from that atmosphere of imminent threat. And after having left them at the bus to Mar del Plata, she had gone out of the station and headed for her car. In the late afternoon, as everyone knows, a fever goes up. Green, reddish, the atmosphere, burning hot, is contaminated by something uncertain, indefinable. At this point Elisa falls silent, cuts a piece of bread, impales it on her fork by the crust and, imparting a circular movement to it, wipes it around the white plate to soak it with oil: the golden seeds collect around the bread, drawn by the suction that, like a sponge, the bread exerts on the bright-colored juice. The piece of bread, moved by the hand that is firmly grasping the fork, traverses the entire surface of the plate but for the rim. When Elisa takes it away to raise it to her mouth, the plate remains empty, gleaming, with a few scattered seeds

surrounded by a bright gelatinous circle. The kitchen is in a
fairly cool semi-darkness. Not a breath of air stirs the blue
canvas curtain that separates it from the porch. Pierced by the
sun, the curtain projects on the colored tiles a blue shadow full
of transparent veins. Without ceasing to chew, Cat contemplates the thick lips on which the oil has left its trace, the
bronze face on which the sweat has begun to streak the black
mascara, the black hair pulled back, the tanned neck, as
lustrous as all the visible skin which emerges, like the shoulder
and the arms, from the stiff, immaculate white dress. The
piece of bread reaches the mouth that opens and sucks it in;
immediately, just as the fork descends and with a tinkle comes
to rest on the rim of the plate, the muscles of the bronze face
begin to move in the rhythm of chewing. Elisa opens her eyes
a little and moves her head forward as she swallows. Yesterday, late in the afternoon, without going any farther, as she
was crossing the deserted street, at the corner by the central
market . . . But no; no. She falls silent once again. Seeing Cat
waiting expectantly, she lowers her eyes and fixes them on the
empty plate. Amid the silence, Cat picks up the cigarettes,
puts one between his lips and lights it, setting the matches
back down on the table. He shakes the match several times till
the flame goes out. A stream of smoke, straight, cylindrical,
turbulent, erupts, aimed directly at Elisa, who raises her eyes,
stares straight into Cat's for a fraction of a second and then
immediately, shaking her shoulders and her head at the same
time, she gives a troubled, modest smile.

"You ought to shave," Elisa's voice says.
Cat rubs his hand over his cheeks, gives a little smile and
half opens his eyes. In answer, he makes a quick gesture with
his lips, consisting of pursing them a little and making them
protrude. It is as though the porch were impregnated with the
late afternoon heat. The two orange-colored canvas deck
chairs, placed facing each other, are sheltered, however, from
the sun. Their bodies are flattened against the canvas and as the

chairs are set low, the two of them must sit up a little if they want to see each other. Elisa's head remains slightly erect; Cat's remains flattened against the canvas. The hem of the white dress has crept up almost to the tops of her tanned thighs. On her right knee a superficial injury, a mere scratch, has left a series of dark, dry crusts. Elisa leans her head back against the canvas of the deck chair once more and closes her eyes again. Her hands, crossed over her lower belly, rest there calmly. Cat sits up and scrutinizes for a moment her bronze legs. He gets to his feet and goes over and kneels down alongside the white dress. Then, brusquely, he brings his head down against her thighs and begins to lick them. Without opening her eyes, Elisa places one of her hands on Cat's head.

"No. Not yet. Not yet," she says.

When the lighted cigarette end is crushed against the white plate, still full of traces of oil, it produces a minute sound, audible nonetheless in the silence that envelops the kitchen and the house. Elisa gets to her feet and begins to clear away the dishes and the tableware. Maintaining the same attitude as when he stubbed the cigarette out, he contemplates her. Elisa clears away the plate with the stubbed-out cigarette, takes away the tableware, and puts the plate on top of the other dirty dishes; she picks the dirty table settings off the table and puts them on top of the plate. On the blue and white checkered tablecloth, full of crumbs and bits of bread, the only things remaining are the glasses, the empty bread basket and the bottle of white wine with a bit still left in it. When Elisa heads toward the sink to put the dishes and the tableware in it, Cat empties the bottle into his glass, and getting to his feet, immediately raises the glass and downs the whole of it in one gulp. Elisa turns around and stands there looking at him from the sink: the table with the blue and white checkered tablecloth, the empty space between the table and the kitchen stove, into which Elisa's empty chair has been pushed a short distance away from the table, separate the two bodies, Cat's with the empty glass in his hand halfway between his mouth and the table, Elisa's leaning against the stove, her arms apart from her sides so as not to rub her dirty fingers against the white dress that is now criss-crossed by a number of horizontal wrinkles, straight and rigid, at the level of her lower belly. Cat picks up the second glass and the empty bottle from the table and making his way around it at a slow and lackadaisical pace sets them down on the stove. Elisa goes on looking at the point beyond the table where Cat has been standing alongside his chair, facing in the direction of the blue canvas curtain whose center appears to be slightly inflated by a luminous spot. Turning slowly, until he is facing Elisa's motionless prof.le, Cat bends his head down. As he does so his broad, flat, pink tongue emerges from between his lips surrounded by his blond beard, at least a week old. At the precise moment that his tongue touches the tanned skin of her shoulder and gives it a quick lick, Elisa abruptly moves aside.

"Not yet," she says.

Cat has retracted his tongue, closing his mouth. He is nonetheless still motionless, with his head bent down, as though he were leaning his chin against an invisible body. The luminosity that comes dimly through the blue cloth of the curtain scatters in the kitchen in which the white walls gleam faintly, in such a way that the semi-darkness blends paradoxically with that diffuse brightness. For a moment nothing happens, or apparently nothing happens: there are only the two motionless bodies and the paradoxical semi-darkness that on close examination may even be slightly yellow.

"Let's go sit on the porch," Elisa says. Her voice continues to echo for a moment after having impelled Cat to turn quickly around and begin to walk, without a word, toward the black door separating the kitchen from the remainder of the house. From the next room he takes down from the wall a folded deck chair and after tucking it underneath his arm goes back through the room in the opposite direction and walks

through the doorway leading to the kitchen, only to note that
Elisa has disappeared and that the blue canvas curtain leading
to the porch is still moving, since Elisa has pushed it aside so as
to leave the kitchen. Cat unfolds, not without effort, the
second orange-colored canvas deck chair, facing the one that
Elisa is sitting in, and sits down in it. Elisa is looking at the
beige horse that is shaking its head at the far end of the yard,
underneath the trees.

"And do you think it's safe here?" she asks casually.

"It's possible," Cat says.

"For my part I don't think it's safer here than on the
island," Elisa says.

"That's possible too," Cat says.

Elisa shakes her head from side to side several times.

"In a word, it doesn't matter in the least to you, one way or
the other."

"That's not impossible either," Cat says.

"I understand, I understand," Elisa says.

Cat's only answer is to stick his tongue out and move it
obscenely back and forth several times across his upper lip.
Elisa smiles, shrugs, and closing her eyes, leans her head back
against the orange canvas. Her arms are resting on the rough
wooden arms of the deck chair. Cat contemplates her for a
moment and assumes a similar position. There is not a breath
of air, and not a sound reaches the porch: the entire afternoon
heat is a single transparent block of mineral, hot and compact,
in which everything, hollowed out inside, is at once close at
hand and unreachable. Each object, solid and still, in its place,
in the block, no more accessible to the fingers than a ship
inside a bottle. Without opening his eyes, without the rest of
his body undergoing the slightest movement, Cat removes
his right hand from the rough wooden armrest and quickly
scratches his chest, at the level of the sparse blond down
growing between his nipples. His hand descends again and
remains half closed, palm up, on his right thigh.

"You ought to shave," Elisa's voice says.

Cat's hand moves upward once again. He rubs it over his
cheeks. He smiles, placidly, half opening his eyes. He makes a
quick gesture with his lips, consisting of pursing them a little
and making them protrude. Elisa's head, slightly raised up,
lies back against the orange canvas again. The hem of her
white dress, which has crept up almost to the tops of her
thighs, affords a glimpse, between her legs, of the close-fitting
black panties clinging to her pubis. Her bronze hands rest, one
on top of the other, on her stomach, against her white dress.
Elisa closes her eyes. Without ceasing to gaze at her parted
legs, Cat sits up, remains motionless for a moment, and finally
gets to his feet and goes over to kneel down beside Elisa. He
brusquely nuzzles his head against her bronze thighs and
begins to lick them. Without opening her eyes, Elisa places
her hand on Cat's head.

"No. Not yet. Not yet," she says.

Cat stands up and goes back to his deck chair, collapsing in
it. Through the shade on the porch, which does not cool it,
there swiftly passes something that effaces it, for a moment,
and that, at almost the same time, restores it.

Elisa is lying in the bed, face up, naked: her head resting on
the flat pillow, her right hand, with the fingers held apart,
gently covering her navel, her left hand with the palm
showing, on her forehead. Her breasts, spread out over her
chest and stretched backwards, because of the horizontal
position of her body, are as tanned as the rest of her, except for
a narrow strip that goes from the lower part of her hips to the
tops of her thighs and in the exact center of which the black
triangle of her pubis is located. Her right leg is stretched out
over the edge of the bed, so that her left buttock is practically
in the air and it is the left foot, resting on the floor, that
contributes to keeping her body on the bed. Her entire
body—except for the narrow white strip—has the reddish-
yellow tinge of lustrous bronze. The position obliges Elisa to
keep her legs parted. Unbuttoning his white shorts—a dingy

grayish-white because they are dirty—and letting them slide
down along his legs, ridding himself of them, trampling on
them with his right foot first and holding the left one back,
then immediately going through the same operation with his
other foot, Cat, at the other end of the bed, whose body also
has a strip, a wider one, of whitish flesh, observes the vertex
formed below by her legs spread apart: a reddish slit. The
black hair gives way to a very narrow area in which the
vertical slash shows, fleetingly, between two protuberances,
its reverse. Fold upon fold, superimposed, flexible shutters of
windows placed, one after the other, along the long red
corridor. Folds and folds, and then other folds, and still more
folds, Cat seems to think, as he begins to walk, unhurriedly,
toward the bed. And so on, ad infinitum.

IV   In order to get out of the dream in which
I am, so to speak, entangled, I must strain
with my entire body, because it is my entire body that is
trapped in it. That is the state I wake up in, standing alongside
the bed. For a moment I can't make head or tail of anything.
My entire body is still, in many ways, pervaded by the dream,
which went like this: lying in bed, in the process of waking
up, I am thinking of the blurred photograph of San Enrico
Imperatore that I have seen, in a blur, in the dream, my back
against the damp sheet, vaguely hearing the sound of the fan
and at the same time that I am thinking it, I am dreaming that I
am lying in bed, in the process of waking up, thinking of the
blurred photograph of San Enrico Imperatore that I have
seen, in a blur, in the dream, my back against the damp sheet
and vaguely hearing the hum of the fan. I have had to pull
very hard, and many times, toward the outside, in order to be
able to get out and still, even so, now that I am standing, in the

semi-darkness, listening to the vague sound of the fan, my
legs are trembling still, numb, still, with sleep, or because of
the dream, and my heart is still pounding just a little. I fling
myself, once more, face downward, onto the bed, flattening
my face against the damp sheet. And all of a sudden, morning
comes: the ceiling, overhead, unexpectedly speckled with
sun. The sheet, twisted, damp, grayish, hurts my back. I find
myself obliged to rid myself of the waking state as well, with
an imperceptible effort, and pass on, again standing on the red
tiles, to an ambiguous, intermediate state, where everything is
no more accessible to my fingertips than a boat inside a bottle.
My fingertips touch, at most, the polished glass without
knowing beforehand that it was there and they experience,
instead of the expected roughness, a uniform, monotonous
smoothness. The smell of the coffee that I am unhurriedly
making, in the kitchen, gets me out, in the beginning, of that
dull delirium, but it too, after a few minutes, settles down
inside me and loses its strength. The calls and the voices of the
bathers, which reach me intermittently, do not modify, even
for a moment, even once, anything about anything. The flow
of the nameless thing inside which I am wandering aimlessly
is, though transparent, slow and thick. My eyes have nothing
to look at. And with the cup of coffee in my hand, the
smoking white cup, I go from the kitchen through the black
doors, from one end of the house to the other; it is slightly
cooler, still, than it is outside, and I finally reach the room at
the front, and opening the window, begin to contemplate the
little beach on which some thirty bathers are exposing themselves to the sun. There are men, women, children. Some of
them are stretched out on multi-colored towels, face up or
face down, others seated, others going into the river or
coming out, running or walking, others moving in the water
at a horizontal to the shore, forming white plumes in the
caramel-colored river. The fat man, with his white helmet,
with his regulation whistle hanging from a cord around his
neck, keeps his distance from the bathers, toward this side of

the yellow sand, close to the two cement grills, sitting underneath a tree. He greets me with a slight wave of his arm and I
answer with a nod. The small crowd at the beach, in front of
me, despite the tanned bodies that move and palpitate, and
even twist and contort themselves at times, despite the liquid
tumult they raise with their belly flops, despite the cries and
shouts and bursts of laughter that ring out and resound as if to
prove definitely that at this moment they are life and nothing
else apart from them is, they nonetheless are not, to my eye,
and to my ear, and to my fingertips, as accessible as they
should be. And it is now, at this very moment, that I see the
green boat making its way upstream and cutting diagonally
across the river to land. It touches shore downstream beyond
the beach, and also beyond the fat man whose helmeted head
turns around toward the boat just as Tilty, after having
dropped the oars inside the boat, rises to his feet slowly and
laboriously, his body twisted like a root and his arms spread
apart helping him to keep his balance. He is now coming
toward the house, carrying on his left shoulder the two
cubical bundles of fodder, which make him bend over toward
the right, toward the ground. His faded khaki shirt, his straw
hat with a round brim, his trousers, faded and much too wide
for him, leaving his ankles showing as though the pair of
trousers had belonged to someone who, despite being older
than he, had been shorter, or as though they had been bought
for him before the rapid spurt of growth of a fifteen-year-old,
the tattered espadrilles, and above all the twisted body, his
head buried between his shoulders, against which the two
bundles of fodder are pressing down on his left shoulder, give
him that air of a marionette stubbornly determined to move
forward, with steps so clumsy, so hesitant, so slow, that they
force him to make visible contortions not only of his body
and his legs, but also of his right arm that is dangling to one
side, so that it would seem as though the medium in which he
is doing his best to make his way along is not air but a thicker,
denser element, working against his efforts and not helping

him. I go to the rear entrance to let him in. I now have before
me, at a distance of a foot and a half from my eyes, his dark
and sweaty face and I listen to his slight panting. As he utters
his slow "Good day," he looks anxiously over my head,
toward the rear of the yard, in the direction of the beige horse.
I relieve him of his burden. Being rid of its load, his body does
not assume a normal posture: on the contrary, it would
appear that the bent-over position forced upon him by the
weight of the fodder had given him, temporarily, a more
natural posture which dissolves when I remove the bundles
from his shoulders. Carrying one in each hand, skirting the
half-rotted tires and the batteries scattered all over the backyard, passing alongside the rusted corrugated tin oil drums, I
head toward the beige horse. It immediately recognizes the
presence of Tilty, who halts next to it and begins to pat it and
stroke its muzzle. As he pats it, his eyes, looking the palpitating, beige body over, meet alongside its muzzle and betray his
obsession: that the hand with the pistol not appear, suddenly,
silently, and that it not slowly place the barrel against the
horse's head. That the detonation not ring out. Then we untie
the bundles and scatter the fodder on the ground, around the
beige horse, which begins to eat. The tops of the trees, pierced
with light, let through many luminous spots onto our bodies
busy at their task, and are also projected on the ground and on
the beige hide of the horse. The red pail is filled twice with
fresh water, as the pump motor roars in the sun. Tilty cleans
up the ground around the horse, removing its excrement and
making a pile of the fodder too scattered to attract the beige
horse. Then I give Tilty something to eat in the kitchen: a can
of hash, cheese and water biscuits that we wash down with a
glass of wine with seltzer. Before leaving, he takes with him,
in a little transparent plastic bag that I take out of the cupboard
in the bedroom, some ice cubes.

"I'll take it out to train it this afternoon or tomorrow," I say
to him.

He nods in approval. He'll be back day after tomorrow. I

see him to the back door, and out to the deserted sidewalk of
the irregular, sloping dirt street that leads to the beach and
down which he is heading toward the boat. From where I am
standing, on the empty treeless sidewalk, I can see, toward
the end of the street, four or five cars parked in the shade,
but the open space onto which the street gives takes in
neither the beach, upriver, nor, downriver, the place where
he has left the boat. It is an open space between the trees of the
two sidewalks whose tops come together above the street,
affording a glimpse, as at the end of a corridor, and beyond the
foliage pierced by spots of light that imprint themselves on
the sidewalk and the street, of a bit of blue sky, and a little
stretch of empty river, behind which there can be seen, its
bank descending steeply, half worn away, stunted, tangled,
dusty vegetation, as though motionless and lifeless, the island.
The cries and shouts of the bathers reach the deserted sidewalk. The twisted body that walks along without, apparently, advancing, toward the area of shadow that separates the
deserted sidewalk from the beach and the river, toward the
empty cars parked in complete disorder along the shoulders,
lingers for a moment in my memory as I head for the far end
of the yard, skirting the rusty, corrugated tin oil drums, the
old tires stained with dried mud and the scattered batteries
half-buried amid the scorched grass. It is still there: frugally,
mistrustfully chewing, moving more slowly, now that it sees
me coming, its jaws from which threads of a whitish slaver are
hanging. More slowly still, until it stops moving them: the
lower one shifted slightly toward the right, the upper one
toward the left, so that they are not exactly on top of each
other and its mouth remains half open baring its big unusually
white teeth and its gums of a bluish pink. Solid, compact,
opaque, without meaning, determined to exist, and prolong-
ing it, its life, by way of its mouth. For a moment nothing
happens: merely the look, that keeps us riveted to the spot,
each of us in our own place, and immediately the animal,
which has remained motionless and just a bit in profile as

though it were made of a dense, yellowish smoke, begins
again, slowly, to chew, in such a way that its lower jaw moves
from right to left and from left to right, while at no time does
its upper jaw remain precisely on top of it. It is as if it were
chewing its own mistrust and as if it were not the green
volume macerated by its own saliva, but my worrisome,
enemy presence that was what it was trying to swallow. The
halter around its neck that keeps it tied to the tree stretches out
now, and remains tense, as the horse gives a swift leap to one
side: the spots of light projected on its smoke-yellow body
move a little, change, as it does so. It is still moving, within
me, when, leaving behind the space strewn with batteries and
tires, I walk across the porch, passing alongside the orange-
colored deck chair and the chair seat on which the glass, the
bottle, and the white bowl are sitting, and go inside the house,
shaking the blue canvas curtain that separates the kitchen door
from the sun-drenched porch. The house is slightly cooler
than the outside air. It is not, even though I am inside it, any
closer at all than it was when I was standing on the deserted
sidewalk watching it move hesitantly toward the area of
shadow or than when I was watching, at the far end of the
yard, amid the trees, the smoke-yellow spot shake itself and
make the leather strap that ties it to the tree become taut. The
white walls, the black doors, the red tile floor and the few
articles of furniture next to the walls, the big table, surrounded by chairs with straw-bottomed seats in the living
room, with the commode to one side, the beds in the three
bedrooms, the wardrobes, the night table with the fan not
running, the little library, the refrigerator, everything, as I
wander aimlessly about the house, would seem to be in the
process of coming out, laboriously, from something black,
formless, nameless. Finally I see the ashtray of fired clay, on
the floor, in the main room, and squat down. Alongside it, on
top of the red tiles, the black mark is stamped. It too has just
emerged from, just come out of, the blackness, or is like a trail
that the blackness has allowed to pass through one of its

cracks. It has no history. It is a blackish spot on a colored tile, next to an ashtray of fired clay, in a white room, in this instant in which a particular light is flowing past. I get up: I know that they are disappearing, despite their calm, I know that we are sinking down, imperceptibly, so as to be reborn, in an interval that it would be ridiculous to call time since I know that it doesn't have a name and could answer to none. I emerge, we emerge, from the unthinkable submersion, as from a swamp. And my legs, laboriously, the left one, the right one, the left now, the right now, are taking me through the black doors, as though for a reason, to the front window which, as I can now see, overlooks the beach. The fat man is strolling, in his bathing trunks and with his white helmet on his head, amid the bathers stretched out face up or on their bellies, on multi-colored towels spread out on the sand. The beach attendant's bulky, tanned body walks along, skirting the bodies stretched out, the baskets, the bags, the mounds of clothes carefully piled up on the ground. The beach attendant also watches the bodies that are splashing about in the water, close in to shore. Farther away, in the middle of the river, Tilty's green boat is heading downstream. At each stroke of the oars, the boat, which appears to be motionless, emerges for a moment from its immobility, only to fall once more, almost instanta-neously, back into it. Two bathers enter the river at a run and a young woman, blonde, tanned, in a sky-blue bikini, comes, dripping water, in toward the beach. A little farther off, parallel to the beach, someone moves along churning up a liquid, whitish tumult, with his vigorous arm and leg strokes. The little kids sit and play in the water, close to shore, as two others, about twelve years old, chase each other, going in and out of the water, running and prancing: the one who's ahead of the other is holding in his hands a big multi-colored rubber ball. The one who's chasing him enters the water and his feet, as he hits it, raise a whitish vortex. The one who's ahead has given up the tactic of suddenly swerving, of feinting, of pretending to change direction and is running, like the other

boy, two or three yards in front of him, through the water,
parallel to the beach. Then he makes a sudden leap sideways,
in such a way that his pursuer, impelled by the inertia of his
own running, goes on for several yards more before reacting.
But the one who is carrying the ball has doubled, thanks to his
surprise move, the lead he had. He runs swiftly out of the
water and keeps running—threading his way amid the bodies
stretched out on the bright-colored towels, the bags and the
baskets and the mounds of clothes neatly piled up—in the
opposite direction from the river. The pursuer is even
blocked, involuntarily, by the beach attendant who is moving about amid the bathers, alternately watching the beach,
the water, the bathers, the boat, the island; every so often he
even takes a quick look in my direction, above the head of the
youngster who is coming at a run toward the window, in a
straight line from the water. He crosses the beach, and when
he reaches the empty space, covered with sparse ash-colored
grass, which separates the beach from the house, he suddenly
stops. His pursuer will never catch up with him now, even
though he goes on running. The one who has arrived first
throws the ball in the air in front of him, and before it touches
the ground kicks it upward with the end of his foot, a kick so
energetic that the effort causes him to fall in a sitting position
on the ground. His pursuer falls on top of him and they roll
over and over, wrestling with each other, on the grass. The
multi-colored ball bounds beside them, comes to rest on the
ground again, and then begins to roll swiftly toward the
beach, stopping alongside the feet of the blonde woman in the
sky-blue bikini, who is standing next to her bags, drying
herself off with a white towel. I leave the window: I carry off
with me, still, as I begin to cross the room again, heading
toward the black door, the empty space in front of the house,
the yellowish beach, the two young boys rolling over and
over on the sparse grass, the bathers stretched out on their
towels of every color, going in or out of the water, the
beach attendant in his white helmet, the smooth, bright,

caramel-colored river, without out a single ripple, and behind, its bank gently descending, the dusty vegetation, half worn away, the island. I go through the empty space that the black door, standing wide open, leaves, and go into the main room. I open the drawer of the commode. Inside, underneath the papers, the pencils, the corkscrew, my fingers come across, unintentionally, the revolver. The box of bullets, lying open, with several of them missing, has let two or three of them fall out, and they lie scattered about in the bottom of the drawer. I close the drawer again.

I closed the drawer again and went and threw myself on the bed. I lay there face up, my head leaning on my hands placed on top of each other above the pillow, my elbows on either side of my head bent at an acute angle. No light was projected on the ceiling overhead, but the room against the window of which the trees on the sidewalk let their thick branches droop, motionless, was enveloped in a greenish sort of luminosity that was a similar sort of semi-darkness. Then I fell asleep, waking up again almost immediately. It seemed to me at least that it had been almost immediately, but when I got up I realized that my midday sleep had been a little longer because something, impossible to define, showed that a certain time had gone by. An hour perhaps, or half an hour, maybe, or forty-five minutes, or an hour and a quarter, or an hour and a half maybe. I went out onto the porch and stood there for a moment in the sun, till the black car arrived. So I knew for certain that it was Saturday. I helped Elisa take out the two big cardboard boxes full of white envelopes, the telephone book, and the food for the weekend. Among the envelopes was the book that Pigeon had sent from France. The work for the agency consisted this time of the following: copying the telephone book in alphabetical order, I was to write down the addresses on the white envelopes and then return them to the agency. They would take charge of putting something inside the envelopes and of having them delivered by mail. The time before, I was to fold in four a sheet of paper with a printed advertisement for a supermarket and put it in the envelopes, and they had taken charge of writing the address on the envelopes and of sending them off. We left the box with the envelopes in the main room and sat down to eat. Elisa slowly prepared a tomato salad on the work counter. I seized the opportunity, at every moment, to grab hold of her, so as to get her going, to get her worked up, but she gently pushed me away, as usual, without saying either yes or no, but only: "It isn't time yet." When siesta time came, we sat down on the porch, which was no longer in the sun, and again she said to me, "It isn't time yet." We sat there for a long time without saying a word, each of us in our deck chair, until she herself, standing up and smoothing her white dress at the level of her belly, said to me, half closing her eyes and without turning her head toward me: "I think the time has come." I followed her to the bedroom. She threw herself on the bed, naked, face up, and waited for me. "You'll see now what's going to happen," I said to her, "you'll see what I'm going to do to you now, so that you'll see." I flung myself on top of her. It had seemed to me that I was going to be able, this afternoon, even if it were only once, and just for a moment, to touch bottom. But I touched nothing. There we were, moving, groaning, sighing, one inside the other, as always—that was the reason why we met every time we could—and when we finished, panting, stretched out one on top of the other, in low spirits, as though worn out, we had not gotten much farther ahead, that was certain; we were just the same as at the beginning and the farthermost point that we had reached was infinitely closer to the beginning than to the end. We lay there alongside each other, smoking. Then I got to my feet, put on my shorts, went to the kitchen to have a glass of water, and when I came back I stood there looking at her from the foot of the bed: she was lying face up, naked, her head resting on the flat pillow, her right hand, with the fingers held apart, gently covering her navel, her left hand on her forehead, with the palm showing.

Her breasts, spread out over her chest toward her ribs and stretched backwards, because of her horizontal position, were as tanned as the rest of her body, except for a strip that went from the lower part of her hips to the top of her thighs, in the exact center of which the black triangle of her pubis was located. Her right leg was stretched out over the edge of the bed, so that her left buttock was almost in the air and it was her left foot, resting on the floor, that was contributing to keep her body on the bed. Her entire body, apart from the narrow whitish stripe, had the reddish-yellow tinge of lustrous bronze. The position obliged her to keep her legs parted: the vertex formed down below by her legs spread apart bared a reddish slit. The black hair gave way to a very narrow area in which the vertical slash showed, fleetingly, between two coarse-grained protuberances, its reverse side. Fold upon fold, superimposed, flexible shutters of windows placed, one after the other, along the long red corridor. Folds and folds, and then other folds, and still more folds. And so on, ad infinitum. "You'll see now what's going to happen," I said to her again, "you'll see what I'm going to do to you now, so that you'll see." But nothing, again: the same moans, the same mutual convulsion, without getting anywhere, so that when we were finally lying alongside each other, again, smoking, not speaking, we hadn't, as the saying goes, gotten one bit farther ahead. Then Elisa got up and fixed a pitcher of lemonade. We wandered about the house naked, each with our glass of lemonade that she had just refilled from the pitcher sitting on the blue and white checkered tablecloth, still strewn with the now-hardened crumbs of bread from lunch. Finally I put my shorts back on, saddled the beige horse, and went off to train it. The mistrust with which it saw me coming turned to fury, and even terror, when I began to saddle it and especially when I mounted it. We started off slowly however, at a nervous trot. Then we galloped along the shore, downstream, leaving behind the white house, the beach on which the bathers were taking their late afternoon dip; we went toward the great red background of the sky, where, beyond the low hills, the islands, the water and the villages, there rises, deserted, burning hot, the city. The beige mount trembled between my legs; and the air, for the first time in many days, hit me hard in the face with great hot gusts. We rode swiftly over that mute stretch of ground in a silent war with no other precise aim than to observe each other and take each other's measure. And when we came back, at a gallop first, then at a slow trot once we were closer to the house, the bathers stopped in their tracks and turned their heads to watch us go by. We went into the backyard, driven mad by the mosquitoes, drenched with sweat and our hearts beating hard. I dismounted and freed him of the saddle. And now, as I come out onto the porch, freshly bathed, freshly shaved, with a glass of white wine in my hand, toward Elisa who, as she drinks, sitting in the orange-colored canvas deck chair, smiles at me vacantly, with her eyes, from above her own glass, I realize that, from the blue semi-darkness, denser than the remainder of the yard, piled up underneath the eucalyptus trees, a beige patch, moving and immutable, leaving off chewing for a moment, slowly, prudently, in profile, is contemplating me.

V   In the beginning there is nothing. Nothing. The smooth, golden river, without a single ripple, and behind, beyond the yellow beach, with its windows and its black doors, the roof of Spanish tiles reverberating in the sun, the white house. Slowly reining in his beige mount for a moment at the top of the bank, Tilty looks, without blinking, for a moment, in the direction of the house: the left part is submerged beneath the bushy-topped trees along the road that slopes down to the river. The rest gleams in the sun. A human figure, sitting at the foot of a tree, at the end of the beach, near the grills, is, though immobile, the only sign of life in the mineral light. Tilty sees it a second after having appeared at the top of the slope, coming out from among the trees on the island, and after having contemplated, without blinking, beyond the smooth golden river, without a single ripple, the white house.

The front feet of the beige horse touch the water, and the shadow of rider and mount, made smaller by the afternoon sun, is projected, faintly, on the river. The air is slightly cooler than at the top of the slope. Imperceptibly a little wave eats into the riverbank and dampens it. The smell of the water rises, all of a sudden, to Tilty's nostrils.

From the front feet of the beige horse an aquatic vortex rises, and the river, convulsed by the animal bulk that is moving forward slowly, emits a continual noise and splashes that sparkle fleetingly in the sun and dash, at times, against Tilty's face, who pulls his legs up over the horse's haunches and remains almost in a kneeling position on its back. On the other side of the river, beyond the beach, Cat's naked torso appears, framed in one of the windows. The white façade of the house gleams in the blinding sun.

When he passes by him a short distance away, leaving the beach behind, the fat man with a white helmet on his head, sitting underneath a tree near the grills, greets him with a nod. Tilty imitates him without turning his head, continuing to look steadily in the direction of the window in which Cat is smoking, in silence.

Someone has begun, some time ago, to kill horses. He comes at night, taking advantage of the darkness, when everyone is asleep, and fires a shot into the animal's head. He goes all about the countryside, the islands, at one point along the river today, at another tomorrow, killing innocent creatures. He is, according to Tilty, sheer evil. And there are nine of them now.

"Ten," Cat says. "They killed another one last night, in Rincón."

Tilty raises to his mouth the oval slice of salami, interlarded with bits of white fat. He chews slowly, with his mouth half open. His eyes, which lie close to his nose, are not looking at anything, though they see the alert, shiny face, the cheeks covered with reddish stubble at least a week old, of Cat, whose muscles, including those of his temples, move in all directions, owing to the violence with which he is chewing his own slices of salami.

Tilty raises to his mouth a second slice of salami, oval, interlarded with bits of white fat. He chews slowly, with his mouth half open. The hard, dry meat, with a strong taste, though it puts up a slight resistance to his meticulous, relentless teeth, gives way immediately and little by little turns, in his mouth, into a softish paste in which there no doubt remain a few persistent, leathery filaments. He finally swallows. Behind Cat, who also chews slowly and continuously in the kitchen, the blue canvas curtain lets through luminous veins of light that form a halo around his head. Tilty raises his glass of red wine, takes a swallow, and sets it back down on the blue and white checkered tablecloth. A drop of wine, which has slid down the outside surface of the glass, falls on the tablecloth, on one of the white squares, and leaves an irregular, violet-colored stain. Tilty and Cat watch it for several seconds.

Upriver, the green boat begins with imperceptible jerks, feeble at first and after a certain time more cleanly, to cut through the water on a diagonal and approach the shore: it leaves behind it a superficial wake, smooth, more luminous than the large smooth, luminous, caramel-colored surface.

It has been moving in a straight line upriver, along the middle of the stream; in an imperceptible way at first, in the luminous expanse, it has deviated from its slow trajectory, and is now moving, obliquely, rigidly, the rower, with his back to his goal, bending rhythmically backwards and forwards, the wake that it is leaving behind bending in a gentle curve, in the sunlight, toward the shore.

The bundles of forage placed one on top of the other on his right shoulder, press against the left side of his face, against his ear and his jawbone, and the forage makes his skin prickle and burn a little. But they are not too heavy, or if they are, Tilty, seeing the white façade of the house dancing inelegantly in front of him in the sun, and leaning out the window, Cat's sunburned torso, and on the other side the bushy-topped trees that intertwine their branches above the road and form a short tunnel of shadow beyond which the sun reverberates once more, the whole beginning, in the morning light, to dance clumsily to the rhythm of his own steps, is thinking about many things at once with the exception of the load that he is carrying, of many things at once and above all of the fact that there was not raised, the night before, slowly, the hand with the pistol, that it did not lean, gently, against the beige head, that there did not ring out, suddenly, the detonation, reaching even the islands.

No: it is still here: alternating restlessness and calm, shaking its tail every so often, its ears pricked up, its big nostrils snorting, alert now that it knows that he is here, letting go of the bundles of fodder. When Cat bends down to pick them up Tilty can even see its legs, the luminous perforations of the dusty foliage that leave dappled markings on its back.

To the rear, somewhere, the pump motor hums in the sun: it is a monotonous sound, of pulleys, of tin plate, and it fills, red-hot, the morning, above the shouts of the bathers. Tilty feels, as he strokes the horse, its warm skin, above its multiple tense muscles, and the gratitude, a mixture of confidence and relaxation, that the animal's whole body offers him. After letting out a prolonged, unconscious sigh, Tilty goes on scattering fodder at the feet of the beige horse.

It is not a good thing to leave it inactive for too long a time, there underneath the trees, in the backyard. It can get too nervous; it can go mad. No animal can bear isolation and inactivity. Its brain begins to drift; its muscles weaken. It begins to go around in circles, without a beginning or an end, without a precise goal. It is much better to go out every so often into the open countryside, to run, in a straight line, toward something, to move along swiftly, to expend as much energy as possible, to get somewhere. And so he says: this afternoon, or tomorrow, he will go out to train it. Tilty, carrying in his right hand the little transparent plastic sack full of ice cubes, enters the shade of the trees, dense, with almost no light filtering through, and his own shadow, that had been heaped up at his feet on the sidewalk of beaten earth, grows blurred.

Forward now: and now backward. Forward. Now. Now backward. Again, now, forward. Now backward once again. Once again? As the boat moves downriver, Tilty's twisted body rows rhythmically: when the oars, emerging from the water, close to either side of the bow, move backwards through the air, at the height of the gunwales, Tilty bends forward, and when the oars, entering the caramel-colored water, move forward, laboriously, Tilty's body, tense all over from the effort, leans rigidly backward. In imperceptible jerks, from the white house, over whose lateral façade the thick branches droop, half hiding it from sight, the bathers, in swimsuits of every imaginable color, sauntering about on the tiny sloping beach, move off. The whole, beneath the smooth blue sky and the yellow spluttering of the sun that is still rising, is reduced in size, discontinuously, with each stroke of the oars, the whole in which each thing slowly grows smaller, contracting, without losing, however, either its proportion within the whole or its sharp focus.

Not a single sound is heard in the town. The last electric lights, the lanterns in the cabins on the outskirts, have long since, little by little, gone out. The only lights left shine feebly from the street lamps, on the corners, motionless, for not even the breath of a breeze stirs the night. At each intersection a dim circle of light illuminates the middle of the road and grazes the four corners: everything else sleeps, submerged in a dense darkness that the enormous trees—taller than the houses and stretching endlessly upward, along the edge of the sidewalks—make even thicker. Not a sound: of either man or animal. All at once, in the darkness, something, a shadow, moves. It is a slightly less dense shadow, vaguely standing out in the blackness, in a street near the main square onto which the tall wall of the church projects yet another shadow. A moving shadow, unlike the other shadows in that sultry night in which nothing moves. It gradually fills, as it shifts about, the interstices, patches, holes of light that here and there block the dense shadow formed by the trees and the houses in the middle of the block; it fills them and, immediately, moving elsewhere, empties them again. No sound accompanies this moving from place to place. When it reaches the corner, where the circle of light of the street lamps cuts the sidewalk in two, the shadow halts for a moment, clings to the wall, blending with it, and disappears. Everything is motionless once again: the circle of light illuminating the middle of the street and cutting through the right angle formed by the sidewalks at the four corners, breaking off at the culverts and the curbs, is still there; the immense trees of the main square, the church in shadow, the electric bulbs in the lamp posts scattered about the square that barely light vague, partial portions of the trees are still there; the black, hard leaves that stand out against the black outlines of the trees silhouetted against the sky in which the damp mist hides the stars are still there. For an incalculable time, seconds, minutes, hours, a time whose duration is in the last analysis of lesser importance or impossible to measure since the interstices that intersect it—if interstices intersect it—answer to no sort of scale or measure, nothing happens in the town, fast asleep and except for the imperceptible interruption and the imperceptible starting up again that no human ear, even if concentrating its attention to the maximum, could have, even vaguely, heard. For a good while nothing happens: and then, slowly, flexibly, the shadow detaches itself from the wall near the corner and ventures out into the light: what appears is a man, without any definite identifying feature, a man in whom everything is vagueness and caution, in the sharply defined line that separates the area lighted by the street lamp and the shadow. The man crosses the street and reaches the public square, taking very long strides that make no noise on the sandy ground. He appears to hesitate for a moment, pondering what direction he should follow or calculating, rather, the itinerary on which he will find himself less exposed to the indiscretion of the light, and finally starts walking diagonally across the square: his steps are long, regular, rhythmic, resolute, and the general attitude of his person varies between the obvious desire to pass unnoticed and an air of false naturalness intended to allay the suspicion of any possible passer-by. He is crossing the square diagonally, he is crossing the square diagonally, more or less visible amid the dim lights and the areas of shadow, at a regular pace. Now he sees him reach the corner opposite the square, leap quickly over the culvert, cross the street, and disappear once again amid the shadows of the side street. Now he sees him arriving at the white house. There is not a sound coming from the house. The windows open to the stifling darkness of the early morning hours allow no light to come through; and the house is as though suffocated, as though crushed between the immense black trees along the sidewalk. Now he sees the blurred figure opening the big door at the rear, and sneaking, without making the slightest sound, into the yard; and he sees, at the other end of the yard, toward the back, toward the trees, the beige patch that is beginning to move about anxiously. The man's figure, blurred, vague, as it advances, slowly raises its hand to its trousers pocket, and swiftly, with a resolute movement, takes out the pistol. He is now almost alongside the animal, which is moving about, hesitantly. The hand, slowly, raises the pistol, aiming toward the horse's head:

no. No: it is not possible; leaning forward, as he rows, Tilty shakes his head. No: it is not possible; the hand with the pistol must not be raised, from out of the darkness, nor the detonation ring out, transforming the night. The sun beams upriver, and on pushing himself backward with all his muscles tense, moving the oars forward underwater, Tilty sees the white house, half hidden by the trees, and the bathers moving about, reduced in size now because of the distance, on the yellow beach or at the water's edge.

Because of the storm that darkens the morning, the river is as though turned to steel and so calm that the wake which the green boat has been leaving behind it remains unchanged, in the same place, showing the boat's trajectory. It can be said that not the slightest breeze is stirring: the trees, a little greener, a little more motionless, that half submerge the house, also appear to be thicker and denser in the air that has turned pitch-dark. In the lowering sky, smoke-gray clouds form in endless chains with a thick edge, like steel lacework. Only the fat man, the beach attendant, is standing on the beach, close to the water's edge, his arms folded across his bare chest, his bare head showing his tanned bald spot. He has turned in his direction now and is watching him get out of the boat. A flash of lightning blanches, for a fraction of a second, the black morning in which the storm would seem to have deposited, at random, here and there, after days and days, a little reality.

One in each hand, the bundles of fodder balance each other and allow him to walk forward, rigid, his arms held slightly apart from his body and his hands holding tightly onto the place where the ends of the wire around the bundles come together. A flash of lightning, prolonged, greenish, drains all the color, momentarily, from the landscape, like bad stage lighting.

The house appears to be deserted, empty: the open windows afford a glimpse of the semi-darkness inside. Tilty turns his head toward the fat man, who has turned around toward him, still on the riverbank, so as to watch him cross the space that separates the green boat anchored a little farther from the beach, downstream from the white house.

Turned toward the left, Tilty's head—whose eyes meet those of the beach attendant—is lifted slightly; the round-brimmed straw hat, that has taken on a shape that fits the contours of his skull, tilts, following the movement of his head, leaning, rigidly, backward.

At the same time as he turns once again in the opposite direction, so that he is once more facing the white house, Tilty's head comes back down again so that the straw hat once more assumes its horizontal position.

He has just barely glimpsed, as he turns his head again, the gesture with which the fat man has answered his greeting: it consisted of removing a hand from his chest, raising it to shoulder height, with the fingers apart and the palm turned outward, and waving it for a moment, feebly, in that position: a pale flash of lightning flares and goes out.

In the morning, darkened by the imminent downpour, the white façade gives off a dull splendor: as he slowly approaches it, with the two bundles of fodder, one in each hand, held by the knot where the two ends of the wire meet, as he slowly leaves behind the green boat anchored on the shore, having turned his head for a moment, as a greeting, toward the beach attendant who must still be watching him from the water's edge with his arms folded on his bare chest, Tilty begins to make out the vacant spaces of the windows that afford a glimpse of the pale half-light inside. His espadrilles, worn to shreds, slap rhythmically on the bone-dry sand. No shadow follows him or precedes him. His body, clearly outlined in the dark, transparent air, moves forward rigidly, balanced between the two bundles of fodder that sway imperceptibly at his sides, approaching the white house on whose lateral façade there intertwine, enormous, the branches of the trees. But his head, stuffed inside the broad-brimmed straw hat, is sunk between his twisted shoulders: though it has no hump, his body nonetheless has a strange shape from his mid-chest up. It is as though his imperfect bust belonged to another body, to another man, and had been coupled, hastily and without coinciding completely with it, to Tilty's body. And he continues to walk on slowly, carrying the bundles of fodder, one in each hand, the two bundles at the same height, as though the level of his shoulders were compensated by the unequal length of his arms and also of the sleeves of his faded shirt. His movements are slow, regular, exterior in the darkened air, his entire silhouette outlined by a glittering gray nimbus against the lowering, smoke-colored sky. A flash of lightning blanches, for a fraction of a second, the dark air. From somewhere, two birds, chasing each other with irregular darts and thrusts, always at the same distance as though they were the fixed parts of an unmodifiable set and being made to shift places by a single mechanism, cross the sky before Tilty's eyes, which follow their trajectory as they vanish in the trees that bend down over the lateral wall of the white house, disappearing amid the leaves. As he advances, Tilty's body leaves vacant, and more and more vast, the space that separates his body from the green boat, the empty space

full of a dull and uniform light with a watery transparency.
The space that separates his body from the boat gradually
stretches out: exterior to the calm outside of the whole,
opaque and rough, forming part of the rough and opaque
masses—trees, the beach attendant, grills, the boat, the white
house—scattered as though at random and helter-skelter
between the lowering, smoke-colored sky, and the yellowish
earth, in the transparent air, as if by miracle, Tilty's body,
with each movement, does not leave its imprint in that air,
multiplying itself to the infinite in an infinity of motionless
poses, along the entire length of its trajectory. Now the sparse
grass, standing slightly straighter because of the imminence of
the downpour, crackles beneath the espadrilles worn to
shreds, and the space that separates Tilty from the house is of a
pale green that contrasts with the ashen yellow of the beach. A
peal of thunder, the sound following the flash of pale light that
has illuminated the darkened air for a few seconds, makes the
entire space shiver for an instant: a slight tremor causes, for a
fraction of a second, the pupils of Tilty's eyes to vibrate,
whereupon he resolutely steps up his pace: beneath the trees,
the black car, parked almost directly into the ditch at an
oblique angle because of the steep slope of the cambered
street, increases little by little in volume, discontinuously, as
Tilty approaches the house. Now the espadrilles slap on the
hard sidewalk and Tilty, beneath the immense treetops that
darken the air, goes past the two black windows that open out
in the side wall of the white house. A flash of lightning
blanches the air, for a fraction of a second. Tilty goes past the
black car and leaves it behind him: when he emerges, rigid,
exterior, walking at a regular pace, at the back door, a clap of
thunder, far in the distance, begins to make its way
earthward.

VI He begins to enter, slowly, as into a swamp, the tanned woman, who takes him inside her with a concentrated silence, her eyes closed, her mouth half open, her upper lip drawn back revealing four opaque teeth, the cavity of her mouth enveloped in a reddish semi-darkness. His mouth clings to her half-open lips. His hands, which search first for her thick, soft breasts, glide sideways to her ribs and meet at her sweaty back, touch each other for a moment and move down lower to her buttocks, taking possession of them: his hands knead and squeeze the soft flesh, inducing the woman to arch her body in such a way that it is no longer supported by the bed—apart from her head resting on the pillow flattened by the motionless kiss—except for her shoulder blades and the soles of her feet: the rest is in the air, in tension, holding up the body of Cat who, as into a swamp, has made his way inside her.

The rhythm has become regular now: the upper part of their bodies, from the waist up, is motionless, Cat's face flattened against Elisa's left shoulder, Elisa's emerging above Cat's left shoulder, their eyes closed, sweat giving their skin a uniform luster, the chest and belly of each of them flattened against the other's, the bed accompanying with a rhythmic creak the regular movement that their bodies are engaged in from the waist down: Cat's going up and down, up and down, in and out, in and out, the woman performing a circular movement of her abdomen that accompanies and complements Cat's movement, his buttocks falling and rising, giving him the complexity of a system of combined pulleys and pistons in which a slight, recurrent irregularity of motion not only is not out of place but contributes to lending a certain harmonious complexity to the whole.

The woman's moans, whose frequency is prolonged and whose intensity gradually increases, resound above the monotonous background of Cat's panting until, all at once, the circular movement of the woman's belly and the repeated movement up and down of Cat's buttocks, cease, for the space of a few seconds, before the final writhe, a violent flailing of hips that is repeated three, four, five times, accompanied by a series of outcries, laments, obscenities, sighs, exclamations that fill the ashen air of the room.

On his knees, Cat sinks his chin between Elisa's parted legs, amid the black hair of her pubis. Standing alongside the bed, Elisa is holding her body rigid and bent slightly backward, so that it is her belly which juts out, while her bronze shoulder is at a more or less oblique angle to her waist. Her shoulders are perhaps shaking because her hands are stroking Cat's head, buried between her thighs, and because of the position of her body, her arms are stretched out as far as they will reach so as to touch his fair hair.

On the bed, Elisa, on all fours, her face nearly touching the wall, her hands leaning on the pillow, is waiting, without impatience, for Cat, who is moving toward her, on his knees, from the other end of the bed, to begin to part, with sweaty hands, her buttocks, the lower part of which reveal a horizontal whitish area, the one contrast on her bronze-colored body. When, following an arduous search, Cat finally enters her, Elisa emits a hoarse, deep, prolonged moan, and slowly lets herself fall, face downward, till she is lying stretched out on the bed, with Cat clinging to her like an iron filing to the surface of a magnet.

Unhurriedly, Elisa lets fall into the transparent pitcher, full
of water up to just a little above halfway, spoonfuls of loose
sugar which she takes out of the white sugar bowl. When she
stirs it with the spoon, with vigorous movements, the water
becomes cloudy and then, as it settles, while Elisa is cutting the
three lemons into four pieces each, it regains something of its
original transparency. Then it is the dropping of the lemons
inside that agitates it once again. Finally Elisa takes ice out of
the refrigerator, drops a number of cubes inside the pitcher,
and begins briskly stirring the mixture again. Cat picks the ice
tray up off the kitchen table, fills it with water, and puts it
back in the refrigerator. There is not a sound in the entire
house, save for the tinkle of the spoon, the flow of the water
pouring into the ice tray, the door of the refrigerator opening
and closing, the nearly imperceptible swish of their bare feet
gliding over the red tiles.

By late afternoon, the bathers have come back again:
arriving on foot in a steady stream if they are from the town
itself, or by car if they are coming from the city. They have
proceeded to spread their multi-colored towels out on the
sand, depositing next to their clothes and their beach bags
heaped up in a pile, cigarettes, matches, their afternoon snack,
jars of cream and bottles of tanning lotion. In order to avoid
the unbearable midday heat, they had taken refuge in dark
rooms, protected from the sun by thick curtains of blue, red,
orange canvas, by awnings with broad stripes, green and
white. Some of them slowly venture down to the riverbank
and contemplate, beyond the smooth, caramel-colored
stream, the vegetation of the island, stunted and dusty, dotted
here and there with large calcined flowers. Others barely take
the time necessary to remove their clothes before they head
for the water at a run and enter it, raising a din of aquatic
sounds and loud splashing. The fat man, with a white helmet
pulled down tightly over his head, threads his way, attentive,
bored, amid the bodies lying stretched out. Cat raises his glass

of lemonade, takes a long sip, and walks away from the
window toward the kitchen: he is stark naked, but seen from
outside, from the beach, he looks in no way different from
before since the lower part of his body, from the waist down,
is not visible from there.

Cat picks the lemonade pitcher up off the blue and white
checkered tablecloth, strewn with the already hardened bread
crumbs from lunch, and fills his glass again. A little piece of
ice, whose shape of a cube has melted down considerably,
slides with a tinkle out of the pitcher into the glass. With the
glass in his hand, Cat heads toward the blue canvas curtain
that separates the kitchen from the porch and pushes it back a
little with his free hand, so as to look into the backyard: the
back of one of the orange-colored deck chairs, the rusted
corrugated tin oil drums, a portion of the ground strewn with
batteries and tires half-buried and rotting away, stained with
dried mud, and farther off, in the very back, underneath the
trees, the yellow-white horse which, at the very moment that
Cat pulls the curtain aside, sneezes with a violent shake of its
head. Cat lets go of the curtain that continues to move, rough
and rigid.

For some inexplicable reason, Elisa has placed her watch on
her left wrist; more inexplicable still insofar as she didn't have
it on when she came back from the city, and insofar as she now
finds herself naked, sitting on the bed, her back leaning
against the pillow rolled up into a ball, between her back and
the wall, and holding a cigarette that she is smoking between
the index and middle fingers of her right hand. On the night
table, next to the turned-off fan, is her empty glass. On seeing
Cat come into the room, Elisa raises her eyes from the book
that she is holding in her left hand and murmurs:
  "Will you pour me a little more lemonade?"
  She closes the book and lays it down on the night table: it is
the one that Pigeon has sent from France. Elisa shakes the ash

off her cigarette onto the little plate that contains the remains
of the mosquito coil. Without saying a word, Cat puts his
own glass down on the night table and picks up the empty
one. As the window that overlooks the street is closed, the air
in the room is sultry and seems as though it were mixed with
an indefinable odor. Everything is enveloped in a yellowish
half-light.

"Does it still burn?" Cat asks.

Elisa smiles and shakes her head. She picks up the glass full
of lemonade and takes a long sip, and then puts it back down
on the night table. The glass, which still has a little lemonade
in it, now occupies exactly the same place as the empty glass
did, the one that Cat is now carrying off toward the kitchen.

Cat picks the pitcher of lemonade up off the blue and white
checked tablecloth strewn with the already hardened bread
crumbs from lunch and fills Elisa's empty glass. Two little
pieces of ice slide with a tinkle out of the pitcher into the glass.
Cat puts the pitcher, now nearly empty, back down on the
table. The sides of the pitcher are streaked with cold drops and
the glass looks misted over down close to the base. Through
the glass there can be seen, piled up on the bottom, the pieces
of lemon, their pulp no longer anything but a series of lifeless
and colorless filaments. Leaving the full glass on the table, Cat
walks over to the curtain of rigid blue canvas, and with the
back of his outstretched fingers separates it a little from the
black door frame in order to have a look at the backyard
through the opening; the light from outside illuminates his
face, eaten into by his reddish beard. Outside are the deck
chairs of orange-colored canvas, the rusted, corrugated tin oil
drums, the ground strewn with tires and batteries half-buried
amid the bone-dry grass, the yellow-white horse chewing
fodder, at the far end of the yard, underneath the trees.

When he turns around, after letting go of the blue canvas
curtain that is still moving at his back, Cat sees Elisa enter the

kitchen, coming, naked, barefoot, and with the glass in her hand, from the bedroom. With a movement of his head, Cat makes a sign in the direction of the backyard. As if she hadn't seen him, Elisa goes on walking toward the table. Now both of them come over, from the opposite ends of the room, to the table covered with the blue and white checkered table- cloth on top of which, alongside the full glass and amid the already hardened bread crumbs from lunch, stands the pitcher of lemonade.

"How thirsty you are," Cat says, seeing Elisa pour herself her third glass of lemonade. Elisa puts the empty pitcher back on the blue and white checkered tablecloth: in her glass, a little more than halfway full, the grayish liquid is still cloudy, filled with bits of lemon pulp and incompletely dissolved grains of sugar that twist and turn about in the middle of a minuscule whirlpool.

The four words, that keep echoing strangely in the kitchen, and that have rung out clearly accompanying the sound of the liquid as it poured into the glass, receive no reply. It is because of their sudden, harsh sound that it becomes noticeable that, for a few seconds, not one noise or so much as a single voice comes from the beach.

They are standing on either side of the table, naked, Cat with his back to the blue canvas curtain through which the afternoon light still shows, though more feebly, Elisa with her back to the black door that leads to the inside bedrooms, leaning over toward the glass half full of lemonade, not paying attention to the hesitant smile of Cat, the odd reso- nance of whose words little by little disappears from the yellowish air, from hearing, and finally from memory.

When her hand touches the glass, the fingers grasp the cold outside of it, and lift it, tilting it, in the direction of her mouth, as her head is tossed slightly backwards. Her naked body, of lustrous bronze, alongside the table, quivers imperceptibly when the glass touches her half-open lips and the hand that is grasping it begins to empty it into her mouth: a complicated muscular movement attests to the passage of the sweet-and-sour liquid down her tense throat.

The glass is now horizontal, almost empty, her head thrown back, her hair black and smooth, loose and short, touching her bronze shoulder and Cat, who has remained motionless, watching Elisa's throat quiver as the liquid goes down, turns abruptly and, going over to the blue canvas curtain with the yellow light still showing through it, separates it a little way from the black door frame with the back of his left hand so as to look outside: the deck chair of orange-colored canvas, the rusty, corrugated oil drums, the space strewn with tires and old batteries half-buried amid the scorched weeds and, farther on, at the back of the yard, the beige horse whose long neck stretches toward the ground looking for something to graze on.

When he withdraws his hand and turns around again, the blue canvas curtain continues to move at his back as do the veins of light projected at his feet, on the red tiles. His bare feet tread on the reflection in movement, which fleetingly imprints itself on them, and then leave it behind as Elisa, who has straightened her head to an erect position, now stretches out her hand with the empty glass so as to leave it on the blue and white checkered tablecloth.

A shout comes, all of a sudden, from the beach, broken, discontinuous, emerging from its nothingness without, to all appearances, seeking a precise destination, a neutral vocal emission that someone brings forth out of the blackness not in order to say something but to see how, in violent jerks, quavering, hesitant, a shout comes into being.

On seeing him arrive with the tack the beige horse, without rebelling, becomes uneasy. Slight movements of its head, as though it were chasing away non–existent insects, the motionless tail that betrays its expectation and the gaze that is fixed on any point of space except on the human figure that is approaching carrying in its hand the riding gear, allow one to surmise that since Cat has left the house, put on his espadrilles on the step, picked up the saddle and the reins from underneath the trees and begun to walk toward the animal, making the leather creak and the metal rings of the reins tinkle, the beige horse has put itself on the defensive and for a moment has ceased to do anything except to be mistrustful. Its aura is, as Cat can attest when he comes within range of it, not only still warmer than the remainder of the air and possessed of a particular odor in which chewed hay and fresh dung are recognizable constituents, but also thicker and giving off, as though in gusts, a bewildered hostility.

Not without rearing up, the beige equine has finally given in, allowing itself to be saddled. Accepting the saddle with swift movements of its head and violent jerks of its entire body, all it manages to do, when he mounts it, is to take two or three nervous steps backwards, flexing its hind legs a little and placing its back in a position slanting slightly backward. It straightens up again and obeys the reins unwillingly, beginning to take short steps, half off to one side, tossing its head every so often and thrusting its chest out as though by so doing it were attempting to deaden an unexpected impact. It passes through the rear door of the yard, crosses the sidewalk, goes past the black car covered with whitish dust parked heading almost directly into the ditch, underneath the trees, and begins to go down the cambered, shady street toward the river.

The little beach stretching out to his left, turned to chaos by the late afternoon bathers, is now only a new recollection sinking into his memory and a sound of voices, laughter and splashing heard behind him which gradually fades away as the beige mount trots along the riverbank toward the almost orange-colored and greenish horizon behind the stunted trees scattered here and there over the yellowish strand.

The blue shadow of horse and rider, enlarged, follows them swiftly, gliding across the sandy ground full of crumbly craters that fall to pieces at the fleeting blow of the horse's hoofs. With his feet fitted into the stirrups, Cat's legs flank the horse's belly and his back remains rigid, jolted by the regular trot that imparts sudden shudders along the entire length of his body. With rapid, repeated goads in its flanks with his heels, and loosening the reins a little, Cat spurs the animal into a gallop. The beige horse abruptly changes the rhythm of its running, as though it had shifted, not to another speed, but to a new dimension of which a gallop is no more than a screen that conceals—unlike the trot where each detail is more visible—the infinite effort of each movement thanks to which each detail and all of the whole change place in space, in infinitesimal and brusque increments.

With its neck stretched toward the water, its front hoofs submerged in the river, the beige horse noisily slakes its thirst, as Cat, leaning forward, holding the loose reins with one hand, strokes the ash-colored hairs of its mane with the other. The calm sky, which is slowly turning red, gives the water, in which it is reflected, a violet tint. Without a sound, the river flows along smoothly, slowly, and the horse's pink tongue breaks the surface with skill and restraint. Cat raises his head and contemplates the space round about him; there is nothing, nothing. The smooth river, without a single ripple, the yellow sand, and on the other side, in the twilight that the mosquitoes are beginning to disturb and that the approach of nightfall does not cool off, empty, the tangled, stunted vegetation at the water's edge, two weeping willows growing on a slant with their foliage dangling limply down toward the river, the yellow bank that imperceptibly slopes down to the shore, half worn away by the water, the island.

VII

It is earth, air, fire, water. And the old batteries and old tires, and the oil drums too. They are blinding. The animal that contemplates me, circumspectly, from the far end of the yard, now that I am coming out onto the porch, having just bathed, just shaved, with the glass of white wine in my hand, walking toward Elisa, who gives me a vacuous smile, from the deck chair, as she drinks, is no doubt a little more real than I am, slightly more concrete—and no doubt it knows it. There is an immense calm: from the beach, in the blue light plagued by mosquitoes and by a shrill chorus of cicadas, no voice, or almost none, carries this far any more, at this hour: the few sounds, the muffled shouts, linger on in the sultry night air without a breeze, attenuated by a silence that is louder than all the voices and all the sounds. They are blinding, because they hide nothing. One's gaze rebounds, becomes fixed once again, and rebounds yet again, in the space of February, the unreal month, that arrives in order to place, like a number standing for all of time, the evidence on the table. Not things, but lumps, transitory knots that come apart, or slowly come undone as they interweave and that immediately, in the blink, so to speak, of an eye, begin interweaving once again. I dismounted from the horse, tied it to a huisache bush, and went in among the stunted trees that spring up from the yellow earth. The sandy soil, full of crumbly craters that fell to pieces from the pressure of my espadrilles, gradually began, as I went farther away from the water, to be covered with sparse grass, until I entered the underbrush: it reached at least as far up as my knees. It kept crackling underneath my feet. There was no other sound to be heard except for the rustle of my footsteps amid the underbrush which, when I stopped, stopped in turn, but not before still resounding and echoing for a few seconds more in my memory before it was dead silent once more. Each crackle of my espadrilles on the scorched leaves, emerging from nothingness, began to vibrate and resonate for a moment only to be buried, yet again, amid endless intervals of silence, before being reborn once again, in nothingness. Walking along slowly, stopping every so often, I left the dense underbrush behind and came out onto a field of esparto grass; between each tall, dark green plant, the narrow sharp-pointed leaves, so long that they grew a little way upward and then doubled back toward the ground, the whitish soil, less sandy and firmer than that closer to the water, seemed to glisten in the last light of late afternoon or to reverberate still from the accumulated heat of the day or of the entire summer. The open field was in front of me: the thick, dark plants, with sharp-pointed leaves, which no longer cast a shadow, separated by two or three yards of empty space between them, scattered about at random, though giving the impression of an illusory order, the white earth hardened by the persistent February light, stretching out in this way to the horizon, the ash-gray, featureless sky above, and behind, the memory-machine reducing to a pulp the recent crackling of my footsteps on the scorched underbrush and lowering it to the bottom. For a few seconds nothing happened: my gaze, that bounced at random against the dark plants, whose leaves, as sharp-pointed as knives, looked as though they were enhaloed by a tenuous radiance, did not encounter, in the vast open space, any precise point on which to focus itself, came and went, bounding back and forth from the dark plants to the whitish earth, from the whitish earth to the ash-gray sky, from the ash-gray sky back once again to the tall, dark plants. There was nothing to indicate, nothing behind, in front, higher up, that there might be, in some other dimension, or among things themselves, an invisible something whose manifestation one might some day hope for. The old-style infinite was now nothing more than an indefinite juxtaposition of things of which it was not possible for me to perceive more than a few at the same time—and there was no sequel whatsoever to that perception, unless it were in one's fallacious memory. From that naked, scorched earth that was the only lesson I came by. And in this frame of mind I retraced my steps, mounted the beige horse and the two of us started back toward the house: at a gallop first, at a trot a little later on, leaving behind the violet sky and the deserted riverbanks, beneath the gaze of the last remaining bathers, when, arriving from the open countryside along the water's edge, we turned off a little way before reaching the beach so as to go up the cambered street and come into the backyard, amid a cloud of mosquitoes and the chirring of the cicadas. The yard was deserted; on the porch, there was nothing but the deck chairs of orange-colored canvas, both empty, and farther in the background, between the two black doors—the one to the kitchen covered by the blue canvas curtain—, the chair of rough-hewn wood with a straw seat standing against the white wall. In a sweat I removed the saddle; the beige horse didn't even deign to pant. I freed him of the saddle and the reins, brought him a little fodder, and stroked his neck and his muzzle several times: outward gestures whose purpose was to drive away, from myself more than from my mount, a vague uneasiness, a tell-tale sign of jealousy or hatred. Then I tore myself away, as best I could, from his aura, consisting of a strong odor and warmth. I crossed the yard strewn with batteries and tires, went up onto the porch, entered the house. The kitchen was empty, but from the bathroom there came the sound of an open faucet: Elisa, in her white dress again, was combing her wet hair and smiled distractedly at me in the mirror. I put my hand, gently, on her bare arm: the hand working the comb through her black hair fell and came to rest on the white washstand. We remained motionless for a moment, looking at each other in the mirror; the contact of my hand on her bare arm, which was still giving off the cool dampness of her recent shower was not, however, from the point of view of a possible experience, any more revealing than the one that I could have obtained by stretching out my hand and touching the mirror at the place on its surface where Elisa's arm was reflected. Smooth or rough, mineral or carnal, the result was no clearer or the penetration deeper; at some point, the horizon of the contact became, no matter what object it touched, smooth, uniform, and without any great meaning. Elisa shook her arm free and went on combing her hair, and at that point I turned around and went out of the bathroom. In the living room, I squatted for a moment alongside the cardboard boxes and plunged a hand into the white envelopes that the jolting of the car had disordered as it transported them. I took out the telephone book from among the envelopes, quickly glanced through it and left it on the table. I opened the drawer of the commode, pushing aside the papers, the corkscrew, the revolver, the bullets that had fallen out of the square cardboard box rolling around in the bottom of the drawer as my hand rummaged about, I took out two or three ballpoint pens, and covering the revolver and the bullets with the sheets of paper again, I closed the drawer. Without sitting down, I tried out the pens on the back of an envelope: they all wrote. I took a pile of envelopes out of the cardboard box and put them on the table. I sat down to work. I copied the name and address of the first subscriber onto the first envelope. As I was copying the seventh one, Elisa came out of the bathroom, and sat down across from me, on the other side of the table. But she stood up again immediately; she said that there was almost no cold white wine left, and that she was going to put two or three bottles in the refrigerator. I stood up too: I left the ballpoint pen on the telephone book, opened to the letter A, went into the bathroom and shaved. I kept seeing, in the mirror, how the little electric shaver removed, along with the white lather, my week-old reddish beard, and how my skin remained smooth, tanned, almost copper-colored, in the place where my beard had been before. Before taking a shower I passed by the kitchen. Standing at the counter, Elisa was opening a bottle of white wine with the corkscrew. She removed the cork from the opener and left it on the table. When I went through the living room again, heading for the bathroom, I noticed that the drawer of the chest was half-way open and closed it. Underneath the shower, for the space of a few seconds I didn't think about anything: that the water was falling, enveloping me in its dense sound, of which it could not be said that it was interfering with the transmission of any message. Finally I turned the shower off, dried myself, went and looked at myself in the mirror again, thinking that after all, what the mirror was reflecting so clearly was, doubtless, me, my very own self, and putting on my shorts, slipping on my espadrilles, I went through the living room in the direction of the kitchen, feeling the air, the night air, again, warmer than my skin from which the coolness of the shower was disappearing, leaving only the dampness. In the kitchen I poured myself a glass of white wine, dropped an ice cube into it, and then put the bottle back inside the refrigerator. There reached me, from the distance, from close by, from the whole length of the riverbank, the chirring of the cicadas. I headed for the porch. Walking across the lighted kitchen, before reaching, before having even touched the blue canvas curtain which separated the kitchen from the porch and which, motionless and rigid, kept anyone from receiving the slightest impression from the outside, I saw the porch with its red tiles and the orange-colored deck chairs, the oil drums, the yard strewn with old batteries and half-rotted tires amid the bone-dry weeds and above all, at the rear, underneath the eucalyptuses, continually shaking its tail and head so as to chase away the mosquitoes that must, without a doubt, be plaguing it, the big palpitating yellowish body, denser than I was, more solid,

more immersed in life. I went through the blue canvas
curtain, came out onto the porch with the cold glass in my
hand, and smile now at Elisa who, in turn, sitting in the deck
chair, as she takes a sip of wine, gives me a vacuous smile from
above the glass. The beige horse, for a fraction of a second, has
remained motionless on seeing me coming, and it now begins
once again to switch its tail and shake its head, contemplating
me. There is an immense calm: from the beach, in the blue
light, plagued by mosquitoes and by a shrill chorus of cicadas,
no voice, or almost none, carries this far any more, at this
hour: the few sounds, the muffled shouts linger on in the
slowly deepening dusk, without a breeze, attenuated by a
silence that is louder than all the voices, and all the sounds.
One's gaze rebounds, becomes fixed once again, and
rebounds yet again, in the space of February, the unreal
month, that arrives in order to place, like a number standing
for all of time, the evidence on the table.

"How far did you go?" Elisa asks.

"Not very far. Along the riverbank," I say.

Elisa shakes her head and sits there in silence, in a thoughtful
mood.

"I went a little way inland, on foot," I say.

Elisa makes a gesture that consists of violently shaking her
shoulders and her head at the same time, clamping her teeth
together and breathing in this way, producing a sort of
prolonged, moist hiss: that attitude is meant to demonstrate
her repugnance and her terror. Open countryside, she says,
and in the daytime above all, in the sunlight, makes her feel
panicky. She always has the impression that *something, something* is hidden among the weeds, merely waiting for someone
to walk by in order to show itself openly.

"Something?" I say. "What do you mean, something?
Something that what?"

Something, yes, that's right, Elisa says: something that
suddenly appears, something alive, or dead, amid the weeds,
or in the distance, in the sunlight; and above all, something in

a state of decomposition: there's no dearth of that in the countryside, right?, Elisa says. In open country, amid the weeds, lots of things, isn't that so?: poisonous snakes even, bones, predatory animals of all sorts and, above all, right?, above all, carrion, bodies decomposing, out of which a murmur suddenly emerges. As though *something*, I don't know, she says, *something* had risen to the surface from the depths of the earth.

My incredulous smile makes her shrug her shoulders, and falling silent, she takes a long sip of white wine. She sits there staring into empty space, with her eyes opened wide, her upper lip hidden by her lower one, which becomes fuller, protruding a little and showing its deep red inner surface. A mosquito lands on her forehead, takes off and comes back and lands on her cheek, falling motionless on it. A fraction of a second goes by; all of a sudden, Elisa's free hand lying on the armrest of the deck chair comes up, open, and slaps her cheek with her palm. Too late: the mosquito, heaven knows how, or when, has taken off again, a fraction of a second before her hand reaches her cheek, and disappears. Elisa's hand moves downward once again. Everything is already black, clearly outlined, against the air of a uniform dark blue, in which nothing sparkles or moves except for the beige form from which there emanates an opaque brightness, like that of rust, and from which one intuits, amid the sporadic, cautious movements, the damp, almost lilac-colored eyes, focused every so often on the spot on the porch on which I am standing, turned toward Elisa. I take a drink of wine: the icy, acid liquid, of a yellowish green, gradually disappears from the glass as it goes down my throat, until it is gone altogether; I tilt the glass a bit farther above my lips and the little piece of ice that was still in the bottom comes sliding down the cold surface of the glass and into my mouth through my half-open lips. I take the glass away from my mouth and begin sucking the little piece of ice, shifting it, with my tongue, from one side of my mouth to the other, making it hit against my teeth, reappear for a moment, held tightly by my teeth, between my half-open lips. I finally spit it out now, aiming it toward the ground of the backyard. And where does it come from? I ask Elisa, without looking at her, turned toward the earthen backyard, where does that fear of coming across, in the countryside, nowhere else but in the countryside, those forgotten bodies decomposing in the inclement weather, come from? She doesn't know. She doesn't know, she says, but that's how it is. It is now beginning to become hard to discern her gestures clearly in the semi-darkness. I can still see her features, and above all, the coarse white linen dress that, in the blue air that is now turning black, emits a sort of phosphorescence. Our voices are now audible above a vague, intermittent murmur that the town projects into the growing darkness, a murmur in which the buzz of mosquitoes stubbornly hovering around us stands out, and the strident chirring of the cicadas, more constant and louder, although it distracts one's attention less, owing doubtless to its monotonous persistence. She doesn't know, Elisa says. She doesn't know, but that's how it is. If a murderer, she argues, wanted to get rid of a corpse, where would it occur to him to make it disappear? In the countryside.

"Or in the river," I say. "Two nice heavy blocks of cement, one tied to each foot, and bye-bye."

Elisa doesn't appear to have heard my suggested alternative: no, to her way of thinking, the right place is the open countryside, among the weeds. She explains her reasons with obsessive minuteness. The urban man will bury the evidence in the country, at night, among the weeds, thereby believing himself freed from it forever—leaving it behind, in the depths of the earth, which is the place where, as we know, the past lies. The next day, however, Elisa goes on, twirling her glass now between the palms of her hands, her gleaming white dress and her face barely discernible in the clammy growing darkness, the next day the dogs of the neighborhood are bound to come, to discover the ground that has been stirred up, and begin to dig, till they bring the evidence into the light of day. No, as she well knows: it's better not to venture out into the countryside, so as not to be the one responsible for discovering, and, in the name of everyone, disclosing the horror. Elisa falls silent. It is now altogether dark and from the town there comes, though muffled, a sound that is like a last lingering trace of fever. She must not see, from where she is sitting, my incredulous smile or my repeated headshaking. The empty glass is growing lukewarm in my hand. Shall we pour ourselves a little more wine? Yes. Elisa hands me her empty glass; though I can hardly see it I become aware of her gesture because of the creaking of the deck chair and the sudden monosyllable with which she answers my proposal, spoken with the slightly agitated voice of someone who is making a brusque movement while speaking. My fingers lightly touch hers as I take the luke-warm glass. I go into the kitchen. When I turn on the light and open the door of the refrigerator, leaning over to take out the bottle, placed vertically on the lowest shelf of the inside panel of the door, I can hear Elisa's voice at my back. I straighten up, with the bottle in my hand, and close the door, turning around and looking closely at Elisa, who is standing next to the blue canvas curtain; her stiff white dress, full of horizontal wrinkles at her belly, stands out, in a more intense way than her tanned skin, smooth and sweaty, and her black hair, against the blue background of the curtain. Hey, Cat, her voice has said. It has sounded odd, as if it had been uttered after a long hesitation, or as if it were the prelude to a question that had been postponed for a long time, or a discourse full of resolutions and arguments worked out after long reflection. But now that I observe her, as I stand with the cold bottle in my hand next to the refrigerator, waiting expectantly and questioning her with my eyes, Elisa, motionless in turn against the motionless background of the blue curtain, lowers her head and murmurs: no, never mind. It's nothing. I then pour white wine into the glasses, filling them halfway, and then I get ice cubes out of the white bowlful that Elisa has put in the refrigerator, and drop one into each of the glasses. When I turn around, with a glass in each hand, Elisa has vanished from the kitchen: the blue canvas curtain is still moving in the black door frame. When I, in turn, go through it, I find Elisa standing on the edge of the porch, looking out toward the far end of the yard, enveloped in dense, already black shadow. My eyes, accommodated to the light in the kitchen, make out nothing—or almost nothing—in the homogeneous blackness of the far end of the yard; but the light, coming from the kitchen, which the blue curtain lets through, shows the faint outline of objects and, above all, a trapezoidal section of the red-tiled floor. It is on this lighted section that I am standing as I hold Elisa's glass of wine out to her. Elisa turns around and takes it from me and goes to sit down in one of the deck chairs. I take the other one. We sip, for a moment, without saying a word to each other, swallows of white wine. Every so often, the tinkle of ice can be heard. Now that darkness has fallen the mosquitoes have settled down again, though a few are still buzzing about us. Clumsy, bewildered movements, the almost metallic sound of a tail that swishes back and forth now and again, come from the spot in the darkness, underneath the now invisible trees, where the beige horse is tirelessly grazing. What I fail to understand, I hear myself saying, is her fear of the country-side, when so many times I've seen her go into the river, as calmly as could be, even at night. Into that black water whose very contact is so frightening or where very often one feels the presence of live things that brush against one's skin, that prickle, and that even bite. That black water, I repeat, into which one makes one's way blindly. And yet, no, with water, she answers me, there's no problem. None.

"The thing is that everyone"—I hear myself say—"seeks in his or her own way, and finds, a particular thing that thereupon becomes impregnated with its own magic. Don't you think so?"

The light—a dim one—coming from the kitchen lightly
grazes Elisa's profile: one of the sides of her nose and part of
her cheekbone and the cheek on the same side glow slightly.
When she moves her head in an absent-minded, though
affirmative gesture, the light on her face shifts several times,
illuminating, fleetingly, her temple, the visible part of her
ear and the black hair hanging down over it. She now leans
her head back, which remains motionless against the canvas of
the chair, and the spot of light imprints itself on the white
dress, at the level of her bosom. And so there you have it, with
water, in the daytime or at night, she repeats, no problem. She
gives herself a sudden slap on the face—a fruitless one
perhaps—so as to crush a mosquito that must have landed on
her cheek. The sound of a car starting up in back, underneath
the trees, along the incline of the cambered street, is heard: one
of the last bathers, surely, who must have stayed on the beach,
having fallen asleep as night fell, or perhaps on the island,
from which he must have come back stroking slowly through
the blackened water. Humid, warm, the dark air—or, rather,
I myself—am set to trembling by the harsh sound with which
the engine takes off and which turns, almost immediately,
into a monotonous rumble from which there reaches the
porch in dense shadow the image of an illusory continuity.
By paying close attention I can perceive, nonetheless, the
infinitesimal break that interrupts, regularly, the line of
sound. The car must now be maneuvering so as to turn
around and head for the center of the town, and farther off,
the asphalt highway that leads to the city: the constant
changes of speed of the engine and the whine of the tires that
bite into the dust of the street and slide allow the progress of
the maneuvers to reach the porch. The beams of the head-
lights that suddenly pierce, beyond the entryway of the
yard, a cloud of whitish dust, the slow rotation of whose
particles, thanks to the intense brightness that cleaves it, can be
seen, amid the fleeting shadows interwoven with them, indicate that the car's rear end is finally facing the river and that

now, as is shown by the rapid movement of lights and shadows within the huge cloud of whitish dust, it is going up the cambered street toward the center of town and, farther on, the asphalt highway leading to the city. The car goes by the rear entryway, leaves it behind, and I see, through the interstices of the privet hedge that separates the back of the yard from the sidewalk, the two red points of the tail lights moving rigidly away in the air that is once again pitch black. Now there is no other sound to be heard, except for that of the engine, which dies away little by little: gradually moving off, it still permits one to perceive, every once in a while, the decreases in speed, the accelerations, the gear changes, the braking called for by the unevenness of the terrain it encounters en route. Now it is an almost inaudible sound. And now, finally, it is impossible to know whether the hum that one thinks one perceives is the last feeble filament of sound that the engine is sending forth, from a point no longer imaginable, or whether it is the muffled repercussion of its purr in one's memory. Now there is again a complete silence of which the shrill sound of the cicadas does not appear to be an interruption but rather, in view of its monotony and its uniformity, a different dimension that is all its own. And suddenly, once again, Elisa slaps herself, fruitlessly, perhaps, on the cheek. We drink, in the semi-darkness, at almost the same time, brief swallows of wine, without speaking. Elisa sighs; she raises her hand as though to give herself a third slap, but her hand stops before it reaches her cheek and begins to wave back and forth, forcefully, at the level of her face. She stands up, still waving her free hand in front of her face. On standing up, she has made the deck chair creak and now the light that the blue canvas curtain allows to come through from the kitchen strikes her foot—shod in the sandal with the strips of leather coiled around her calf that keep the bronze ring over her instep taut—, the side of her calf, and the hem of her white dress that comes halfway down her thighs. A ray of light filtering through the narrow opening separating the canvas curtain from the black door frame now touches, in turn, her blurred profile, making her nose stand out, the end of it giving off a sort of glow, and above all the thick, fleshy, closed lips, that pucker a little and move slightly, without parting. Elisa remains for a fraction of a second in that position, until she makes a curious movement, consisting of shaking her entire body, and her shoulders in particular, as though, in an anachronistic way, or a paradoxical one, rather, she had received, in the scorching night, an ice-cold breeze, and then, abruptly, she crosses the narrow space that separates her from the blue canvas curtain and, pushing it aside with the same hand that is holding the glass, enters the kitchen, receiving against her body, for the space of a few seconds, the full force of the light coming from the kitchen onto the porch, that the curtain, returning to its initial position, though still shaking, intercepts once again. What follows is a strange, nameless state, in which the present, *which is as wide as the whole of time is long*, seems to have risen, from who knows where, to the surface of who knows what, and in which what I was, that in and of itself, in no way amounted to much, now knows that it is here, in the present, knows it, without being able however to pursue its knowledge any farther and without having sought, in the fraction of a second prior to that state, by any means whatsoever, to catch a glimpse of it. This state is going away now; and now, in the darkness, the sounds, the murmurs, the chorus of cicadas, the barking of a dog at the other end of town, begin, gradually, to come unbound from each other, to separate, building up, out of the black, compact mass of night, levels, dimensions, heights, various distances, a structure of sounds that produce, in the uniform blackness, a precarious, fragile space, whose distribution in the blackness continuously changes shape, duration, and one might even say, to put it into words somehow, place. But now it is gone: it is as if an errant wave, a phosphorescent image of many colors combined in a harmonious way, had been reflected, on passing, for a few instants, through me, and had then continued on its way, leaving me in that other firmer, more permanent state, in which everything is within reach of my fingertips, with the same accessibility as a ship inside a bottle. I am drawn out of this drowsiness, after a few minutes, by the sounds coming from the kitchen. When I leave the blue canvas curtain behind, which goes on quivering and must be letting rays of shifting light pass over the floor of the porch, I find Elisa busy at the cutting board: with the kitchen knife she is slicing from a huge hunk of raw meat, little pieces that she is slowly dropping inside a hollow dish. The little strips of flesh are gradually accumulating in the bottom of the dish. Elisa, who has beamed at me, on hearing me come in, a quick smile, without interrupting what she is doing, has turned her head back around again so as to keep careful watch of her movements as she cuts, from the big chunk of meat which gradually diminishes in size, the little strips of a more or less regular thickness. The knife gradually reveals the reddish insides of the meat, criss-crossed by a filigree of nerves and fat, until the metallic knife blade hits, and shows, the bright convex surface of a white bone.

VIII

In the beginning there is nothing. Nothing. On one side the smooth, golden river, without a single ripple, the island with its bank that gradually slopes down to the water, the stunted, dusty vegetation, on the other the two windows and the black door, the roof of Spanish tiles, the white house, and in between the empty stretch of yellow beach, sloping almost imperceptibly down to the river, on which the sunlight, like a huge yellow conflagration traversed by white filaments, flows, rebounds and reverberates.

Sitting on the ground, his naked back leaning against the tree, the beach attendant is reading, in the total silence of siesta time, the comic book that is resting on his sloping thighs as though on a lectern. When he raises his head, his gaze, instead of becoming fixed on some precise object, seems, rather, to dissipate, to vanish in the empty space of the beach that ends, in the distance, in a stunted, ashen-colored wall of trees from which there stand out two weeping willows bending toward the river; that motion, mechanical, somnambulistic, is repeated every so often, it lasts for a few seconds and, once completed, his head leans back again and his gaze continues to peruse the juxtaposed squares filled with colored images. When he reaches the last square of the right-hand page, the beach attendant turns the page and fixes his gaze on the uppermost image of the new page; without taking his eyes from the colored squares for a second he scratches, mechanically, the sparse and graying hair on his chest, between the bulging, flaccid nipples, alongside the regulation metal whistle hanging from the blackish string around his neck, and then he lets his hand fall to the ground, the back of it lying ignored on the scanty, ash-colored grass. The tree beneath which he has seated himself so as to protect himself from the afternoon sun, lets through its drooping, whitish foliage luminous patches of light that imprint themselves on everything on the ground around them, on the colored images of the comic book and on his motionless body, barely disturbed by the slight, regular intake of his nearly imperceptible breathing.

The substance of which that light is made—the light that flows and bounces off the deserted space of the river and the beach, off the great semi-circle of trees that surrounds, without moving, the beach, off the white house—gives the impression of being, though arid, transparent, and seemingly fills all the air with a yellow and white spluttering, scattered in such a way that the sky itself, in which not a single cloud is to be seen, pales by contrast to that light, the sky in which the sun, too strong for the eyes to bear, affords a glimpse of a flaming surface that moves and changes as if it were a living organism, filling the entire sky around it with scintillations.

The beach attendant, going on from one image to another, fills in the breaks with his memory, not seeing the blazing light that flows over the yellow stretch of beach or, on the other side of the smooth, golden river, without a single ripple, at the top of the bank, the horseman who has just appeared, coming from the interior of the island, and who has reined in his mount for a moment, seeking with his eyes, no doubt, in the caramel-colored water, the ford where he will cross to the other side.

Now he sees him: he has gone into the water, on the other bank of the river; the horse feels its way along, cautiously, adapting itself without hurrying, without surprise, to the change of element, to the water that must be surrounding its front hoofs in lukewarm swirls.

The comic book lies open on the ground, alongside the trunk of the tree. The vivid colors of the sketches inside the panels stand out in the shadow of the tree, and the light that filters through the leaves and is projected onto the printed figures, in a fragmentary way, seems to make the colors fade a little. The beach attendant has stood up to get a better look at the rider who has raised his legs and crossed them on the back of the horse, which is now almost in the middle of the river, proceeding along the ford, with the water reaching up as far as its midribs. Horse and rider seem to know by heart that passage which the months-long drought has made even more accessible. The beach attendant knows that in order to reach the other shore without crossing the deep part, so as to be able to let the horse continue on foot without obliging it to swim and the rider to plunge into the water and grab it by its tail, they must not advance in a straight line from one bank to the other, but instead veer off on a slight diagonal upriver, so as to follow the path of the ford. The expression of slight expectancy on the beach attendant's face gradually gives way to a vague smile, as though slightly astonished, when he notes that the trajectory of the horse has shifted a little upriver and that the waterline around its ribs has begun, imperceptibly, to move downward.

The delicate hoofs of the horse touch shore making its entire body, imperceptibly, and for a fraction of a second—thereby marking the passage from one element to another, change gait so to speak—hesitate, shiver; and the drops, the swirls of water spinning around its hoofs or flying off its body, sparkle for a brief moment in the air, as though they had suddenly stopped and then immediately gone on again, before falling on the sand and disappearing.

The beach attendant who now sees the horse halted a few yards from the white house, has sat down again. The comic book is still lying on the ground, alongside him, open, receiving, like the beach attendant's tanned body, the filtered sunlight of the tree, whose dusty crown, in the mid-afternoon sun, reveals its gray, scorched leaves which, without falling off, crackle every so often, like dry leaves in autumn or like wood in the fire. From where the beach attendant is sitting, the windows can be seen, but they do not afford a view of the inside of the house: so that as a result it is the sight of the horseman, who has stopped a few yards from the house, his gaze fixed on one of the windows, and the movements of his head, that causes the beach attendant to deduce that Cat Garay must be looking out of one of the windows, and that he is no doubt the invisible speaker conversing with the rider mounted on the beige horse.

You can't say, the beach attendant thinks, that he's a hunchback. Not at all. But his head, damn it, his head, with its straw hat, looks as though it's embedded between his shoulders of uneven height, as if he'd gotten a heavy hammer blow perfectly calculated to make it sink down in between his shoulders without cracking it into a thousand pieces, or making it disappear altogether into the hollow of his thorax, but not well enough calculated, on the other hand, to avoid making his shoulders uneven in height, seeing as how the left one is much lower than the right one, so that his head tilts, rigidly, a little to the left. Apart from that, the beach attendant has been unable to perceive any other abnormality in the tall, skinny body, covered by a shirt and a pair of pants of an indefinable color, but he deduces that the uneven height of his shoulders must result in a conspicuous inequality in the length of his arms, or rather, a difference as to how far down they reach when he lets them hang down alongside his body, unless the left one is some two inches shorter than the other one. He must be fifteen, sixteen years old, the beach attendant thinks, and he must have come here from the islands. He must have crossed any number of islands and fords, he must have trotted along for an hour or two in order to reach the white house in front of which he has now stopped, in the midday sun, moving his head in the direction of the invisible person he is talking to, who is leaning, doubtless, on the black window-sill: horse and rider, and the shadow of horse and rider, down below, on the sparse, ashen-colored grass, in the afternoon sun that clouds the entire air with a sparkling whitish dust.

Going off at a slow trot, the beige horse, keeping its head erect nonetheless, the rider rigid although giving the impression of an intense precariousness, begin to climb up the incline of the cambered street, until they enter the shadow of the trees, becoming for a few seconds more tense somehow before disappearing.

Now there is no longer anything in the great open space. The beach attendant is stretching out his hand, his gaze not following his gesture, toward the comic book lying alongside him, on the ground. His hand pats the sandy ground two or three times, coming closer to the book, but his gaze continues to be riveted on the big open, empty expanse, in which the glare of the sun that reverberates particularly on the façade of the white house, against the roof of Spanish tiles, sends forth yellow and white rays that seem to split up all space into infinite parts. The sun overhead, paradoxically clouding, rather than brightening, the sky, and then, down below, the vast empty expanse, as far as the semi-circle of trees in the middle of which the white house is seemingly embedded, the smooth, golden or caramel-colored river, without a single ripple, the low, dusty island. The yellow stretch of beach appears to be traversed by those white and yellow rays, vertical, oblique, that keep changing the dimensions, the location, within the whole, of an image shattered or broken down, rather, into infinite fragments, not like a puzzle but more like a moving imprint, that keeps building itself up or destroying itself, successively or simultaneously, beneath the gaze that perceives, without becoming aware of them or without entirely understanding the continuous modifications.

The hand now touches, finally, the comic book lying to one side, on the ground, and picking it up, begins to raise it toward the heavy, tanned, sloping thighs that are to serve as a lectern. The rustle of the pages, the crackling of the paper is added, at times, to the intermittent crackling of the grayish, scorched foliage. Although he does not reach the point, far from it, of wondering about it, and although words have little or nothing to do with the question, when the beach attendant finally places the comic book on his sloping thighs and bends his head toward the panels that nearly overflow with colored images, something about the motionless, scorching hot atmosphere allows him to entertain the vague doubt whether really, in successive points of the vast, open, gleaming space, a few minutes before, horse and rider have been filling it up, little by little, with their compact musculature, or whether those moving volumes that are already fading from his awareness, in which the colored images are taking their place, are nothing but an illusion of his memory, and that nobody, nothing, at no time has ever been in the vast, unstable empty space in which the light ceaselessly deteriorates.

The first horse, a roan with a bluish-white tinge, had been found on the island, some eight months before. It was part of a fairly large herd, whose owner was a man from the city, named Dr. Croce, who had sent it to graze on the island in the care of the overseer of his property in Rincón Norte. The overseer found it by chance, among some clumps of grass, and since it had been lying there dead for at least two weeks, the crows, the ants and the vermin of the island had picked it almost clean; there was almost no flesh left and the overseer, who recognized it from the remains of hide still adhering to the skeleton, didn't realize what had happened till some time later, when the killer began committing one crime after another. The overseer went back to the place where the skeleton was now bleached almost white and noted that the bluish-white roan also had a hole in its temple. At first the overseer had thought it had been an accident or a sudden disease that, in two or three days, had done the animal in, but when he went back to the island and squatted down to have a close look at the skeleton he saw the hole in the skull clearly and no longer had any doubts. He sent word to his boss. Along about then everybody who lived along the riverbank was rather upset. The second victim had been another bluish-white roan, again in the Rincón area, but this time not on the island, but in a little open field between Rincón and Colastiné, on the other side of the highway, after La Toma, to be exact. It was one of the two or three horses belonging to Coco, the butcher, the youngest of all the ones he had, a colt almost, that he was preparing to race. For months that animal had had a soft life: it ate only corn, and Coco treated it better than he did his own family. Every so often he put it out to pasture in that little field so that it wouldn't get bored by being kept cooped up in the corral, and because being fenced in makes horses very skittish. Now, for a colt there is nothing worse than that sort of nervousness: it gets scared over anything and everything, and there is no way to get anything through its head. So Coco had it put out to pasture every so often in the open field, with the other horses, some five hundred yards behind the butcher shop. That was where they found it one morning, almost exactly a month after the overseer of Croce's herd had found the first bluish-white roan on the island. It was a Sunday and Coco had let it loose in the field on Saturday afternoon so that its nerves would calm down a little before he began training it. The other horses looked on from a distance, and it appeared as though they were unwilling to come any closer. They were frightened. For a good while, and even though they were gentle, tame animals, they wouldn't let anybody approach them. Perhaps the killer had mistreated them. Impossible to know: the one thing certain was that they were frightened, terrified rather, as though they had seen something that night, something unexpected, terrible, that had forever deprived them of their innocence. With Coco's bluish-white roan, things got complicated. Everybody's first thought was that a vendetta was involved. A few days before, Coco had kicked Videla out of the grocery store with a bar that he'd opened up next door to the butcher shop, because apparently Videla, in his cups, kept telling anybody who would listen that he'd known Coco since he'd been just a kid and that Coco, who had never amounted to anything, had raked in dough by robbing the poor, extending them credit and taking advantage of the bad years to force them to sell their fields and their animals at a loss. There was a certain amount of truth in all that, but when all was said and done, Coco had gone a little too far by treating Videla the way he had, above all seeing that Videla was a poor man, much older than Coco, and couldn't keep himself from drinking. Coco didn't swear a deposition against him or anything else, but simply went directly from the little pasture to Videla's cabin and began to abuse him so as to get a confession out of him. But Videla kept denying it. If, as Coco had just told him, the roan had been killed with a firearm, where would he, Videla, get a firearm when he didn't even have room enough to die in, and how could he know that the horse was in the little field if everybody knew very well that most of the time the animals were penned up behind the butcher store? Moreover he, Videla, had been in Fochi's tavern, across from the Beba, in Colastiné Norte till very late that night. The youngest of the Lázaros had brought him back to the cabin on his motorcycle, at the crack of dawn, because Videla was in no condition even to walk. That was true; the youngest of the Lázaros corroborated Videla's story: he had left him at the door of his cabin around two in the morning, so drunk that he had his doubts that he would have been able to proceed on foot to the little field to fire a shot at the horse and then go back home to his cabin in full daylight. The trip back and forth was over three miles. Coco finally ended the confrontation, although his suspicions were not laid completely to rest until, some ten days later, a third horse, one with four white feet, turned up with a bullet hole in its head, near Cayastá. This time, the killer had been merciless. Not content to shoot it, once it was dead he had slashed it all over with a knife and pulled its entrails out. The horse with the four white feet had been the one animal that a poor old man, a Creole who lived near Cayastá, owned. He almost burst into tears when he went to report the killing to the police. According to him, and apparently it was true, since he was a very poor but highly respected man who had worked till very recently in the public slaughterhouse and who lived on his pension, it couldn't be a case of a vendetta because as far as he knew, not a soul who lived around there had ever had the slightest run-in with him. The killer had shot the horse dead in a small corral, located a few yards from his cabin, just as day was breaking. Since the old man was very hard of hearing and was sleeping at that hour—his wife had gone to spend the night at the cabin of a sister of hers who was sick—he hadn't heard anything and hadn't discovered the horse till the next morning, as he was about to saddle it up to go into town, to collect his pension, as a matter of fact. Instead of that, he was obliged to go on foot to Cayastá to report the killing to the police. The chief of police of Cayastá, a man named Lorenzo, hadn't even bothered to come have a look at the animal; he had the old man's declaration taken down for a brief statement in writing and closed the case. But that same night, another horse was killed, this time in Vuelta del Dorado, that is to say, halfway between Santa Rosa and Cayastá. Two horses in twenty-four hours was two too many and rumors began to circulate all the way up and down the river. The most absurd things were passed along the grapevine: that there was a plague that the horses transmitted and that the authorities didn't want to say anything so as not to alarm the population, that it was a series of criminal acts the police themselves carried out as a pretext to jail certain inhabitants of the region who did not agree with the government, and even that there was a group of revolutionaries who engaged in maneuvers in the fields along the river and had killed the horses by accident. Other rumors had it that someone had killed a horse in La Toma in order to take vengeance on its owner, and that later on he had found himself obliged to kill the other two for the sole object of keeping people from suspecting him. In view of the distance between the various places in which the crimes had been committed, many people asserted that the killer, in order to get from place to place, doubtless had to use a car. But this argument didn't hold water. Although La Toma, being located between Rincón and Colastiné, is fairly far from Cayastá (some thirty miles), the distance between Cayastá and La Vuelta del Dorado is short enough so that a person would be able to commit the two crimes on the same day without the need for a car. If by chance the killer lived somewhere that was approximately halfway between the two places, the problem of getting around was relatively easy to solve. It could be done by car, on horseback, on a bicycle, on a motorcycle, and even in a boat by way of the river. The distance between La Toma and Cayastá wasn't at all important, because the killer had had ten days to move from one place to the other. It was when the horse with the four white feet belonging to the old man from the slaughterhouse was killed and all those rumors started to make the rounds that the overseer in charge of Dr. Croce's herd decided to go back to examine the skeleton being bleached white on the island. He discovered in the skull the entry and exit holes of the bullet and immediately sent word to his boss who lived in the city and who came down to his property by the river the very next day. There was no longer any possible doubt: from somewhere along the riverside, someone was coming out at night, for some reason, to kill horses, and as far as the last ones were concerned, he wasn't content to take their lives but, with a sort of enraged cruelty, savagely hacked them open and pulled their entrails out. The fourth horse, the roan of La Vuelta del Dorado, for example, had been nearly decapitated after having been shot to death, and the body of the animal had been slashed all over. The horse's owner, the gringo Haroldo, a dealer in hides, came to Santa Rosa and telephoned to the city—to a brother who was an employee at police headquarters, it would appear. Around two o'clock in the afternoon a van arrived from the city, with four policemen dressed in civvies. They took photographs of the animal, went about making inquiries among the neighbors and stayed till late at night eating a barbecue in the patio of the dealer in hides, by lantern light, and listening to one of gringo Haroldo's peons play the accordion. They never came back again. Never. Not even a week later, when, one morning, two horses that had been hacked to pieces turned up in the same corral, in Colastiné Norte. They were two old draft horses, two ashen-colored Percherons that looked like twins, suffering from countless ailments, which served their owner, a farmer, to transport carob beans or melons from the field to the shed at harvest time. The farmer was old Lázaro, the father, it so happened, of the young lad who had been having a few drinks at the Fochi bar, opposite the Beba, with Videla, the night when Coco's bluish-white roan was killed. Two horses finished off at one time, on the same night: old Lázaro ended up in the hospital, and they very nearly buried him with his Percherons. What attracted people's notice this time was the fact that the killer had committed that crime much farther down the river than the last two. Lázaro's three sons began to investigate on their own, going and coming all along the riverbank, and took turns mounting guard at night in the pasture, because the best horses—all of them draft animals, but young and healthy ones which pulled the flatbed cart to the city—were all there and their lives had been saved because on the night of the crime they had just happened to be delivering a load of carob beans to the public market. Two or three days after having been discharged from the hospital, old Lázaro had a visit from Coco and Haroldo the gringo who came to him to propose forming a sort of commission of disaster victims and petitioning the government to send a police patrol. During these same days too a yellow car began going up and down the riverbank, with two reporters from *La Región* who visited one farm after another, questioning the people who lived there and taking notes in a little notebook. That week two articles on the subject came out in the paper. People read them and commented on them and said that there were lots of mistakes in them, that this or that part fell short of the truth, that another was distorted and that, for example, no mention was made of the third horse that they'd killed, the one with the four white feet that belonged to the old man from Cayastá. What the articles did get right was the fact that there appeared to be nothing in common between the owners of the various horses, and that if the killer wanted to do harm, it wasn't the owners he wanted to do it to but the horses themselves. That the evil deed was done against the horses and not the owners was obvious by the way in which the man vented his cruelty on the poor animals after having shot them to death. If he had wanted to cause the owners damage the shot would have been enough: but those savage gashes that he proceeded to inflict on the corpses clearly proved that the killer had something against horses. Something else that the articles brought up, which many people along the river had already been wondering about, was whether the killer was just one man or whether on the other hand several were involved, or whether the killer or killers acted on impulse or with malice aforethought. Certain details could lead to the conclusion that he had acted on impulse: the fact, for example, that he had killed old Lázaro's two Percherons who were suffering from any number of ailments when, if he had really wanted to do Lázaro harm, the two young horses that were in the city that night would have better suited his purposes. But other details could also allow premeditation to be suspected: was it pure chance, for instance, that the killer had done his dirty work in Cayastá on the very night when the old man, who was hard of hearing, had been alone at his farm because his wife had had to go spend the night at the farm of a sick relative? And how, for example, could the killer know that the bluish-white roan of Coco's was out in the pasture if he hadn't known beforehand that Coco took it out of the stable once a week so that the colt would calm down a little. And he had done in the roan on precisely a night when by chance there was nobody in the hide dealer's warehouse. In any case, it was a person who was very well acquainted with the comings and goings of the people who lived along the riverbank, who was posted on the movements of each one of them, and who must also know a great deal about horses, to be able to approach them as he did and fire at them almost at point-blank range or actually hit them point-blank with a bullet in the temple. In a word, the articles in the paper did not

say what the people along the river had been wondering
about for some time: whether the man made preparations,
slowly and carefully, for each killing, or whether in the
middle of the night, unexpectedly, wherever he might be, he
was overcome by the urge to go out in those fields with a
firearm in his hand and shoot horses in the head. As for the
patrol they finally sent from the city, it was a red jeep that
during the day went on a few patrols around the countryside
but at night, when it would have been really necessary, it was
seen parked in reverse underneath the neon sign of La Arboleda, the motel in Giménez, where there were bar girls and
sometimes some sort of show. At any rate, the patrol was
good for something, since the killer didn't go into action for
two months. In the beginning, everybody waited, from one
moment to the next, to discover more mutilated horses
somewhere along the river in the morning. But since nothing
happened in the first week, or in the second either, in the third
a less close watch was kept. The patrol—the red jeep—was
sent out from the city on some days but not on others. The
owners of the horses who in the beginning mounted guard
every night near the pastures, began to go off to bed earlier
and earlier on the third or fourth week, so that after a month
they again left the horses all by themselves the whole night
long. The fear vanished, the men's at least, since the horses
continued to be nervous and a stranger could hardly get near
them. The proof of that nervousness was provided one
Sunday by a horse from Helvecia—one of the gentlest, which
for that very reason its owner, an Arab who ran a general
store, lent to some friends of his son's, who was studying in
the city and had invited his classmates to spend Sunday in the
country. The first one to mount it, a girl, could hardly stay on
the horse. Nervous from the moment he felt her on top of
him, the animal bolted when she loosened the reins to let him
trot, and beginning to buck he finally threw her against a tree.
They had to take her for emergency treatment to a clinic in
the city, and she died that very night. Anybody who knew

even a little bit about horses could see: the state of those animals was obvious. They reared easily, they tried to bite their riders, and they seldom allowed themselves to be mounted by strangers. And people didn't seem to realize that the cause of all that was the crimes, and that the horses could smell in the air that a plot against them was being hatched in the dark. So when at the end of a month in which nothing had happened people's vigilance was relaxed, the only ones to remain on the alert, who were not at all persuaded that the danger had passed, were the horses. Anyone who had ever set about watching horses for even a little while would have realized that the animals knew that something was in the offing. Ever since the beginning of May, which was when Dr. Croce's bluish-white roan had been discovered in the undergrowth on the island, picked clean by the carrion falcons and the ants, all along the river the horses seemed to know a little bit more than the men. Lázaro's Percherons had been killed in mid-July. In the two months that followed, amid storms and freezing weather, nothing happened: and the truth is that it was not easy to remain outdoors all night keeping watch on the pastures in the middle of the frosts of July and August, which covered the open countryside with hoarfrost, or at the time of heavy squalls of fine rain that lasted for a week and during which the countryside and the rivers were deserted and people huddled around the hearth inside their cabins. It was in the middle of September, the sixteenth—to be more exact on the night of the fifteenth to the sixteenth—when there was hardly any more talk of the subject along the river, that another horse, a honey-colored one, turned up in a field in Rincón, stone dead, with a bullet in its head and its body full of deep gashes. That same day an article turned up in the paper, and it was even accompanied by a photo of the horse. Its owner was a man from the city who had a country house in Rincón, just a short way from the beach. When he was in the city, he let his horse loose to graze in a pasture on the other side of the road. It was in that open stretch of ground that the killer

had shot it dead and then slashed it all over. The man came
from the city that very day and his blue car was seen going
first to the pasture in which they had found the horse, and
then to the weekend house two or three blocks from the
beach, and finally parked for a long time in front of the police
station. A police officer was seen leaving by the front door and
going back in by the rear entrance, closed off by a curtain, that
opened out onto the next street, bringing three or four bottles
of beer. The late-model blue car was parked along the culvert
opposite the police station for about two hours. Finally the
man came out accompanied by Horse Leyva, the chief of
police. They shook hands and the man got into the car and
headed off for the city. Horse stood there on the sidewalk,
watching the car raise a cloud of whitish dust with its rear
wheels. He remained in the doorway for a long time, as
though lost in thought. Then he ordered the jeep brought
round, and sitting alongside the police officer who was
driving, began to go from one cabin along the river to the
next, interrogating people. He gave two or three of them
some rough treatment. He gave one of the Salases—Jesús's
son, who according to what people said was cheeky enough
to defy him—a black eye and took him down to the police
station. Apparently they found a revolver underneath the
mattress of his cot and a cardboard carton of bullets with at
least half a dozen of them missing. They kept him in the police
station in Rincón for three or four days and then, one night, it
seems, they took him out and brought him to the city.
Someone who happened to see him as they were taking him
out by the back door says that in those three or four days they
had badly manhandled him and Salas had apparently confessed. But such rumors didn't convince anybody. On the one
hand, even though Salas was an odd sort who lived all by
himself in his cabin by the river and was on close terms with
nobody, not even his family, which was fairly large, he had
never had any trouble with his neighbors, and though people
circulated the rumor that he had a screw loose nobody could

complain that Salas failed him, and on the other hand the fact that anybody had confessed while being interrogated by Horse Leyva didn't prove anything, since everybody knew that Horse was a torture specialist, and it was even said that every so often they brought him from the city—at night and in secret—a revolutionary, so that Horse would make him sing. In any event that was how the situation remained for a month: Salas the madman was apparently responsible for all those crimes and since he had confessed everything all over again in the city they had handed him over to the police headquarters in Las Flores. The victims, except for Lázaro and the old man from Cayastá, had made a cash gift to the chief of police—or at least that was what was being repeated all along the river. And in *La Región* another article had appeared in which it was said that Salas was the presumed killer. That was what it said: "the presumed killer." They were taking no chances. This reserve was no doubt owing to the fact that everyone was well acquainted with Horse's reputation, but since he was the protégé of the politicians there was no way to deny directly either the methods or the results of the investigation. Horse cruised proudly up and down the riverbank in his red jeep, or if the weather was nice he sat after his siesta in a wicker chair in the doorway of the police station and sipped mate with a police officer. Sometimes he sent another police officer to the slaughterhouse, very early in the morning, and got them to give him the entrails that came out steaming from the belly of the animals, so as to have them grilled at the back of the patio at midday underneath the trees, as he read a comic book or listened to a transistor radio in his office. And it was also rumored that every so often, at night, a private car pulled up to police headquarters, out of which they removed a handcuffed man, so that Horse, with his special methods, would make him talk. Since one early morning, when sudden shouts apparently rang out in the town, people said in undertones the next day that a revolutionary who had been a traitor to the city had cried out two or three times when they took him out of the car to make him go inside the police station. In any event, when Horse arrested Salas and sent him to the city, the business of the horses wasn't repeated for some time, three months at least. There were a number of possibilities: either Salas was really the killer of the horses and hence when he was put in jail no other crime could be committed, or else Salas was innocent and the killer took advantage of his detention in order not to go on killing horses so as to add to the suspicions about Salas, or else the real killer, out of prudence or out of fear of falling into the hands of the chief of police, had decided to wait for a while for the surveillance to become less strict before going into action again. This last possibility turned out to be closest to the truth: because around three months after the last crime, on Christmas Eve, another horse was killed: Leyva's own sorrel, on which he occasionally turned up in the town, when he was off duty, and which he kept in the back yard of the police station so as to feed him at the community's expense. The killer had taken advantage of the chaos of Christmas Eve, with its bands of musicians, its skyrockets, and its drunkards, and above all with the fire at the municipal library, that for the time being no one could say whether it had been intentional or accidental. On Christmas Eve, once midnight had struck, people coming out of midnight Mass said they saw, on the other side of the plaza, through the two small windows that overlooked the sidewalk, two showers of smoke and sparks and flames coming from the community library. Someone went off at a run to tell the police, and fifteen minutes later practically the entire town was in the public square, in front of the library, helping the police officers—the city firemen had been summoned by telephone and had arrived just as the fire had already been brought under control—or else watching the flames coming out of the windows. Practically nothing was left, so to speak, of the library, which was a little room full of books piled up on shelves that covered two whole walls. The cause of the fire was not very clear: it might have been a short circuit or an accident caused by a skyrocket or a firecracker, or, as was discovered later, a criminal act. Because when the police officers returned to the station, around two-thirty in the morning, they found Horse's sorrel dead and covered all over with deep gashes, right in the middle of the yard. Horse had gone straight home from the library, without stopping by the police station, and one of his men went to tell him about the remains of the body. Everyone was a bit feverish that night, because of the wine or the cider, perhaps, or on account of the fire; at any rate when Horse arrived at the police station it was full of people—the yard in particular—and people who hadn't dared come inside for fear that in an access of rage Horse might not let them leave, contemplated the dead animal in the yard from the sidewalk. Horse didn't wait till the next day, no indeed, to begin his investigation. He immediately rose to his feet from alongside the horse, where he had placed one knee on the ground so as to examine more closely the havoc that the killer had wreaked with a knife on the animal's body, and turning around began to look closely at those present, trying to see if the murderer was among us. For several minutes nobody blinked, not wanting to make the slightest gesture that might arouse Horse's suspicions. All of us were standing in the dimly-lighted yard on the ground soaked with the blood of the sorrel, whose greenish entrails could be seen dangling halfway out of one of the gashes. Then Horse came out to the sidewalk and began to scrutinize one by one those who hadn't dared come inside: his hands were blood-stained and he was holding his arms away from his body so that his hands wouldn't brush against his shirt or his trousers, with his cartridge belt around his waist and his revolver on his right hip. Since apparently he discovered nothing suspicious about those present, he shouted an order to one of the policemen to get the jeep out, and at that moment those of us who were in the yard or on the sidewalk seized the chance to get as far away from the police station as possible while the getting was good. Ten minutes later not a soul was to be seen

in the streets, but from their beds everyone could hear the red
jeep as it drove back and forth between one end of the town to
the other, with the motor left running when every so often it
stopped outside one or another of the houses. All the townspeople must have been thinking more or less the same thing as
they lay in their beds: that it had now been proved beyond a
doubt that Jesús Salas's son was innocent, or that on the
contrary there was a possibility that there was more than one
murderer of horses, an eventuality that they had turned over
in their minds for months and that was now proving to be the
right one. There was also the possibility that there were not
just two but many killers, that that mania for murdering
horses had become a sort of epidemic and that each one of us,
for one reason or another, had set out to kill horses till not a
single one was left alive anywhere along the riverside. A
neighbor for many years, a father or a brother, a childhood
friend, suddenly became suspect. There were several instances
of violence: one night a fisherman leaped with a knife on his
own son, who was coming back from a dance and who,
having seen a girl home after it was over, entered his house by
way of the corral, located behind the house, instead of coming
in through the front as usual. Both of them were injured in the
mix-up, the son with a deep gash in his side which very nearly
pierced his spleen, and the father with two or three contusions
on the face which sent him to the hospital. An atmosphere of
general mistrust hovered over the town. In the café, for
example, nobody looked anyone else straight in the eye, nor
did anybody bring up the subject of horses. And if the red jeep
happened to go by the door of the general store with a bar
counter where the men gathered to have a beer or a vermouth
with bitters at noon, after work, or as night was falling,
nobody opened his mouth again for a good while and it was
more than likely that a few minutes later, on some pretext or
other, everyone had already gone home, leaving the bar
counter of the general store deserted once more. Something
else that began to become more and more frequent were the

anonymous accusations received by the police, and even ones made in person. In no time at all the red jeep was seen leaving the police station at top speed and returning with someone who was placed under arrest and then released a few hours later. From Christmas on, for at least a week, the jeep came and went nonstop all along the river, with Horse Leyva sitting next to the police officer who was driving. If anyone got on the wrong side of Leyva as he was about to interrogate him, the chief of police took him to the station and kept him locked up for two or three days. The best thing to do, after Christmas, was to make oneself as inconspicuous as possible. It was plain to see that Horse wasn't about to drop the subject of the killing of his sorrel. Not only had it subjected him to an enormous financial loss and sentimental grief, because he was prouder of that horse than he was of his sons, but it had also made him look ridiculous in the eyes of the authorities in the city, since in view of the new crime Salas's guilt seemed questionable and the judge was about to be obliged to open the case again. On Christmas Day the yellow car of *La Región* was seen driving through town and stopping in front of the police station. On the following day, the 26th—because there is no newspaper on Christmas Day—another article appeared that ended, rather hesitantly, by saying that the "person previously arrested," that is to say, Jesús Salas's son, ought to be let out on bail until the evidence against him was more persuasive, that the new "criminal act"—that is, the fact that the sorrel belonging to the chief of police had been hacked to pieces—"cast serious doubts on his presumed guilt." Nonetheless, Salas did not get out until January 27, and as ill luck would have it, two nights later another dead horse turned up in Santa Rosa, a pinto dray horse that its owner, a baker, used for delivering his bread. When Horse learned of this new crime, he drove off at full speed in the red jeep, heading toward Santa Rosa. He went straight to the baker, who had not wanted to report the crime because in his opinion the whole story of the horses was nothing but politics, and after examining the pinto stretched out on the ground, dead and with its entrails spilling out, Horse began to interrogate its owner, as the baker later recounted repeatedly, as to whether he had seen any suspicious-looking individual prowling about the bakery, whether in recent days any stranger had appeared in the town, whether he had in mind any person who might have a grudge against him for some reason, and whether he was aware that refusing to report the killing to the police was so serious a criminal act that it might have the gravest of consequences for him. Before returning to Rincón Horse stopped by the police station in Santa Rosa and had a five-minute conversation with the chief of police. When he got back to Rincón, at around five in the afternoon, on entering the police station he found Jesús Salas's son, who, on learning that another crime had been committed, had given himself up voluntarily. Horse paid almost no attention to him: to calm his nerves a bit, however, he ordered Salas to wait in the yard. It was eight or nine that night before he let him go. Since Salas was in no position to protest, he contained himself and patiently bore the long two- or three-hour wait, not counting the time that he had been cooling his heels in the police station until Horse came back from Santa Rosa. In the case of the baker's dray horse, the inquiry had been a waste of time: if the murderer had been made of dust, of smoke, he would not have left fewer traces. A police officer who had jokingly commented on the day following the killing in Santa Rosa that maybe it hadn't been a case of murder but of suicide was ordered by Leyva to hand over his sidearms and was placed under arrest for forty-eight hours. At least that was the story that made the rounds in the town. The agitation and the mistrust mounted, even more than after Christmas. It was said that people's weapons were going to be confiscated, that it was possible that the army would intervene or that a police detachment from Regional Headquarters would be sent to set up camp and patrol the riverbanks. The various civic associations in Helvecia, Santa Rosa, Cayastá and

Rincón put out communiqués. In fact, many red police cars
were seen criss-crossing the region after the 27th. One morning, some three days later, he was in his house, calm as
anything, when he heard a knock on the door and when he
went to open it he found himself face to face with two police
detectives in civvies who had come from the city and who
interrogated him for about two hours. They had asked him a
whole bunch of questions, staring him straight in the eye, and
had even gone so far as to rough him up a little. But he
couldn't tell them anything: he always went straight from the
chicken ranch where he worked to his cabin without even
dropping in at the tavern of late to have a drink with friends.
The detectives from the city had a discussion with each other
each time he answered a question, so as to decide whether they
thought that what he had just said was true or false. They
came back again and again to the subject of outsiders. They
wanted to find out at all costs whether he had seen strangers,
individuals who were not from the region, show up in the
town, in a car or on foot. He hadn't seen anybody. Finally,
around noon, the two detectives had left. This had been on
Tuesday morning, precisely the day that he hadn't gone to the
chicken ranch because an inspection had been scheduled and
he wasn't registered at the Department of Labor. Tuesday
night, then Wednesday night, and bam! Thursday night,
another horse hacked to pieces. Can you imagine? That was
why everything had been in more or less of a hubbub that
morning: the red jeep kept coming and going from one end of
town to the other and the owner of the horse . . .

On noting that the beach attendant has raised his head a
little way, looking in the direction of the white house that
looms up at his back, the man interrupts his account for a few
seconds, but when his eyes fleetingly meet those of the
bathing attendant, who has turned them once again toward
his, as though to show him that his attention is free again, the
man goes on speaking and moving his head in such a way that

the light that filters through his woven straw hat is projected, moving ceaselessly, on his lean, sunburned face.

The fact is that the bathing attendant has seen, beyond his conversational partner's head protected by the straw hat, the only resident of the white house come out—from the front wall of it, as it were, since the door, owing to the placement of the house, is scarcely visible—dressed in nothing but a pair of shorts of an indefinable color and now, as his interlocutor resumes his account, he sees him walk slowly and nonchalantly, his head drooping, his body tanned by the sun all summer long, across the deserted beach, toward the water.

. . . the owner of the horse, in a single morning, had crossed the town on foot three times, going to and from the police station. They had given him the news in the café at noon, when he left the chicken ranch. The horse of the night before was a white one, the most beautiful horse in the region, not yet even three years old, one they were getting ready to race at the Las Flores track. Like the others, it had been left in a dreadful state, and apparently things were much more complicated this time because the animal was insured. And to think that he had seen it just the day before, late in the afternoon, as they were bringing it back after having taken it out for a training session in the open countryside, going down the streets of the town at a slow trot! A few hours later, the horse was stretched out in the yard, with a bullet in the head and all its entrails spilling out: the owner, they said, had apparently fired the groom, and thrown several punches at him as well. The groom went home with his face and his shirt covered with blood. All this had happened in the town since the night before. No, as he kept saying, kept telling his wife: for some time now, everything had been going badly. All along the river, men came out at night, armed with a revolver and a knife, to kill horses, and nobody along the river who owned a horse could sleep in peace, and even people who didn't have a horse couldn't sleep, since it was also possible that the person sleeping in bed with you, or in the next bedroom, was getting up at daybreak without making a sound so as to head across the countryside with a knife and a pistol.

His skin tanned, his hair ash-blond, his head drooping, Cat is crossing the deserted beach in a straight line, heading for the water, leaving the space that he has filled for a moment with his body behind him, and as he listens to the long monologue being delivered by the person with whom he is talking, the beach attendant thinks he perceives, for a fraction of a second, repeated to infinity, in the space between the white façade and the point now occupied by Cat's body, the image of that body in each of the walking positions that it has assumed in its trajectory.

As Cat walks on toward the water—the space that separates him from the riverbank gradually growing smaller and smaller—in the sparkling light, the beach attendant, who out of courtesy toward his conversational partner must, so as to prove that he is paying attention to his account, look him almost continuously in the eye, tries every so often to meet Cat's gaze to greet him, so that his furtive glances toward him, cast whenever the man he is listening to is momentarily distracted, show him Cat closer and closer to the water's edge without its having been possible for him to see him move, in such a way that to the visual decomposition of Cat's body into all the movements of walking, there is now added the illusion of a progress by way of discontinuous jerks that abruptly shorten the distance that separates Cat from the riverbank.

The man has stopped speaking and is looking closely at the beach attendant's face to see the effects of his long account: his own face reflects the anxiety of the narrator who, empty now of his account, seeks to discover in the expression of his hearer whether his words have come close to their intended aim, and whether the look on his face attests to the efficacy of his narration. His eyes open, somewhat shaded beneath the brim of the straw hat, search the round face of the beach attendant, who tries to assume a reassuring expression. Yes, in fact, the beach attendant's expression appears to mean: as a matter of fact, this entire story of horses is more or less as you have just told it, it is approximately in that way that there must have come about the things that, moreover, generally speaking, have the meaning that you have given them in your account. And the beach attendant, leaving his expression of acquiescence at the narrator's disposal, turns his eyes to look, furtively, out of the corner of them, at Cat, who has stopped at the river's edge and, with his hands resting on his waist and his elbows at a distance from his body, has raised his head and observes, in the afternoon silence, the middle of the river.

The man in the straw hat and the white shirt has also turned his head, in the same way as the beach attendant, whose expression of acquiescence has changed to a total absence of expression and both direct their gaze toward the fair-haired man who is, little by little, without making any sound, entering the water: his ankles, his knees, a large part of his thighs disappear and now, all of a sudden, his body emerges, taking off upward first and then bending back down toward the surface, and plunges forcefully into the river, producing, in the sun-drenched silence of siesta time, a liquid uproar and a tumult of drops that detach themselves for a moment from the liquid mass, gleam fleetingly in the air, and then fall back again.

Under the dusty shade of the tree that protects them from the light of February, the unreal month, the two men look at the river, in which concentric waves are moving toward the banks of the river, gradually growing wider and wider, until Cat's head violently emerges on the empty surface, dripping water, the nape of his neck turned in the direction of the beach and his face toward the low-lying, dusty, calcined island.

His head disappears again beneath the water and in its absence new concentric waves grow wider and wider, even more swiftly, as they move toward the riverbanks, which still quiver from the first ones.

This story of horses has changed the whole region, says the man in the straw hat. As he speaks he shakes his head and the bits of sunlight filtering through the sun-seared foliage and the interstices of the hat move from place to place on his severe, sunburned face and his white shirt. There must be, the beach attendant answers, a lot of politics involved in all that. The man in the straw hat shakes his head as the beach attendant tries, without succeeding, to repeat his statement. No, the man in the straw hat says, it is like a plague that men succumb to and that kills horses by means of an interposed person. As he is uttering the words "by means of an interposed person," several yards away, in the river, Cat's head comes to the surface, shaking from side to side and dripping water, his head turned this time toward the deserted little stretch of beach, toward the two men talking together underneath the tree, toward the white house.

The beach attendant has noted his indecision on seeing him come out of the river, dripping water, his feet agilely though slowly thrashing the caramel-colored water, his arms dangling alongside his body. The beach attendant watches subtly on seeing him coming toward them, and almost simultaneously the man in the straw hat has fallen motionless, rigid, in a ceremonious attitude, characteristic of the man from the countryside when confronted with the offhandedness of the city dweller. The beach attendant knows, however, that the conversation will be a conventional one, that Cat, who has offered no greeting as he went by on his way down to the water, has found himself obliged, on coming out of it, to approach and exchange a few words with the only two individuals visible anywhere on the beach.

He stops two yards away, outside the tenuous patch of shade, full of luminous perforations that the tree projects on the white sand, on the sparse, ash-colored grass. His hair, a smooth vortex clinging to his skull and temples, is still dripping drops of water on his shoulders, his neck, his forehead. The sparse blond down on his chest is flattened against his skin. His dip in the river has, so to speak, darkened his several days' growth of beard. He has made a gesture of greeting before stopping by raising his right hand a little way, up as high as his chest, and then immediately letting it fall again. The beach attendant and the man in the straw hat reply in unison, the beach attendant's voice slightly graver than that of the man in the straw hat, which, by contrast, has seemed more servile. The dual reply, and the courteous gestures that have accompanied it appear to awaken in him, the beach attendant notes, a certain surprise mingled with embarrassment. For a few seconds the ritual dialogue following the exchange of greetings is difficult to get started again. It touches on the drought, the terrible heat, the white horse that from time to time trotted quickly along the water's edge and that they had discovered in a yard in town that morning, full of deep gashes, with its greenish entrails spilling out and a bullet in its head. The conversation turns to the subject of the bathers: they appear in mid-morning, the afternoon heat drives them away, and as dusk is falling they turn up again. The conversation finally dwindles, is interrupted by long pauses, and can't get going again. The three men stand there in silence, with their eyes too wide open and a half-embarrassed and half-polite smile that takes the place of the impossible conversation. Their voices, whose tone has been almost confidential, except for that of the man in the straw hat, which is slightly higher in pitch than that of the others, linger as if echoing in the air, less as voices than as sounds to which the heavy, sultry air offers an excessive resistance, preventing their departure and their dying away.

Now that Cat and the man in the straw hat have disappeared, one of them as if breathed in by the façade of the white house, the other going at a slow, almost painful pace, up the gentle incline that leads to the sidewalk protected by the dense shade of the trees, the beach attendant has sat down again, picking up at almost the same time the comic book that was lying alongside the trunk of the tree and resting it on his sloping thighs that serve him as a lectern.

For several minutes, absorbed in his reading, the beach attendant who, seen from a distance, would have given the impression of being a man fast asleep or made of stone, divorces himself completely from the reality that surrounds him and sits there with his legs bent, his head leaning forward, his eyes calmly perusing the colored pictures. Then he raises his head and remains for one or two minutes with his eyes staring into emptiness, thinking of nothing in particular, without even the memory filled with garish colors of his recent reading or any other memory from farther back in time taking the place of the colored images in the clear center of his conscience. His body, soft and slack, as though it were made of sand or cotton nonetheless appears to have been abandoned, or to have fallen, rather, into this emptiness. He doesn't even blink: his open eyes, which see nothing, do not appear to reflect any thought either. He is completely empty, and his faculties, in suspension, or without any tension, rather, seem to have left him in this state of oblivion; like a marionette, motionless and entangled in all its many strings, whose arms and legs have been left lying on the floor. Then the beach attendant shakes himself, as though coming to with a start, sits up straight and leans his back and his helmeted head against the tree trunk. His hands lie on top of the colored pictures of the comic book placed on his heavy, sloping thighs which serve him as a lectern.

From the depths there comes, for no apparent reason, a memory: in the days when he was still the champion of the

province for the number of hours spent in the water, fifteen
years back, the beach attendant had been in the river for
seventy-six hours. He was thoroughly familiar with that
river; and the little streams and brooks that flowed down
from other areas to empty into it, or that flowed out of it,
traced a series of capricious curves forming islands in the
middle, and then joined the powerful current once again. It
was in this current that he had been for seventy-six hours, not
in one of its branches but in the very middle of the great river,
whose banks could barely be made out. Floating, drifting, in
the deep, caramel-colored water, in the October dawn, without anything around him except the water, seen from its
surface level, above which there appeared nothing except his
head, somewhat drowsy from the current. Those seventy-six
hours were barely the beginning of his prolonged stay in the
water; it was his third dawn in the river. He had seen, on the
water in motion, the greenish sun and the red moon, day after
day, become visible on the horizon, climb slowly upward in
the sky, gradually go down and disappear. The beach attendant calmly did the dead man's float with his face to the sun or
to the starry sky. He knew that on the banks of the river the
curious must be standing on tiptoe so as to try to spot him in
the middle of the water, whose current, to which he offered
no resistance yet at the same time did not help along with his
efforts so as not to tire himself out too much, was making him
drift downriver, like a tree trunk; every so often, a boat, with
two or three of his fans inside, approached cutting across the
river on a diagonal and stopped a few yards away, for just a
few minutes, long enough to offer a few words of encourage-
ment, to which he replied with vague smiles and vacuous
expressions, avoiding speaking so as to save his energy. Then
he would watch the boat go away with the same painful
smile, like that of a sick man or that of an invalid, until the
river banks swallowed it up. The patrol boat circled about in
the vicinity and from time to time, there leaned over the
gunwale toward him the head, covered by a cap or a hat, of

one of the organizers or a journalist: two or three times it had been his own wife who, smiling, had held up one of their children for him to see. He answered everything with his vague gestures, his vacuous smiles. It was when they left him all by himself, when nobody approached him, that he felt the best: allowing himself to grow drowsy, to be slowly carried along by the current, his face to the sky, the beach attendant, without surrendering himself, however, to any one definite dream, saw many precise, well-outlined images file past in his mind, images that came and went and seemed to bear little relationship to each other. And the water clinging to his body, forgotten, swirling all about him, moving continually, changing, always at eye level, slightly ruffled, flowing southward and carrying him along with it, as though it were playing. It had been like that for seventy-six hours: now, on the deserted river, dawn was breaking. The patrol boat, which had accompanied him all night long, had gone off for a moment toward the riverbank, so that he was alone, seeing the sun, or a segment, rather, of a reddish color, make its way through the vegetation of the islands, staining the sky around it. There were still stars out, though they were barely visible now. The beach attendant's drowsiness was due less to fatigue than to the continuous ebb and flow of the water rocking him back and forth. The rising sun began, all of a sudden, without the beach attendant having had time to perceive the transition, to be reflected in the water: a line of moving, copper-colored, feeble points that began to dance in front of the beach attendant's eyes, changing size, color, place. At times they formed a wavering line, set to quivering by an imperceptible undulation, but almost immediately the line broke up, turning into that indistinct number of dancing points. The beach attendant had his eyes riveted on them. He saw them as being located just a little way away from his retina, or his attention, or his consciousness, in a state that was not that of complete wakefulness yet neither did it have anything to do with sleep, but even if he had had the idea of looking away and beginning to think of something else, which did not occur, it would have doubtless necessitated a much greater effort than that required for a similar decision in an ordinary situation. Nor was there any doubt that the water was calmly carrying him southward. But it was also taking with it the reflection, so that the distance that separated them remained constant, as did his angle of vision, which produced the illusion of perfect immobility, like that of the bird that enters the aura of the serpent and remains riveted to the spot as it watches it dancing. Without moving, without even blinking, the beach attendant contemplated the ray of light and saw it change from oneness to multiplicity and from the many to the one from one thousandth of a second to another, without his ceasing to be continually rocked back and forth in that undulatory movement which was transformed into a sort of whirlpool of twinkles when the line of light broke up, and which made him drowsy. And at a certain moment—in his memory the beach attendant could not say when—, the line did not become one again: in the light of memory, one could rationally argue that the sun, which the beach attendant had ceased to see, had doubtless risen slightly higher in the sky, thus modifying its reflection in the water, which might very well be the correct hypothesis, since it seemed to him that he remembered that the sky above his head had grown paler and the stars were no longer visible. What is beyond question is that all around him the surface of the water had turned into a series of points of light, indefinite in number and perhaps infinite, very close to each other but not touching each other as was proved by the fact that despite their continual twinkling an extremely thin black line could be seen between one and the next. As far as his eyes could see, that is to say, the entire visible horizon, the surface that surrounded him, where it was no longer possible to distinguish the water from the river banks, seemed to have been pulverized, and the infinite number of particles that jiggled before his eyes lacked the slightest cohesion. He might have compared what he saw to a garment covered with sequins had he not seemed to recall that sequins are sewn on in such a way that they partly cover each other, almost like the scales on a fish's body. Those points of light, on the contrary, did not have the shape of any one body, but were, rather, an infinity of minuscule bodies, like a sky dotted with stars, with the difference that the black empty space between the points of light was an extremely thin little stripe, barely visible, or rather, a very fine black circumference, because the profusion of luminous points that surrounded him transformed the black space that encompassed them into a circumference. From that precarious space there emerged, rigid and motionless, the beach attendant's head, which floated tensely and on an inclined plane and which seemed to be surrounded by those points of light, some of which sparkled even in his hair or on his three-day growth of beard. The beach attendant, who had almost literally spent his whole life in the water, had never seen anything like that. And, all of a sudden, at the crack of that October dawn, his known universe lost its cohesion, reducing itself to dust, transforming itself into a vortex of formless, and perhaps bottomless, corpuscles, where it was no longer all that easy to look for a place to stand on, as it was possible to do in the water. His feeling was less one of terror than of astonishment—and above all repulsion—with the result that he tried to remain as rigid as possible, so as to avoid all contact with that ultimate and meaningless substance that the world had turned into. There was not a sound to be heard, or if there was one, a murmur, a rustle, palpitations, or an almost inaudible tinkle perhaps that might allow one to surmise that those corpuscles were colliding, the beach attendant wasn't listening to it, absorbed as he was in contemplation and in the conclusions that he might draw from the spectacle taking place before his eyes. The engine of the patrol boat, emitting a muffled purr in the first light of day, didn't draw him out of his contemplation either and seeing it come closer, cleaving the surface with its white prow—all contaminated too with points of light—the beach attendant wondered how in the devil he could make any progress in that disconnected, changing, unstable medium, drifting in empty space. Without showing any signs of panic, unhurriedly, he brought his arm up to the surface and stretched it out toward the patrol boat, making vague motions with his hand to indicate that they should haul him out, but as they were lifting him up, with straps that they had placed underneath his armpits and were pulling on from the boat, the beach attendant continued to keep himself rigid, silent, his eyes still riveted on that pulverized light that constituted the entire visible horizon. From the patrol boat they had taken him to a clinic, because he appeared to have lost altogether his power of speech. The doctors attributed his state to excessive fatigue—and it was true that the training had been intense and the beach attendant was no longer in his early youth, but the attendant, who confined himself to speaking very little, using gestures and hand motions to communicate with others, knew very well in his heart of hearts that he wasn't exhausted or anything of the sort, but that what he had seen was difficult to explain, and for that reason he preferred to remain silent and appear to be half asleep. It took him weeks, months to get used to everyday reality again, the reality of before his immersion, to seeing a body, a face, an ordinary place, as a complete entity and not as an infinite series of points in suspension, with no relationship between them other than two or three rudimentary mechanical laws. That was how he had lost his title of record-holder of the province for the longest stay in the water. In the beginning they had given him a pension, and then, partly to keep himself occupied and partly too to have an easier time of it making ends meet at the end of the month, he had requested the post of beach attendant—when, years later, the fever was almost forgotten and his feeling of strangeness had turned into a sort of second nature, unconscious, solid and incurable.

That memory, which he scarcely thought of any more, had reappeared in successive phases: first, like a sudden flash, without yet being a memory, but only a reminder from his sense of recall that he was remembering something without knowing exactly what: then, in a second burst, he had remembered a whole series of secondary elements which he was unable to individualize because he lacked the principal memory; then immediately, after a moment in which he had again remained empty, as it were, memory had allowed the recollection to surface, clear and neutral, a recollection, like any number of others, that enters consciousness without anything, apparently, having summoned it, like a slide that is projected on a blank wall, mechanically, and then is effaced, and finally, the recollection had gotten the better of him, for several minutes, shutting him up within himself, isolating him from the outside world, taking possession of him and producing in his body a series of transformations, since during the moment in which he was remembering he had had his eyes wide open, his lips clamped against each other and protruding slightly, his hands lying, forgotten and flabby, on either side of his body on the ground, palms upward, half closed on the sparse, ash-colored grass, the chain of associations interrupted and seeing so clearly his head emerging from amid that pulverized light, that for a fraction of a second he had a sort of impression of having been split in two since he thought he was looking at himself from the gunwale of the patrol boat.

In the distance, on the other side of the beach, the two willows bend toward the water; there is nothing, nothing; the smooth river, without a single ripple, caramel-colored, with, on one shore, the low, dusty island, and on the other, beyond the yellow beach on the gentle slope marking where it ends, the white house. The beach attendant takes it all in, in one quick glance, when he raises, distractedly, his head, as he turns the page of the colored comic book that is resting on his sloping thighs, as on a lectern.

To distract himself a bit rather than to make a show of his authority, the beach attendant strolls among them: they have been arriving, in groups of two or three, they have taken off their street clothes, underneath which they were wearing their bathing suits, and they had sat down or stretched out on the sand or on colored towels. Some of them have arrived already wearing only their bathing suits, their cigarettes, matches, and a bottle of suntan lotion in their hand, or in a straw beach bag. Those from the city have left their cars on the shoulder of the tree-lined street that leads to the beach. Now, even though it must be past seven p.m., there are almost thirty of them. The beach attendant will have to collect, as best he can, once they leave, the trash that they will leave behind. Two or three little children are playing at the water's edge, digging in the damp sand. The light of the sun going down, which comes, as though from a bonfire, from behind the town or, rather, from the city, filters, almost horizontally, through the trees, encircling the leaves with a sparkling aureole. The water is violet-colored. The bathers running in and out of it raise white plumes that turn iridescent for a fleeting moment, and then fall back into the current. Stretched out on the ground, the women, with their eyes closed, barely breathe. The men, sitting alongside them, smoke and look, in silence, around them. But there are also the shouts, the cries, the bursts of laughter, forthcoming from who knows who, which on ringing out seem to collide several times with a material that resists them before they die down and disappear. The riverbank bustles with the coming and going of the bathers who, as they emerge from the water, leave damp traces that become beaded with soft little balls of blackened sand, stuck together by the wetness that their feet appear to be sowing with each step. On emerging from the river, their bodies are dripping wet and although not the slightest breeze is blowing, five minutes later they are as dry as though they had never gone into the water, except for their hair, which slowly loosens itself from their skulls and which contact with the water has darkened and smoothed slightly. The women lying face downward lean their chin or their cheek on their hands placed one atop the other, and as their breasts flatten out against the colored towels, they can be seen peeking out a little, whiter than the rest of their skin, along the edges of their bikini tops, just under their armpits, while, owing to the position of their bodies, their waists arch and their buttocks become rounder, more compact and more prominent. Those who are lying face up let their navel in the middle of their belly show and a very light line of down that descends toward their pubis, disappearing from sight underneath the triangular bikini bottom that covers their *mons veneris*. The protuberance of the men's genitals, crammed together by the pressure of the stretch fabric, can be seen underneath their tight-fitting swimming trunks. Those with white skin stand out immediately from the others: either they have forgone coming to the beach ever since the beginning of summer, or else their milky skins don't tan. The skin of most of the bathers, however, goes from the color of tea, or cognac rather, to dark brown. At times, on the lower belly, there can be seen a white line that goes all around the body and suggests the color of the part of it protected from the sun by their bathing trunks. The sand gradually fills up with marks, footprints, holes, mounds, wrinkled papers, empty packages of cigarettes or else peach pits, cigarettes smoked down to the very end leaving nothing but the filter, empty bottles of suntan lotion. An almost continuous aquatic sound, whose intensity changes every so often, produced by the bodies that plunge into the water or run in and out of it, accompanies the voices and the cries that intermingle in the limited space of the beach. A tanned young man, wearing a pair of electric blue swimming trunks, goes past the beach attendant and enters the water, at a run. The beach attendant watches him: the water gradually covers his ankles, his knees, his thighs, and his headway, against the resistance of the water, gradually becomes slower, more difficult. Finally, when the water is almost at the level of his waist, he plunges into the river and disappears. For nearly a minute there is no other trace of him except the change in the surface of the water caused by the dive until, near the middle of the river, his head appears again, explosively, as though blinded, shaking from side to side and dripping water. For a moment, the bather appears to drift aimlessly, until he dives underwater once more and disappears. An interval similar to the first one, in which nothing happens and nothing is to be seen, prior to the reappearance of his head, very abruptly this time too, close to the opposite bank of the river. The beach attendant, who had stopped for a moment to watch him, continues on his way, strolling slowly among the bathers sitting or lying stretched out on the sand. Swiftly directing his gaze toward the white house, he sees Cat standing in the doorway, leaning against the frame, looking toward the river. The bather, at that moment, has come out of the river and is climbing, seemingly with difficulty, up the riverbank of the island. When he reaches the top, he rests his hands on his hips and, thrusting his chest out, begins to contemplate the beach. The horizontal light illuminates the upper part of his body whereas his legs appear to be submerged in the shadow that seems to be mounting, like a blue vapor, out of the earth. The bather places the edge of his hands around his mouth, vertically, his fingertips touching just above the bridge of his nose, so as to form a megaphone, and begins to call to someone who is on this side of the river, in a voice which is doubtless powerful in the immediate vicinity of the place where it is emitted, but which is weakened by the time it reaches the little beach.

IX It has, Cat says, as he tastes the meat, neither salt nor sense. Elisa shakes her head, smiling, and looks at him: the same indifferent, apathetic smile, the half-closed eyes that gaze at her as though from behind a curtain of smoke, the close-shaven cheeks that from time to time give off metallic glints.

Neither salt nor sense, Cat repeats, staring her straight in the eye with that expression that one has no idea whether it is meant as mockery of himself, of others, or a facial tic that has nothing to do with any sort of feeling or emotion, of which he is not even aware. The sound of a car that must be coming slowly down the sandy streets, heading toward the beach, changes Cat's expression: his eyes turn to one side, paradoxically, and become motionless, just as his entire body does, the hand holding the fork suspended halfway between his mouth and the plate full of little pieces of meat on which there can be distinguished here and there a number of green bits of parsley.

They sense, without paying any particular attention to it, as they go on eating, without saying a word, above the tinkling of the silverware against the white earthenware plates, the sound of the engine of the car and hence its route: it has doubtless gone down the asphalt highway from the city, taken the main street to the public square, driven around the edge of it, turned to the left, leaving it, the center of town, and the church behind, continued along the dark streets toward the beach, and now it is going down the tree-lined street, next to the sidewalk with the privet, and its driver, no doubt seeing in the light of the headlamps the black car parked on the shoulder of the street, has gone on a little farther, descending the slope and parking at the entrance to the beach.

In the silence that follows, the sound of the engine, which has stopped now, seems to go on resounding still, in the pitch-dark air outside, or in the ear, or even more to the point, in the memory, until it disappears completely, as though it had been gradually sinking amid the folds of a porous, black, limitless substance.

After that lingering echo of the sound of the engine nothing else is heard, not even the tinkle of the silverware against the white earthenware plates from which the little pieces of fried meat with bits of parsley sticking to them are disappearing, since for a moment Cat and Elisa remain motionless, gripping their forks, their heads bent down toward the plates that their eyes wander over, it would seem, without seeing them.

From the pitch-black beach there reaches their ears, at two different times, the sound of car doors opening and closing, slightly louder than the voices and the laughter of a man and a woman who are doubtless walking along the beach, no doubt looking for a place to sit down, or perhaps intending to go into the water.

Motionless, gripping his fork, his head bent down toward his plate that his eyes wander over, it would seem, without seeing it, Cat pictures in his mind the couple getting out of the car, the man by the door on the driver's side, the woman by the one on the other side, their faces turned toward the water, on the black beach, until the image is effaced and his fork reaches down to his plate.

Elisa too, on hearing the sound of the doors and the voices, has pictured in her mind, for a fraction of a second, the couple that is laboriously trudging through the sand on the slope down to the beach, and as the scene takes shape in her imagination her gaze is fixed on Cat's face, on which a vague, fleeting expression, the consequence perhaps of the attention he has paid to the sounds from the beach, is reflected and effaced as his left hand guides his fork toward the plate on which the little pieces of fried meat sprinkled with parsley gleam.

In the lighted kitchen, Cat and Elisa are finishing their meal, bending over their plates: the tinkle of the silverware against the earthenware plates, the creaking sounds of the chairs with straw seats, the stream of white wine falling, with a liquid murmur, into the glasses, resound in the room in which the red-tiled floor gleams and in which the white walls and the blue and white checkered tablecloth reflect the light. No noise or sound of laughter is coming from outside now, yet every so often, even though several minutes have gone by since the noise that evoked it was forthcoming, the image of the couple getting out of the car, the man by way of the door on the driver's side, the woman by the one on the other side, facing the water, mounts, like a memory now, in Cat's head.

For Elisa, who is clearing the dishes from the table, as Cat lights a cigarette, rocking back and forth in his chair with the straw seat, his extended legs disappearing underneath the table, cut off at mid-thigh by the straight edge of the checkered tablecloth, the image that comes back to her memory differs, despite the common elements, from Cat's: the couple is making its way, in the darkness, with laborious footsteps, through the sand, to the water's edge.

Now the kitchen is empty. The plates, the platter, the frying pan, the tableware pile up in the sink. Elisa, who has finished clearing the table, has just disappeared from the kitchen, pushing aside the blue canvas curtain which separates the kitchen from the porch. Her voice comes from the porch and echoes in the empty kitchen. Cat's answers. No, he doesn't want any coffee, his voice says. What he would rather have, the voice coming from the porch to the empty lighted kitchen goes on to say, is a big glass of white wine, since the thirst that keeps tormenting him, the voice says ironically, refuses to go away. A big glass. One this tall, says the voice, which has doubtless been accompanied by a gesture invisible in the darkness of the porch. Elisa goes back into the kitchen and, skirting the tables and chairs that are sitting, mute, in the middle of the room, heads for the refrigerator. Her bronze body, most of it covered by the stiff white linen dress, slowly crosses the space separating the blue canvas curtain from the refrigerator, built into the white wall, and the red-tiled kitchen stove. Her body, exterior to the lighted space, passes through it. No one could tell, from outside, from her flesh so apparently firm and serene, her head so solid and compact, her gaze so steady and expressionless, that on the inside a multitude of images, of palpitations, of pulsations are continually making their way through her, like a stone that when it is turned over allows one to see the teeming clot of an anthill.

The presence of the beige horse seems to fill, soft and diffuse, the entire backyard; every so often its tail swishes, mechanically, and every once in a while its hoofs strike the ground, producing a sound, as soft as its body, that resounds with a muffled echo in the shadow. Since not the slightest breeze is blowing, the trees at the very back of the yard betray their presence only by the denser blackness of their crowns outlined against the black air. With the glass of white wine in his hand, Cat has halted, looking toward the far end of the yard, in the area of the porch dimly lighted by the glow coming from the kitchen, which filters through the edges of the blue curtain. Elisa has sat down in one of the deck chairs and is looking, as Cat is, toward the far end of the yard.

No matter how hard he listens, with his gaze turned toward the yard in which the presence of the yellowish-white horse hovers like an unpleasant smell, like an effluvium or an odor, no sound, no sign of life reaches him from the beach, except for the stubborn images, two or three of them, always the same ones, whereby he pictures to himself the imaginary couple heading for the water across the black empty space.

The sound of the engine approaching and maneuvering as it comes out at the beach, the voices and the laughter of the man and the woman, the doors opening and closing: considering, calmly, the poverty of the material, it is possible, without talking nonsense, to wonder whether there is still any reason to continue to wait for any sign of life from the beach. From somewhere in the night there has seemed, at some moment or another, to have reached the ear a series of noises apparently produced by a car approaching from the center of town and finally stopping at the entrance to the beach, and by a woman and a man who got out of it, slamming the doors and allowing their discreet voices and laughter to be heard; the memory of those sounds is firmer and clearer than the conviction that there has really once reached the ear, through the darkness, the recollection of the noises, without the noises, which is now floating in silence in Cat's memory and which, now, is effaced once more.

They have remained, for quite some time, on the porch, smoking in the darkness and taking from time to time swallows of white wine. The red tips of their cigarettes rose to their mouths and descended and their glow became more intense with each drag, as their voices, sporadically, intersected in the pitch-black air and slowly faded away. The deck chairs creaked when their sweaty bodies stirred, flattened against the orange-colored canvas which seen from very close up appeared to give off a slight phosphorescence. Elisa has made, in the course of the conversation, reference to an

episode of the evening before: at dusk, just after dropping off
Héctor and the children at the bus to Mar del Plata, she had
walked from the station to a deserted, treeless street, where
she had parked the black car. She had met almost no one in the
two or three blocks that she had covered on foot as she went
from the station to the car: almost no one, and yet it was no
later than seven at night and the sun was still up. When she
reached the black car she had had the feeling that. . . . Elisa has
said on the porch barely illuminated by the dim light filtering
out from the kitchen through the edges of the blue curtain and
falling on the red tiles in precisely the empty space separating
the two deck chairs. And then, all of a sudden, she has stopped
in mid-sentence, saying that no, never mind, it wasn't worth
talking about. Cat didn't appear to have noted the interruption, and had simply emptied his glass of wine in one swallow
and set it down on the floor alongside the deck chair, producing a brief, abrupt sound. Shortly thereafter, they had risen to
their feet and, making their way with difficulty in the darkness, amid the old batteries and rotted tires, they had little by
little approached the yellowish-white horse, seeing with
greater clarity as they approached the dull gleam given off by
the horse's coat. Elisa gently patted it on the neck as Cat,
keeping his distance, commented that the horse's total immobility, like that of a man glued to the wall of a tunnel as a
locomotive goes past him at top speed, was a sign of fear and
mistrust. Not a single one of the horse's muscles seemed to
have moved, as a matter of fact, as they had approached it or
during the minutes that they had been with it. But when they
began walking back to the house, amid the dried-up weeds
that crackled in the darkness, they had begun to hear, once
again, the metallic swishes of its tail and the noise of its hoofs
pawing the ground, as though the entire beige body had
expanded when the strangers left. They went inside the
house, leaving the yard and the porch behind them and
turning out the light in the kitchen as they headed for the
inside rooms. In the living room, as he heard Elisa urinating in

the bathroom, Cat, standing next to the big table, began to leaf through the telephone book and shuffle distractedly through the first addressed envelopes. Then he went into the next room, and without turning on the light, began to look through the open window toward the dark beach: two or three minutes would have to go by before he could begin to distinguish in the great black mass, confused forms of varying thickness, each of them with its particular intensity of blackness, until there would begin to be recognizable the grayish stretch of beach, the river like a sheet of black metal giving off a few dim reflections here and there, the stunted trees of the island like a back curtain without depth whose sinuous upper edge was supposed to represent the silhouette of a row of trees cut out of a large piece of plywood painted black. Cat searched in vain for signs of the presence of the couple on the visible part of the beach; if in fact they heard, as they were eating, the noise of the engine coming from the center of town and perhaps from the asphalt highway and then maneuvering at the entrance to the beach, and after that the sound of doors opening and closing, and the voices and the laughter of the man and the woman, the source of those sounds seemed at present to have been eradicated. But from the window the entrance to the beach is not visible, and a large stretch of it, in the part with the grills and amid the sparse trees, cannot be seen from there. Cat has opened the door leading to the beach and has gone outside, leaving the door halfway open behind him. Walking forward a few paces on the sandy ground he has been able to make out, at the entrance to the beach, slanting downward from the top of the street banked with earth to the slope that leads to the stretch of sand, a big white car that stands out clearly in the darkness. But despite his every effort to penetrate the darkness he has not seen the slightest trace of its occupants.

Just as he goes into the bedroom to get the book that Pigeon has sent him from France, Elisa, who has meticulously stretched the bedsheet taut and carefully placed the pillow against the head of the bed, is taking off, over her head, her white dress. Her bronze breasts shake ponderously, in time to the rhythm of her movements. Elisa carefully folds the dress in two and places it on the backboard of the bed. The straps of her sandals that hold in place the bronze rings resting on her instep are tied together at her calves after crossing each other several times and her thin transparent panties afford a glimpse of a glimpse of a triangle of a more intense and protuberant blackness between her legs. When Elisa turns around to put the dress on the backboard of the bed, Cat notes that her white buttocks escape underneath the panties, which do not manage to hold them in completely: two strips of thick flesh that fold over onto the upper part of her thighs. And when she leans over a little to arrange the dress on the backboard, Cat sees that the transparent fabric of her panties stretches, tensely, over the vertical cleft that separates her buttocks: thanks to an odd effect, the fabric, which loses its blackness because of the tension and becomes even more transparent, appears to contain a sort of diffuse, slate-colored fog, coming up out of the narrow black cleft. Leaning his belly against her slightly protruding buttocks because of her bent-over position, and cradling her drooping breasts in the palms of his hollowed hands, Cat murmurs two or three words in Elisa's ear; she shakes her head and smiles. Then Cat heads for the night table, saying: "Like a horse's, that's right," and picks up the book. As he turns around to leave the room, he halts: on the white sheet that Elisa has just stretched taut there can be seen, in the middle of the bed, one directly next to the other, like two circles of a diameter no greater than that of a ten-centavo coin, two small blood stains.

X   In the beginning, there is nothing. Nothing. The deadly quiet streets, deserted, roasting in the sun and up above, parched, ashen, without a single cloud, full of burning slivers, the sky.

On the roofs of the one- or two-story houses, television antennas gleam, as though they were incandescent. The awnings of the shops, striped, orange, blue, green, polka-dotted, protect, sporadically, stretches of sidewalks from the sun. But their shade is scanty, and since in the downtown area there are almost no trees, and since it is too early in the day—one-thirty in the afternoon at the latest—the rows of houses, straight as a string, but broken off at each intersection, cast over the sidewalks no more than a narrow strip of shade. No coolness comes from the doorways and the shadowed hallways inside through the half-open doors. Dirt accumulates in the doorways of the shops closed for vacation, and on the tile floors inside, two weeks' mail that the postman has slipped underneath the door day after day can be seen. Even the bars are empty: in the darkness inside, apart from a waiter or two, the bartender, the dishwasher, it is rare to see a customer sitting at a table or leaning on the bar counter. The blades of the old black ceiling fans turn endlessly round and round, as do those of the more modern upright fans, placed in strategic corners, tracing periodic semi-circles, feeble drafts of lukewarm air. White laundry is drying on the terrace rooftops; the sun reflects blindingly off the large sheets hung on the clotheslines. In the parks, the February sun withers the trees. The foliage is grayish, scorched, dried up. The unusual silence grows at siesta-time. Behind the windows and the doors left ajar or closed, the city's inhabitants, clad in light garments, snore in their beds without stirring or walk about with a soft whisper of slippers through the darkened rooms that neither fans nor the air conditioning units of the houses of those well off manage to cool completely. Exposed to the sun of February, the unreal month, the city turns to ashes, abandoned.

When she reaches the corner by the market, Elisa stops for a moment on the edge of the sidewalk. She has gone five or six blocks on foot: the edge of her upper lip is beaded with little drops of sweat, as is her forehead on which the thin layer of makeup that protects it has developed a few little cracks. From her straw bag, Elisa takes out a handkerchief rolled up in a ball and gently presses it to various parts of her face: her forehead, her upper lip, her temples, her cheeks. With her eyes half closed, her lips parted and her teeth clenched, one hand resting on top of the other at the level of her abdomen, Elisa looks at the long, straight street stretching out in front of her. Except for a few parked cars, there is nobody, nothing, anywhere along it. After a minute of standing there motionless, owing not so much to hesitation as to a dizzy spell, Elisa steps off the curb onto the street and starts across it. In the middle, the heel of her shoe sinks into the asphalt softened by the heat. The empty shoe remains stuck in the asphalt, and Elisa's body is propelled forward, with her arms thrust out seeking support, preceded by the straw bag that falls to the pavement before she does, its contents beginning to spill all over and even to fly through the air. It is her knees that touch the asphalt first of all, and then the palms of her hands, so that before she realizes it, Elisa is now on all fours in the middle of the deserted street, in her bare feet, since her fall has been so abrupt that her second shoe has come off too, lying lost among the objects that have been flung out of her purse: her dark glasses, one of the lenses of which has broken, her wallet, keys, cosmetics and two or three pieces of cotton. Her knees and the palms of her hands stick to the burning asphalt. Elisa feels the violent pounding of her temples, and her clouded gaze surveys her surroundings. Luckily, the street is still empty. But farther on, in the middle of the block, a man has come out onto the balcony and is standing there motionless, watching her. Elisa, moving about on all fours, begins to gather together her scattered belongings and put them in the bag. Then, by tugging at it, she works the shoe sunk in the viscous asphalt loose and puts it on. Before climbing up onto the sidewalk she glances, furtively, toward the middle of the block. The man on the balcony has disappeared.

The noises of the bus station are now behind her. In the black car, parked in the deserted street, the reddish reflection of the setting sun hits her full in the face as it glances off the rear view mirror. Turning her eyes away, Elisa changes the position of the rear view mirror and starts the engine. Although the sun has begun to go down several hours before—it is after seven—it is still as hot as ever and Elisa can feel the yellow dress, rough and silky at the same time, stuck to her back, between her shoulder blades. And her dizzy feeling, which she had hoped—around noon—would disappear when the sun set, has only worsened. Her mind has turned into a sort of compact, opaque stone, a place where thoughts neither come nor go, and that seems to be unable to establish any relationship with that hazy, burning-hot outside world that fills the whole visible horizon. And in the late afternoon, on trying to cross the street at the corner by the market, she had suddenly found herself, without being altogether aware of what was happening, on all fours in the middle of the street, barefoot, in the midst of the articles that had fallen out of her bag and were scattered all about her on the pavement. Even her dark glasses had broken; and it had taken her a great deal of effort to dig out the shoe, its heel sunk almost all the way into the soft, sticky tar. And, knowing that Héctor and the children no doubt needed her to make the last-minute preparations for the trip, she had been wandering around the city until almost six. There was something about that deserted city, crushed flat beneath the sun, that had made her go around in circles all day long, not looking for anything in particular, from the center to the outskirts and from the outskirts to the center, until the stone of her mind turned dense and opaque, and everything outside grew thick and pasty, without the least clarity, however, having made its way inside. The car takes off, and the two rows of one- or two-story houses not shaded by a single tree, begin filing past toward the rear. She ought, this very minute, Elisa thinks, she doubtless ought to go straight back home, take a bath, rest, but something, she doesn't know what, a force, makes her turn a corner that takes her in the opposite direction from her house, proceed without hesitating down the deserted street, toward the south, and stop the car along the edge of the park. She hasn't come this way looking for anything in particular: neither a person, nor a landscape, nothing. She has parked on the edge of the Parque Sur and is now contemplating, or trying to contemplate, rather, beyond the jacarandas and the *palos borrachos*, the lagoon, almost violet in the dying light. A man and a woman, sitting on a bench underneath the trees, with their backs to the water, interrupt their conversation for a moment to look at her indifferently. But there is nothing, no sign either in the violet water, in the highway that goes by, above the shrubbery, on the other side of the lagoon, nor in the *palos borrachos* whose pink, yellow or white flowers seem flattened by the incandescent air. The couple go back to their desultory conversation. Elisa heads off again. She leaves behind the park, the south of the city, the center, the street she lives on, and then takes nearly the same route again in the opposite direction, until she begins for the second time to drive along the edge of the Parque Sur, the jacarandas and the *palos borrachos*, the yellow, pink and white flowers, that are now beginning to sparkle in the blue semi-darkness of dusk. Once the sun sets, people begin to venture out into the street. Here and there, couples can now be seen strolling arm in arm, families have come out to drink mate on the sidewalk, sitting

in a circle or leaning the backs of their chairs against the wall
on either side of the front door of the house. The steely glitter
of television screens begins to twinkle in most of the houses,
through the windows and doors, thrown wide open, and the
sound of the American serials, with their squealing of tires,
their windows being broken, their syrupy music and bursts of
machine gun fire, come from thousands and thousands of sets
at the same time, filling the hot, darkened air with shudders of
sounds. Elisa leaves the Parque Sur behind for the second
time, and crossing the center of the city—where a few more
people are out and about because night has fallen—and also
leaving it behind, she finally parks in front of the door of her
house. Inside it is dark and very hot. Elisa gets undressed in the
darkness of the bedroom and then opens, one by one, the back
windows. As soon as she reaches the bathroom she turns the
light on. As the water fills the bathtub, Elisa urinates, sitting
on the toilet with her legs apart, her left elbow leaning on her
thigh and her cheek in the palm of her hand. When the tub is
half full, Elisa gets in. The water comes up to her chest, so that
her bronze breasts float, half submerged. With her eyes
closed, her back and her head resting against the sloping inner
curve of the bathtub, Elisa tries to rid herself of her feeling of
malaise, to lighten the compact stone that has taken the place
occupied by her mind, crossed every so often by images that
come all by themselves and that do not seem to belong to
anybody, that evoke nothing, that are not accompanied by
any emotion or any feeling and that do not seem to have any
meaning either, like memories that belonged to other people
and are floating in her head by mistake. Finally she lets herself
slide down and submerges her head in the water. For a few
seconds, the echo of the aquatic sounds that her bronze body
has produced as it plunged all the way into the water lingers in
the lighted bathroom, amid the silence. And when her head
emerges again, with her hair stuck to her temples and to the
back of her neck, dripping water, her eyes, tightly closed,
seem to have more life than when they were staring, open and

fixed, at the ceiling. When she gets out of the bathtub, Elisa
puts on a green bathrobe and a pair of slippers and begins to
dry her hair as she watches television in the darkness of the
living room. A man dressed in a swallow-tailed coat, the
bright parts of whom—his hands, his face, his starched shirt
front, his instrument—appear to be mounted like jewels in
the darkness, is playing a melody on a long silver flute. Where
his eyes should be, there are two dark circles. When the music
ends the flute descends to the level of his chest, his head is
thrust slightly forward in such a way that the shadow around
his eyes is effaced, and on his delicate, almost lipless mouth a
half-smile appears. The man begins to raise the flute slowly,
and just as it is about to touch his lips, the instrument
disintegrates, is pulverized, becomes transformed into a little
cloud of silver dust that sparkles, grows more and more
tenuous until it disappears altogether. The magician bows,
sober and rigid, when the lights in the studio go up and
thunderous applause—no doubt prerecorded— greets his
number. Then, on the local news show, there is mention of a
white horse that has been killed the night before in Rincón.
They broadcast a bulletin from the Society for the Protection
of Animals and the commentator begins to recount the event
in detail. Elisa sets the hair dryer down on the table, and
turning on the light, begins looking for the afternoon paper
that she has picked up as she came in—the delivery boy has
slipped it, as he does every night, underneath the door—and
that she has left, without even glancing at the headlines on the
first page, somewhere around the house. She finds it on the
kitchen table. In the crime section there is a brief article on the
white horse: it is the tenth one that has been killed along the
river in the last few months. More than the death of the horse,
it is the mention of Rincón that has aroused Elisa's interest, as
if the mention of a known place had brought back to her mind
a modicum of reality. But almost the moment she sets the
paper down, still open, on the kitchen table to go turn off the
television that is filling the darkened living room with a blue

glow, Rincón disappears from her thoughts like a dream that
is someone else's and all that is left is the living room in
darkness, her damp body for which even the bathrobe is in its
own way a prison, and the bits and pieces of remote impres-
sions and sensations like memories that there is no way to fit
together so as to form a clear and definite pattern. Elisa
suddenly feels that she is in the present, in that present and not
in some other, surrounded by inert objects that are as much in
the present, or as present, as she herself is, as if the whole,
whose borderlines are vague, had just popped up all in one
piece from a black area, in the same way that a circular
platform on which there is a stage set and actors rises up from
below to the center of the lighted stage. Until after a few
seconds of stupefaction, during which nothing happens,
except for the exteriority against which her comprehension
keeps colliding, her memory, which appeared to be blocked
on the threshold of the lighted area, like an actor whom an
unexpected contretemps keeps from coming onstage, leaving
it empty for a moment, begins to flow again, bringing with it
familiar things that keep filing past one after the other, as
well-organized and as reassuring as the images of a television
program.

   Very early, the light filters horizontally through the slats of
the venetian blinds, turning the warm blackness a light gray
and giving the bronze body, naked, constricted by sleep, a
particular luminosity. On the white rectangle of the bed,
without a pillow, without a top sheet, Elisa is sleeping on her
side, the position of her body making her hip curve upward,
her buttocks jut out, her waist form a hollow and the line of
her back mount straight to the nape of her neck. The thumb
of her right hand disappears between her rounded lips, and
every so often there is heard, in the silent room disturbed by
none of the usual sounds of dawn, the intermittent sound of
Elisa taking a suck on her thumb. The silhouette of her naked
body is duplicated, along its entire length, by a glowing line, a

reflection of the morning light filtering through the slats of the venetian blinds and clinging to the outlines of her bronze body. Her disheveled hair falls over her eyes, so that all that remains alive in Elisa's body are her lips, her mouth emitting those damp sibilant sounds as she sucks, periodically, on her thumb. Below the line of brightness that haloes it, her bronze body seems as though it is plunging into denser and denser zones of shadow, as though it were a thick spot that stands out against the white rectangle on which she is stretched out, and that attains its paroxysm of blackness in the dark line that separates her two round buttocks and that extends, becoming rougher and more uneven, like a wrinkled and enlarged protuberance on the bark of a tree, to her crotch hidden by her placid thighs pressed close together. A car goes past close by, in the street, and the sound of the horse's hoofs against the asphalt and the deafening noise of the wheels break for a moment the silence of the room, causing a shiver to traverse the sleeping body which, when the sound moves off in an undetermined direction, recovers its immobility.

Elisa comes out of the shower in a happy mood, humming. She removes the plastic cap that protected her hair, and wrapping herself in a large-sized towel with green and white stripes, begins to dry herself off gently, pressing the towel against her skin with the palm of her hand so that the porous fabric absorbs the wetness and tossing her head back, so that the skin on her neck grows tense and her eyes half close. But when she goes out of the bathroom, leaving behind the warm steam that clouds the mirror, her head loses its tension and bends forward with her chin resting against her chest above her breasts that slowly jiggle as a consequence of her walking pace which makes her whole body shake.

The bronze ring, resting on her instep, is set firmly in place against her flesh when Elisa finishes winding the leather straps around her ankles several times and ties them securely with a double knot at the calf. The stiffly starched white dress, of rough material, reaches halfway down her thighs and gleams in the semi-darkness of the room. The sun outside, which must be high in the sky by now—it is nearly nine o'clock— makes its presence felt by the horizontal rays of light that filter through the closed blinds. Standing next to the living room table, Elisa checks the contents of her straw bag: her money, her keys, her dark glasses, one of the lenses of which has been broken as a result of her fall the afternoon before, at the corner by the market, cosmetics, two or three pieces of cotton. Picking it up from a chair, Elisa adds her bikini. Her slow, indifferent movements are the only sign of life in the dim, gray, inert room, but the life they possess seems fragile, weak, hopeless. Elisa heads toward the outside door but halfway there she stops, hesitates for a moment, and then comes back and sits down next to the table, leaving the straw bag on the floor at her feet, leaning against the chair leg. With bent head, her face expressionless, Elisa remains motionless for several minutes. Inside her nothing happens. The line of images, of representations, the chain of postcards that flow spontaneously in the darkness has been obstructed some- where and now at the point where ordinarily it becomes vivid there is nothing, nothing is going by, not even blackness or the awareness of blackness; there is nothing more than a colorless emptiness to which not even the word hollow is applicable, since a hollow suggests a form and from Elisa's mind every form is banished. For several minutes no decision, even though it were only that of moving her hand an inch on the table, can be set in motion from that colorless emptiness.

In the treeless street, the morning light is reflected by the gray or white façades of the one- or two-story houses, against the gray tiles and against the dark blue asphalt. Across the way, at this late hour, a woman is washing down the side- walk. She throws soapy water on the tiles and then sweeps it toward the curb. The rhythmical swish of the broom against

the wet tiles is the only sound to be heard in the empty street
and the water that darkens that fragment of sidewalk extin-
guishes its reflection and makes it a contrast to the rest of the
straight, deserted street that stretches to the horizon, immersed in the scorching light that gives the eye no respite.
After hesitating for a moment, recovering from the shock of
that raw brightness, Elisa closes the outside door behind her
and heads for the black car, parked next to the curb. The
woman wielding the broom stops for a moment, looks in
Elisa's direction, and after a few seconds, as though it had
taken her some time to decide, or to remember her duties as a
good neighbor, greets her with a nod of her head. Elisa
answers with a quick gesture, unsmilingly, and gets into the
car. It is so hot inside that Elisa rolls down the windows, opens
the front doors all the way and steps back out onto the
sidewalk, hoping that the unbearable heat inside will lessen a
little. After a few minutes' wait in the sun, on the sidewalk,
she gets back into the car again, closes the doors and starts the
engine. In the middle of the rectangle of the car window, the
woman who was sweeping the sidewalk and hasn't moved,
leaning on the broom handle, looks like a figure in a photograph that shows a familiar scene. When the car starts off,
heading for the nearby intersection, the woman's image
disappears from the car window only to reappear all of a
sudden, a few seconds later, in the rear view mirror.

When she stepped off the sidewalk into the street, in the
deserted late afternoon, the heel of her shoe had sunk into the
asphalt, which the heat had turned into a soft, sticky paste.
Everything had happened in a fraction of a second: she had
taken two or three steps on the soft asphalt and all of a sudden
she had found herself on all fours, crawling in the middle of
the street, on the corner by the market, amid the articles that
had hurtled out of her bag and were strewn all over the
pavement around her. A man was watching from a balcony,
halfway down the block. She had begun to crawl around on

all fours, so as to gather her things together and put them back inside her bag: one of the lenses of her dark glasses had been broken as a result of her fall. Her yellow dress, at once silky and rough to the touch, had two or three little dirty stains, two or three scuffed places, on the side of her right thigh. And on raising her head, after having gathered her things together and stood up, she had noted that the man watching her from up there, from the balcony, had disappeared.

The drought and horses are all that anybody talks about in the market. But the huge area, which occupies an entire block, is less lively than usual, and filled with fewer people. A number of stands are closed. Raw meat hangs from hooks above the counters of the butcher stalls. Kidneys, hearts, tripe hanging in a tangled mass can be seen. On the marble counters bulls' testicles are on display, arranged in pairs. Ribs with thick layers of fat over them are offered for sale, either all in one piece or in sections. There are metal containers overflowing with meat already hacked into pieces and at certain stalls huge whole sides of beef that have not yet been cut into pieces. A small, straight drain runs all along the stalls, serving to draw off all the water from the daily cleaning. In the bottom of it is a stagnant little trickle of blood. From some of the pieces of meat hanging up, dark blood drips at regular intervals. Heads, skinned but whole, of cows, lambs, pigs, fix blind, uniform eyes on the customers who approach the counters. All that meat, which is undoubtedly fresh, gives off a very slight odor that fills Elisa's nostrils when, loaded down with packages, she leaves by the main door and begins to walk toward the black car, parked in the next block. Elisa crosses the intersection: the same one that she has crossed in the opposite direction a while before, coming from the car to the market, and the same one, moreover, where, the day before, as she was about to cross it in the same direction as at present, with no idea how, owing to the fact that the heel of her shoe had gotten stuck in the boiling-hot asphalt, she had all of a sudden found herself on all fours in the middle of the street, gathering together one by one the objects that had fallen out of her straw bag, and lay scattered all about her.

Simone, the man in charge of the Agency, chats with the secretary. Subject: horses. To his way of thinking, the whole story of the horses is only a smoke screen. It is part and parcel, according to Simone, of a government maneuver aimed at justifying mysterious movements of the army and the police. There have no doubt been horses killed, by accident, or in the course of a shootout of some sort, but that whole campaign in the newspapers, on the radio and on television, according to which for months now, periodically, a killer of horses comes out at night to commit his murderous deeds, impelled by an irresistible force, like Peter Lorre in *The Black Vampire*, seems to him, to say the least, a little like a cheap novel.

"Yet that's how it is," Elisa says, savoring the coffee that the secretary has made for the three of them in the little kitchen at the back, participating all the while in the conversation as she goes back and forth.

That's how it is, Elisa says. Above his thick black mustache and his hooked nose, Simone's little eyes follow with interest her reasoning, as do the secretary's, while remaining fixed above the little white cup raised at an angle to her lips.

"Or that *may be* how it is," Elisa corrects herself. "There's no reason to reject the possibility out of hand that someone might decide, one fine day, with no apparent motive, to grab a revolver and go out in the countryside to kill horses."

Simone agrees, half-heartedly. Despite the air conditioning that cools the place, the skin of his dark gnarled face glistens with sweat, no doubt because of the cup of coffee he has just finished drinking. The office seems to be enveloped in the morning silence. The sounds, the voices, the gestures intersect, clear and abrupt, in the cool air of the room. The window, which looks out on a terrace of brick-colored tiles faded by inclement weather, lets in a light dimmed by the shadow of the building that extends to the parapet of the house next to it. But a patch of blue sky is visible from the office. It looks like a sky in the process of disintegrating. The blue is vanishing, eaten away by an infinite number of little white points or of glittering little spots, like a blue china cup covered in places with ashes, and half charred to cinders, after a fire.

Simone puts the boxful of envelopes in the back seat, alongside the one containing the food. Elisa watches him from the shade of the two-story house that protects the sidewalk from the sun without cooling it.

"Everything's ready," Simone says, straightening up and slamming the back door shut. "And tell him that when he gets over his agoraphobia, maybe he'll come have a cup of coffee at the office."

"You're right. He hardly ever goes out any more," Elisa says.

"If the world were to fall to pieces he wouldn't turn a hair," Simone says.

His thick, metallic-looking mustache scratches Elisa's cheeks as they exchange two quick conventional kisses. Elisa gets into the car. Simone's gnarled face appears in the frame of the rolled-down window. "And please, see that he finishes the envelopes on time." Elisa nods, and Simone's face disappears.

In the noon light, the empty city, whose center the car is leaving behind, scintillates beneath the incandescent cupola of the sky of a grayish blue color against which not a single cloud is to be seen on the entire visible horizon. At each corner, the black car slows down, and then accelerates after going through each intersection. Every so often, a human figure can be made out on the sidewalks, in the doorways of the houses, behind the wheel of a car or underneath the awning of a bar. The one- or two-story houses baking in the sun move slowly backwards, in two straight lines, on either side of Elisa. Finally the black car reaches the boulevard and turns in the direction of the suspension bridge. The trees along the walkway in the middle of the boulevard form, over the sidewalk, a thick shadow, but the leaves are too withered to gleam. At the end of the boulevard the trees end, abruptly. There are the two arms of the railway barrier with wide red and white stripes, pointing obliquely toward the sky, the parallel tracks on which the car slows down, and farther ahead, the boulevard that widens and slopes up toward the bridge, leaving behind, on the left, the local television studios, a low modern building with a stretch of yellowish lawn. The car goes out onto the bridge, in a lower gear, and the platform of planks gives a dull rumble. The two yellow cranes rising high in the air near the opposite shore are motionless and the structure of the new highway overpass, made of iron beams that emerge from great blocks of cement on unfinished pillars, rises, unfinished, in the middle of the lagoon, advancing in the direction of the city; there is not a single worker visible in the immediate vicinity. The vast area covered by the lagoon appears to have grown smaller because of the drought, and the shores extend, irregularly, as far as what is ordinarily the middle of the water: in the distance, toward Guadalupe, beyond the pillars of the old railroad bridge—now without a platform—the yellow shores covered with sparse, grayish grass, almost touch each other. The smell of dead fish, of a wild river, enters through the open car windows, overwhelming Elisa, as the car moves toward the exit of the bridge. A white motor boat slowly enters the lagoon, emerging from the small stream that separates the highway overpass under construction from the buildings of the Yacht Club, bits of whose Spanish tile roof can be glimpsed between the tops of the trees that shade it from the sun. The white motor boat leaves behind on the little stream a wake whose edges gradually separate on the surface of the caramel-colored water, heading toward the opposite banks, making the rows of boats—row boats, motor boats, even yachts—moored by their prows along the sandy bank bob up and down as they reach them. Owing to the difference

in weight, in size, in category, the boats pitch with a different
intensity and a different rhythm, as though the cause that has
set them in motion were different for each one, or as though
each one were floating in a particular hermetically sealed
medium, thereby demonstrating the illusory continuity of
the water. The black car finally drives off the black structure
of suspended cables, iron and timberwork, and accelerates as
it comes out on the blue strip of asphalt, to the right of the
white line that separates it into two halves and docilely
follows the layout of the road. As the car continues on—not a
single vehicle can be seen on the horizon—the white line,
which appears to be coming toward Elisa at a uniform speed,
as though it were the ground, the desolate landscape that were
moving, and not the black car, moves at times to the right, to
the left, or most of the time, stays exactly between the two
front wheels, gliding swiftly and constantly beneath the
precise vertex of the hood, as though a powerful force were
winding it up at a point situated behind the black car. The
movement is so uniform that the black car appears to be
motionless on an endless strip running in the opposite direction. On the two plains stretched out on either side of the
highway the grayish dried-out blades of straw, of a regular
height, accentuate, because of their monotony, the impression of immobility. Finally La Guardia appears to the right of
the car, with its brick ovens on the outskirts, its roofs of
Spanish tiles toned down in color by the dust, its yellowish
façades gleaming in the sun, and its main street, a dirt road,
that leads away from the wide, straight, cambered highway
and wanders off into the countryside, toward the river, lined
with two sparse rows of houses and cabins. There is not a soul
in sight in the town: the sun at its zenith has chased the
townspeople inside their houses or, perhaps, under the shade
of the trees in the backyards. When she reaches the highway
checkpoint, where there is a fork in the highway, Elisa slows
down, but the only two policemen to be seen, inside the squat,
rudimentary structure that serves as their office and refuge,

don't even pay any attention to her. The black car accelerates
again. Elisa's feet, criss-crossed by the leather straps of the
sandals whose bronze rings lie flat against her insteps, mechanically work the pedals, and the white dress, pulled up to her
lower belly, shows her bronze thighs whose muscles are
activated by the movement of her feet and calves. The
straight line which goes from the checkpoint at La Toma and
passes by the Arboleda motel, in Colastiné Norte, where
vague, fleeting and confused memories, like those of an
animal, come to her, Elisa drives as though she were asleep,
with her head erect and her eyes half closed, fixed on a
constant, imprecise point, located somewhere in the incandescent air, between the horizon and the car hood. In the
direction of the horizon, the glare of the sun creates mirages of
water as though the highway—from which the white line
that divided it in two has disappeared all of a sudden at the
highway checkpoint—had sunk a little, covered by a luminous, motionless patina above which floats a series of transparent undulating vertical lines that seem to turn the air into
something material. With the first curves that precede, by
several miles, the entrance to Rincón, the highway becomes
more intimate, less desolate, full of villas that peek out from
between the trees, of flower and vegetable gardens maintained with great difficulty by constant watering, and even
enormous *ombú* trees whose tops intersect above the highway,
forming a short tunnel of shade. But the fleeting impression of
coolness ends as suddenly as it has appeared: the black car
comes out onto a deserted, straight stretch, with no trees,
baking in the sun. Some five hundred yards farther on, to the
right, is Rincón, whose first cabins can be discerned on the
outskirts. To the left, just before the dirt road that leads
toward the center of the little town and toward the river,
there is a service station, without a soul in sight. Elisa slows
down, making the turn, and begins to go down the slope that
leads from the paved highway to the dirt road. When she
reaches it, accelerating a little again, from between the back

wheels a dense shower of yellowish dust begins to rise, growing larger as it mounts higher and ending in a roiling swirl. Two rows of oleanders line the street, but the leaves and the pink flowers are dulled by the dust accumulating on them. A little boy, dressed in rags and tatters, slowly crosses the square diagonally, with a bottle of red wine dangling from one hand and a siphon bottle of seltzer water in the other, beneath the *palos borrachos* and the orange trees grown skimpy from the heat which nonetheless cast bits of thin shadow on the yellowed grass. When he spies the black car he stops for two or three seconds, watching it, and then goes on his way, passing between a white globe of the municipal lighting system, balanced atop a pillar, and the bust of San Martín resting on an oblong column whose whiteness has been weathered to a dull gray. Another slow, long and pensive look follows the black car as it goes past the police station: an officer in his shirt sleeves with a white handkerchief tied around his neck to absorb the sweat, is standing on the tall brick sidewalk of the police station, reached from the sandy street by way of a little brick staircase. The high sidewalks, a frequent feature of the center of town, built to prevent buildings from being flooded, seem to be doubly useless now because of the drought. The police officer has turned around to look at the car that is slowly drawing away, enveloped in its cloud of yellow dust, and his sluggish, work-worn face of an animal stultified by the heat, gradually takes shape with facial movements so slow and unconnected, so disarticulated that rather than an expression—properly speaking—they appear to be a series of meaningless grimaces, with no relationship to any hypothetical internal source that would account for the origin of them. Toward the beach, on the outskirts, sidewalks of any sort disappear. There aren't even any roadside ditches. There is only the straight, yellowish strip, with irregular edges lost amid dusty weeds separated from the front yards by some invisible little path and by chain-link fences; a few old brick houses, unwhitewashed, or modern weekend houses,

well kept up and surrounded by shade trees, break the monotony of the street. Elisa makes the turn and sees, toward the far
end of the street, some hundred yards ahead, the big trees that
form a dense arch above the cambered street and the dirt
sidewalk. Through the hollow left by the trees, at the end of
the tunnel of shadow, a patch of blue can be seen, but not the
river. The shower of dust turns into a cloud that literally
covers the black car when Elisa brakes, on a slant toward the
sidewalk, in front of the back entry to the white house.

"Saturday, already," says Cat, who has come out onto the
sidewalk, in shorts and barefoot, and is now looking at her
sandal—the bronze ring—as though it were the only part of
her person that interested him. Tanned by the sun of the entire
summer, his body, almost without down, except for a few
blond hairs on his chest and his legs, stands out against the
vertical stripes, painted in green, on the heavy wooden door.
Elisa puts her bare arm through the straps of the straw bag,
leaving it hanging from her left shoulder. Up until a few
seconds before, she has been holding it against her belly,
clutched in her two hands.

"Yes, Saturday," she says.

Cat slowly shakes his head.

"Saturday," he says.

He goes over and gives her a quick kiss on the lips. His
several days' growth of reddish beard scratches Elisa's cheeks a
little. Cat motions with his head toward the car and, putting
the tips of his fingers together, moves his hand several times at
the level of his mouth, toward his half-open lips, accompanying his gesture with a questioning look, to find out if Elisa has
brought something to eat.

"There's everything," Elisa says, smiling, and turning
toward the black car. Cat points to the two cardboard cartons
lying in the back seat.

"More simony?"

"Yes. The envelopes and the telephone book," Elisa says.

"And what about Pigeon's book?"

"It's in with the envelopes."

"Verrry good," Cat says, parodying the intonation of a schoolmaster addressing a pupil who has recited his lesson properly.

What goes in the refrigerator—meat, vegetables, fruit—gets put away in it; the rest stays in the cardboard carton, in a corner of the kitchen, behind the door leading to the porch: Elisa and Cat put the food away, pour themselves a glass of white wine and go out onto the porch. The contrast between the semi-darkness of the kitchen and the harsh light outside makes them blink. Beyond the porch are the rusted corrugated tin oil drums, one vertical, the other lying on its side, and then come the old batteries, half-buried, and the rotted tires, stained with dried mud lying among the dried-up, dead weeds; and at the far end of the yard, underneath the eucalyptuses, in the part of the lot with no grass—which Cat and Tomatis, Elisa observes, had inexplicably started clearing away one morning, breaking off work as abruptly as they had begun, so that unlike all the backyards in the universe, the back part of this one is cleared and the front part invaded by scrub—dappled by the spots of light filtering through the leaves, the beige horse, which contemplates them, only its tail moving, with a regular, rhythmic beat.

"Don Layo sent it to me to protect it from the killer," Cat says. "But I have the impression that he would prefer that the horse be protected from me. It can't stand the sight of me."

They walk toward the far end of the yard. The tall weeds crackle, hurt Elisa's calves a little; Cat goes on ahead of her for a few yards, his eyes fixed on the horse. Elisa follows him nonchalantly, and when Cat halts two or three yards away from the animal Elisa halts in turn, takes a sip of wine, begins walking again, reaches Cat's side and stops once again. The yellow horse is facing them, standing in front of them with that asymmetry typical of horses: slightly knock-kneed, its legs out of joint, too thick in relation to the volume of the body, and its head, above all, owing to its long neck, which gives the impression of being situated in the wrong place in relation to the remainder of its body, a bit to one side, so that what its head leaves visible is its shoulder blade and the curve of its abdomen, which hides its hind quarters. A fringe of mane, lighter than the rest of its body, falls between its ears, set wide apart. The beige horse, in view of the proximity of its visitors, has become rigid, motionless; only its tail betrays it: every so often, like a pendulum, it appears, spread out behind it, of the same color as its forelocks that fall between its ears, and then disappears again only to reappear a few seconds later on the opposite side.

In the silence of one o'clock in the afternoon, underneath the trees, the beige horse, which Elisa and Cat contemplate, motionless, from two yards away, is motionless, its ears pricked up and separated by the fringe of mane lighter than the rest of its coat, its black nostrils, its eyes that squint a little, its head slightly to one side, thus giving the impression of being situated in the wrong place in relation to the remainder of its body. Its tail, lighter, like the forelocks of its mane, than the rest of its body, betrays it with a metallic swish, appearing, spread out, to the right of its body and then disappearing again.

Cat abruptly raises his glass of white wine to his lips and drains it in one swallow, without ceasing to look, as he drinks, toward the yellowish-white horse, who contemplates them without moving. Elisa too is standing motionless. A slight swishing noise, like grains of extremely fine sand rubbing against each other fleetingly, is heard, and the horse's tail, which has appeared, spreading out, a few seconds before, to the right of its body, then instantly disappearing again, now appears, spread out, on the left side of its body, and once again, instantaneously, disappears.

A ringdove begins to coo. The beige horse's tail, which has spread out, a few seconds before, on the left side of its body, producing a slight, metallic swishing sound, has once again, almost instantaneously, disappeared. Elisa raises her head toward the tops of the eucalyptus trees, looking for the bird, which must have alighted among the leaves, ready to take a nap. But the branches, tall ones, on the eucalyptuses, between which patches of sunlight can be perceived, here and there, appear to be deserted. The grave, low-pitched cooing of the ringdove is heard again, and Elisa, who has started to lower her head, abruptly raises it again, and begins to look in all directions among the leaves, trying to discover the place from which the song of the invisible bird is reaching her ears.

The horse's tail, lighter in color, like its fringe of mane, than the rest of its yellowish coat, has disappeared once more between its hind quarters, after having appeared, spread out, with a metallic swish, on the left side of its body. It is the only thing moving on the compact, asymmetrical body, that is emitting an aura of warmth, a unique odor, to which, doubtless, its own dung and the fodder spread out on the ground contribute, and which is more intense than that of the eucalyptuses, among whose branches, invisible, a ringdove has cooed for the second time.

With the empty glass in his hand, Cat looks fixedly at the beige horse. Beneath the protuberance of its forehead, where the double bony line of its nasal passage begins, the horse's eyes stare steadily back at him. The yellowish body, the tension of which is noticeable, remains perfectly motionless since the alert attitude that it has assumed when it saw them approaching appears to keep in check the slightest tremor. Only its tail, with a certain regularity, moves back and forth, like a pendulum, and now reappears, after having appeared on the right side of its hind quarters, on the left side, spreading out with a dull, metallic swish. A ringdove begins to sing

amid the branches of the eucalyptus trees, at some invisible
point above their heads, in the silence of one in the afternoon,
and after a few seconds' interruption, just as Elisa, who has
raised her head to try to spy the bird among the leaves, begins
to lower it toward the horse, gives another warm, grave coo,
from the invisible point among the leaves where it has settled
down to nap.

"It can't stand the sight of me. Notice the way it looks at
me," Cat says.

Elisa, who is scrutinizing the branches of the trees with her
head raised, looking for the place from which the coos of the
ringdove have come, gives up her search and takes a look at
the horse.

"I feel sorry for him," she says.

"Despite the enormous cock he's got, the big bastard?" Cat
says.

Elisa leans over to one side and leans her head on her right
shoulder to have a look, between the hind legs of the horse, at
the black sac of its genitals.

"I don't notice anything special," she says, straightening
up.

"You must not be the sort of mare he prefers," Cat says.

Elisa turns back toward the house, slowly, disdainfully.

"Paranoid," she says, "and crude besides."

". . . and crude," he says, "besides."

Cat holds her back, grabbing her by the arm, drawing her
toward him, and making her trip. Elisa lets herself fall,
laughing, against Cat's body; owing to the violence of her
movement, a little white wine spills out of her glass and falls to
the ground, where it is immediately absorbed by the bone-
dry earth, leaving a damp little spot. Cat, who has glued his
body to Elisa's back and buttocks, slides his hands underneath
her armpits and begins to fondle her breasts above the white
dress: the palm of his right hand and the back of his left, in

which he is holding his empty glass, rub with a calculated roughness the two fleshy protuberances. The beige horse becomes agitated and begins to draw away: its shod hoofs clatter as they hit the ground, its tail shakes violently, and its head begins to move up and down, and from left to right, so that the warm aura is disturbed and retreats with each movement backward of the yellowish body.

For the third time, after a ten-second interval, the ringdove gives forth with its soft, grave, guttural coo, from the vague point amid the branches of the trees in which it has alighted, doubtless, to take a nap.

When, with the same abruptness with which they began, Cat's violent caresses grow calmer, the beige horse, which has begun to tremble and retreat, stops dead in its tracks, its gaze fixed on the couple which in turn has ceased moving altogether, each of them yielding to the embrace for a very brief moment, during which, all at once, and after a ten-second interval, the ringdove emits its coo for the third time. The cooing resounds in the hot, sun-drenched silence of one o'clock, when the clacking of the horse's hoofs against the sandy ground has barely ceased disappearing completely from the heavy air. The unusual, guttural, soft, warm song of the ringdove, lasting no longer than one or two seconds, has appeared to be, in the course of its brief manifestation, at the very end of time, as though it had been the one force, extremely feeble, that has drawn the entire universe out of its mineral inertia, setting it in motion again after an indeterminate interval of general inability to move, of periodic shipwreck.

For some reason impossible to fathom, Elisa comments, Cat and Tomatis had begun one morning to clear the area at the far end of the backyard, opening up at the same time a path leading in the direction of the pump generator, on the

other side of the house, and leaving the entire front part
covered with those bone-dry weeds, without having even
taken the trouble to gather together the half-buried batteries,
the rotten tires stained with dried mud, the rusted corrugated
oil drums, that were the vestiges of the Garay family's period
of splendor, of the era prior to the death of Garay senior—
prior to Pigeon's departure—, when they could still allow
themselves the luxury of an automobile. Any normal person,
Elisa goes on, as they walk amid the weeds toward the porch
on which the deck chair of orange-colored canvas is reclining
in the sun, any human being other than either Cat or Tomatis,
would have begun by first clearing away the batteries, the
tires and the oil drums and then set about cutting down the
weeds from the edge of the porch to the far end of the yard.
That's not so, Cat says, just as his faded espadrilles touch the
red tiles of the porch: Elisa, who has a slight head start over
him, reaches the blue curtain in a couple of determined
strides. That's not so: the vestiges of the technological era—
the tires, the batteries, the rusted oil drums—ought to be
regarded as a legitimate addition to the landscape, as rightly so
as, for example, the eucalyptus trees that had been planted by
man's hand. So there's no reason, Cat says, following Elisa
into the kitchen, to take them away, and as for the supposed
natural order that according to Elisa the rest of humanity
claimed it was necessary to take into account in judging the
neatness of a yard, it was immediately obvious that such a
claim was absurd. Since space was infinite, it didn't begin
anywhere; each of the points that constituted it was equal to
every other. To begin at any one point amounted to the same
thing as not clearing, behind oneself, an infinite space, only to
find oneself facing the prospect of having to clear, in front of
oneself, another infinite space, or rather, an infinite part of the
same infinite space that began at the blade of the hoe. Cat sets
the empty glass down on the blue and white checkered
tablecloth: it was clear, therefore, that the point at which one
began to clean up, or at which one gave up the job, didn't

matter. One was always doomed to clean up no more than a fragment, and to leave, in any case, no matter at what point one began and ended and also no matter how large the area cleared, an infinite space covered with weeds and underbrush, in whatever direction one looked.

The world was outside of him, inside an enormous diamond, and no opening existed in it that would allow him to enter; he was obliged to resign himself to feeling the smooth wall with his fingers, Cat had said, as they were sitting down at the table, and began helping themselves out of the white dishes on the blue and white checkered tablecloth, slices of the tomatoes that Elisa had cut and seasoned with salt, oil and vinegar on the work counter atop the red-tiled stove. Then he had begun to eat in silence. To her, on the other hand, Elisa had said, there were moments when she seemed to be floating; there was neither an outside nor an inside world. But this happened only at certain moments. Then she had begun to describe, in a monotonous, absent voice, the city: in the late afternoon, when it was ordinarily full of people, there was not one soul to be seen in the downtown area. In the morning, around noon, even on a Saturday, the few shops that hadn't closed were empty, despite the relative coolness coming from their doorways. The dark blue asphalt of the streets melted in the sun. One could even hear the sound of the light.

In the other deck chair, in which he has sat down once again a few moments before, Cat dozes with his eyes closed and his hands resting one atop the other on the crown of his head. His face gleams with sweat. Elisa directs slow, exploratory glances toward that hot, sun-drenched silence that opens out between her and the eucalyptus trees at the far end of the yard, beneath whose shade traversed by rays of sunlight the beige horse is calmly vegetating. The open, rectangular space, longer than it is wide, bordered by a dusty privet hedge, beneath the calcined sky, offers itself to her eyes with such

sharp clarity that for a few seconds it seems to her that she
perceives the exact dimension of every tuft of dried-up
weeds, all irregular in height, from among which emerge the
scattered batteries and half-rotted tires covered with dried
mud stains, each one of the scabs of rust accumulating on the
corrugated surface of the oil drums. And, moreover, the
proper dimension of herself; as though she herself were
nothing but a transparent partition, through which another
gaze, not her own, were looking at that inert landscape of
which her own transparency forms a part. For several seconds
her fixed unblinking gaze remains riveted on the empty
center of the open space, until, all of a sudden, as though it had
been formed, spontaneously, from the emptiness itself, a
butterfly begins fluttering about the backyard, between the
far end of the weeds and the sky, not far above the ground,
hesitantly, its black palpitating wings traversed by yellow
stripes. Elisa's gaze now concentrates on the butterfly, which
begins to fly around in circles, mounting and descending,
continually moving its wings with yellow stripes in a space it
appears to have taken over for itself, one that measures no
more than four or five yards in diameter. As it continues to flit
about, it sometimes descends to the tips of the weeds, brushing against them as it goes by or hovering around them for a
fraction of a second, and then it suddenly flies upward, filling
the empty air, in which its wings striped with yellow gleam
from time to time, with an intricate pattern of straight,
curved, vertical, oblique, helical, horizontal lines, in such a
way that the homogeneous appearance of the emptiness in
which it is evolving keeps falling apart, little by little, until it is
transformed into an infinity of imaginary fragments, as
though the little palpitating body in which the entire life of
the universe appears to have been concentrated, were cleaving, with the cutting edge of its being, the translucent air. Elisa
follows the butterfly's continual evolutions; her gaze sur-
renders to that geometric labyrinth, and for several seconds
even the sensation of her own transparency disappears, as

though she herself had suddenly begun to whirl about in the empty air or as though the butterfly had concentrated within itself not only Elisa's entire exterior, but also her interior, dispersed now and unaware of its new condition within the soft, velvety little body and in the trembling wings with yellow stripes.

Bare naked, Elisa moves forward a little on the bed, on all fours, toward the headboard, looking over her shoulder, paying close attention to Cat's movements as he follows her on his knees, holding in the palm of his half-closed right hand, his reddish, erect penis; the bed shakes a little, as a result of the movement of the bodies seeking a comfortable position in which to couple. The fan, on the night table, periodically sweeps, in a semi-circle, the burning-hot air, in the daytime near-darkness of the room. When Cat, clinging to her buttocks, finally abruptly penetrates her, after poking around with his fingers and the tip of his penis in the folds of her vulva, Elisa lets out a moan, and balancing precariously for a fraction of a second, takes her hands away from above the pillow and presses her palms against the white, rough wall on either side of her head, with her fingers apart. Her forehead grazes the white wall. Cat keeps going in and coming out of her body, with regular movements that change rhythm, speed, depth, so that at times his penis enters as far as it can go, with a slow, calculated push, and then as it comes out again just as slowly every so often, Elisa feels a series of brief tremors that expand like concentric waves through her entire body, causing all of her muscles to quiver as they pass, as the waves of a river set the aquatic plants and the debris floating on the surface to trembling. At certain times, the reddish head touches a crucial point, somewhere, in the depths, a sort of knot that emits concentric circular radiations that gradually reach, through her organs, her tissues, her nerves, her bones and her muscles, the level of her skin, and as the first ones have not yet finished expanding before the red head is already touching the point

again, new radiations are superimposed on the first ones, with
the result that the endless movement occupies the whole of
Elisa's mind and body, eliminating every thought. The entire
universe around her seems totally destroyed, far-distant; of
the man who is going in and coming out, rhythmically, of her
body, of the person whose long, hard, moist organ she clearly
felt up until a few moments before, nothing remains except a
vague, blurred mass, that from time to time touches the point
that sets her to trembling. As the frequency and the intensity
of the radiations that are continually superimposed increase,
more and more numerous, more rapid, more profound, Elisa
keeps gradually raising her head, with her eyes closed, and
opening her mouth wider and wider, she finally sticks out her
tongue, straight, tense, reddish, which begins to wet her own
lips and to vibrate, rigid and pointed, between the corners of
her mouth, until she begins to lick the white wall. At the same
time, her hips begin to move, slowly at first, rocking from left
to right and from right to left, until another circular movement is added to the first, in such a way that the compact
sphere of her buttocks, shaken by the complex rhythm of her
movements, transmits its shaking motions to the naked body
mounted on top of her. With orgasm, their bodies reach the
limit of their tension, which lasts for a few seconds, until,
without losing their rigidity, they let themselves go and fall
back, stretched out one atop the other on the white sheet,
piled one atop the other, like two wooden planks.

Carefully, in an almost kindly way, she makes a pitcher of
lemonade. The afternoon goes by slowly, imperceptibly, and
when nothing is left in the bottom of the pitcher except a
cloudy sediment and wan bits of lemon, Cat, who has been
taking a peek, from time to time, at the horse from the kitchen
through the slit between the blue canvas curtain and the black
door frame, decides to take it out to train it in the late
afternoon, taking off by way of the riverbank and leaving
behind the white house and the beach to which the bathers

have returned, their cries, voices and splashings reaching her, clear and distant, without, however, attracting her attention as she wanders naked around the house, or contemplates, stretched out on the bed, the semi-darkness concentrated on the ceiling of the bedroom. For a few minutes she drops off into a light sleep, which rather than a quick nap is a sort of uncertainty, a little more acute than usual, as to her state—not sure whether it is an illusory waking state or troubled sleep—and from which she awakens, or which, rather, she leaves behind, her mouth dry and her mind a bit befuddled. Then she puts on her scanty two-piece bikini, made of a bright orange stretch fabric with oblique black stripes, takes off her wristwatch, leaving it on the night table, turns the fan off, and going through, one by one, the white rooms with the openings framed in black, a few scattered pieces of furniture and a floor of red tiles, goes out onto the beach through the front door. The bathers are lolling in the setting sun: the smooth river, without a single ripple, is turning violet in the late afternoon, and on the opposite bank of the river, the low-lying, dusty island is motionless and deserted. Its gently sloping bank ends in a reddish edge that the water wears away. Elisa crosses the beach, slowly making her way around the bathers sitting on the sand or on colored towels, and halts at the water's edge: the beach attendant, like a species of sub-aquatic creature, blind and bulky, emerges from the river, ten or twelve yards from the shoreline, showing first his glistening back, around which the water swirls, and then suddenly sticking his head out, giving it a slow, violent shake to remove the water from it. As he walks toward the shore his body emerges, gradually, from the water: his shoulders, his chest, his tense round abdomen, his short bathing trunks clinging to his legs that are relatively thin in relation to the bulk of his body, his rock-hard knees. A whistle hangs from his chest, tied around his neck with a little dark-colored cord. Dripping water, the beach attendant walks past her and greets her with deference. Elisa looks at his feet, tanned like the rest of his body; as he walks along the strip of damp sand bordering the beach, their white soles show as they leave wide and unrecognizable—almost inhuman—imprints. Elisa stands motionless on the shore, breathing in the peculiar odor of the water, a wild smell of decayed vegetation, of aquatic plants, of mud and fish. The din that the bathers' bodies produce as they plunge into the water, the voices, the shouts, the paddling of the littlest children at the water's edge, seem like sounds that are coming from a long way away, as though Elisa were still somewhere else, in deep shadow, and heard them reach her ear after being filtered through the walls, the empty rooms and the air, or even better, as though, shut up in a room in the darkness, thousands of miles from there, she were only imagining them. When she dives in and begins to swim underwater, the sounds vanish from her ears but still linger on in her memory, a little more clearly, it seems to her, than when she was standing on the edge of the beach listening to them, and even a little more clearly than the underwater murmur that surrounds her as she stays on the bottom. Her dip has cleared her head a bit, and when she comes out of the water and begins to walk among the bathers scattered on the sand, the warm air adheres to her skin, as if the dying light, despite its fainter incandescence, had made the air a little more clammy. She feels even better under the cold shower: as though the water were opening, little by little, a curtain in her mind, revealing a minutely detailed, well-lighted stage set of a popular comedy; all the objects are sharply outlined, with their silhouettes standing out clearly in space, recognizable for what they are, their functions definite, and all of them occupying precisely their proper place. When her mind becomes vacant again, there is neither weight, nor opacity, nor anxiety. It is merely the natural interval separating one stage set and another, like the sudden black space that separates, on a white wall, the projection of two colored slides. As she goes on drying herself off in the bathroom there come to her mind memories, thoughts, precise images of persons and

of familiar objects that occupy a natural place in the world
that Elisa does not doubt for a second is the correct and real
one. The easily comprehensible sharpness of the world gives
her a brief feeling of euphoria, which makes itself evident in
the vigor with which, with scrupulous care, she rubs her
naked body dry with the green towel. All of a sudden, a
memory lingers, goes down deeper, occupies the entire
visible horizon, and Elisa gradually recalls one by one its
details, gradually situates it in the museum of her past, all her
attention concentrated on it, accompanying her remem-
brance—which has presented itself to her just because, for no
apparent reason—of the vigorous movements that she is
imparting to the green towel against her damp skin, the color
of bronze. She is not even aware of being in the act of
remembering it. She is slowly entering more deeply into it, as
if she were going into a swamp, and as she sinks down lower
and lower she also does not perceive that her memory is
bottomless, that she could go on adding, if she were of a mind
to, and if memory were on her side, an infinity of details.
Then she crosses, barefoot, on tiptoe, through the white
rooms and gets dressed in the bedroom. Standing in front of
the bathroom mirror, as she slowly brushes her wet black
hair, the memory forsakes her. A succession of images, similar
tó those between one dream and another, occupies its place.
She is in the midst of doing that—brushing her wet hair, as
the drops of water slide down her cheeks and her neck, in the
bathroom where the distant noises from the beach, so close
after all, reach her ears—when Cat arrives, sweating, breathing hard, with that fevered look of people coming back from
the open countryside, absorbed in thought, the expression on
his face neither indifferent nor hostile but instead distant,
fitful. Cat leaves the bathroom as abruptly as he has entered.
When Elisa has finished combing her hair and leaves the
bathroom in turn, she finds him copying names and addresses
out of the phone book onto the white envelopes. "I wonder
what   the   devil   they're   thinking   of   sending   out

inside," Cat murmurs, hearing her come into the room, without interrupting his work. Elisa sits down facing him, on the
other side of the table, and remains motionless for ten seconds:
then she stands up again. Mechanically she does two or three
household tasks and then, once again crossing the room in
which Cat is writing—bent over toward the envelopes and
the phone book—heads for the room at the front, and, throw-
ing the window wide open and leaning on the sill, begins to
contemplate the beach. Many bathers have already left.
Unconsciously, she has doubtless been hearing them go past,
heading for the town or the city, on foot or by car, through
the bedroom window or from the bathroom, whose little
window, set high up, opens onto the porch; though the bathroom, like the bedroom, is located on the side of the house that
overlooks the sidewalk. The bathers who are still there, six or
seven of them including the beach attendant who will doubtless be the last to leave, move slowly along the beach, deeply
tanned, and their silhouettes, paradoxically, stand out more
clearly in the light that has fast faded. The dusk has transformed the visible space into four depthless bands of different
colors: at the top, the broad, greenish band of the sky, against
which the black filigree of the island's vegetation stands out,
amid whose intricate perforations green patches of sky reappear; the violet band of the water, which comes after that of
the vegetation and is full of little spots of smooth brightness
that retain its violet-colored tint, and finally the blue sand,
which portends nightfall, against which are disposed, as
though incorporeal, the moving silhouettes of the last bathers,
whose profiles glow in the absent, scintillating light. When
Elisa withdraws from the window, closing it halfway, the
blue of the beach is already taking over the entire space. At the
back of the house, the black eucalyptuses stand out against a
spot of yellowish red. As she crossed through the rooms, Elisa
has heard the sound of the shower in the bathroom, and now,
settled in the deck chair, in the blue semi-darkness of the
porch, she sees Cat come outside, freshly bathed and shaved,

with a glass of white wine in his hand. For a good while they exchange, in the dusk, until it is pitch dark, an indifferent dialogue, interrupted by endless silences, which they break so as to go have supper. Elisa takes out of the refrigerator a block of cold red meat that she begins to cut up into little pieces and fries in the skillet: the white wine gradually goes to their head, but they are too accustomed to it for the effect to be one of euphoria, and it never goes beyond a slight, almost imperceptible delirium, like a distant maundering or a slight blurring of their vision. During the meal they distract themselves by hearing, by imagining, the sound of the engine of a car slowly approaching from the center of town toward the riverbank and stopping at the beach; they hear the voices and the laughter of a couple getting out of the car and disappearing in the darkness and the silence of the beach. Then for a good while, oblivious of each other, they wander about the house, going outside through the front, to the beach or the porch, roughly touching, observing, or changing the place, here and there, of some object, until finally they join each other on the porch and making the weeds crackle as they walk across the yard to the very back, stop for a few moments underneath the eucalyptuses, near the beige horse which, as it has been doing ever since it came to the house, stops moving altogether and grows tense at the proximity of human beings. The obscure, confused life emanating from the horse, like a sort of warm whirlwind, but at the same time gentle and muffled, forms an aura around it that moves back along with it when the animal moves back and that does not move if it remains motionless. As Elisa is getting undressed to go to bed, Cat enters the bedroom to look for the book that Pigeon has sent from France. Coming from behind her, Cat presses against her naked body and begins to murmur obscenities in her ear; Elisa hears them, absent-mindedly, as one hears rain, continuing the while to spread her white dress out on the headboard of the bed. Before leaving the bedroom, Cat points to two little spots of blood in the middle of the sheet. Blood thou art, he

intones, and to blood thou shalt return. Then he leaves the
room. Before getting into bed, Elisa turns the fan on, lights a
mosquito coil. In the darkness, against the monotonous background of the humming of the fan, lying face up, naked on
the damp sheet, she hears, coming from the kitchen, the
sound of the refrigerator door being slammed shut, a tinkle of
bottles, a chair being dragged across the tiles. With the glass of
white wine within reach of his hand, Cat must be leaning over
toward the open book lying on the kitchen table, as the blue
smoke of his cigarette rises, disintegrating, toward the lamp
around which moths gather, circling round it, blinded, and
smash to pieces by bumping into the table or the walls. He
doubtless is paying no attention to anything around him, all
by himself, holding in the summer night the book that
without him, without his abandonment, would have been
just another object, inert and mute, on the night table, lifeless
and forgotten between the fan that keeps humming continuously and the incandescent end of the coil. Elisa instinctively raises the thumb of her left hand to her mouth and
begins to suck on it; the suction forms a vortex of saliva
around her finger, and the odd sound of her sucking resounds
in the darkness of the bedroom. With no transition, abruptly,
as if the darkness that occupies her mind as she sleeps were
produced by a mechanical switch whose effect is instantaneous, Elisa falls asleep. Two hours later—Elisa doesn't know
that two hours have gone by—she awakens for a few seconds,
sits up a little way and casts a drowsy glance about her: the
lamp on the night table is lighted and Cat, his back leaning
against his pillow folded in two, is lying at her side in the bed,
reading. Elisa forgets, almost at the same moment that she
perceives it, the scene before her eyes, and goes back to sleep.
A mad trilling of birds rouses her from her sleep: through the
half-open window, the morning light is turning the darkness
of the bedroom gray. Cat is sleeping with his face flattened
against the pillow folded in half, his mouth open and twisted,
his buttocks, whiter than the rest of his body, raised in a slight

curve, his right hand stretched out alongside his body, in such
a way that his hand is leaning on the base of his wrist, with his
palm upward and his fingers bent inward, like a claw. Gently,
so as not to awaken him, Elisa gets out of bed and heads for the
bathroom. Just as she goes through the doorway, she hears a
car engine—doubtless the one that they have heard the night
before—slowly ascending the slope leading up from the
beach and beginning to drive off toward the center of town.
Elisa looks at herself, for a few seconds, mechanically, in the
mirror, and then sits down to empty her bowels. She remains
rigid, calm, her soft hands dangling between her bare thighs
on which her forearms are resting, in the clear gray light
filtering through the high little window that overlooks the
porch. Since she has now become used to the excited trilling
that the birds are sending forth from the trees along the
sidewalk, she has ceased to hear it. She has also forgotten
about the sound of the car engine, that she could nonetheless
hear if she paid attention, coming from somewhere in the
town. The detonations that follow sound too far away to
startle her; isolated shots from a revolver or a rifle and the
rattling of a machine gun. They last for several seconds,
interrupted by silences, at once clear and vague, as though,
because of the space that they have traveled so as to reach her
ears, they had been transformed into the shadow of shots, or as
though they had rung out in her imagination or in her
memory.

XI The Chevalier, assuredly, must be wondering, since the others were not him-
self, whether the same thing that was happening to him was
happening to them, that is to say: that each time the members
of the group—his sister Madame de Saint-Ange, the pederast

Dolmancé, Eugénie de Mistival, whose education in libertinage had been the pretext for the orgy, Augustín, Madame de Saint-Ange's gardener and, of course, the Chevalier de Mirval himself—assumed a new position that in the beginning had something sculptural about it, and the new act in common began, yet in the end he experienced the sensation of having gotten nowhere and of finding himself, as before the beginning of it, in the same place. In the excessive show that all of them made of their love of libertinage there was surely something suspect: the verbal ocean in which they submerged their copulations, and, particularly, the routine nature of their expressions, above all, attracted attention. One would have said, to judge from the invariable repetition of their exclamations, that the aspiration to enjoy infinite and ever-renewed sensual pleasure was a mere hypothetical aim and that, when put in sweaty practice, it was subject to the rigorous laws of reality, condemning the participants to a monotony altogether devoid of chance factors, and to the periodic and systematic return of the same sensations. As they were on the point of reaching orgasm, clichés issued from their mouths, ready-made phrases as solid and round as though they had been spitting out their teeth, whose regular and universal form could immediately be recognized: this one was a molar, this one a bicuspid, this one an incisor. To hide the shame of the fiasco, the participants began to speak, theorizing: if they had spent the entire afternoon being inundated with sperm, introducing a gigantic member in a neighbor's anus and savoring the excreta of those charming ladies, it was so as not to destroy the balance of nature and help social revolutions to be carried out to their ultimate consequences. Pedagogical discourses and general principles, meant to edify Eugénie, were repeated in detail following each collective orgasm. The Chevalier must have awaited them with impatience and listened to them with relief: they were minutes of tranquility stolen from the carnal treadmill. Nature, customs, religion, were the favorite subjects of the conversations, aside from the study of minute differences in sexual techniques and practices, aimed at perfecting the moments of pleasure. The Chevalier, who must have ended up praising pure sentiments and confessing that he lent himself to the maneuvers of his friends out of sheer fellow-feeling and good breeding, thereby showing that he had kept himself somewhat apart from the group all this time, was unable to formulate the problem for himself in the terms whereby it leapt to the eye: in the encomium that proceeded, step by step, from copulation to assassination, by way of masturbation, fellatio, sodomy, coprophagia, masochism and sadism, his sister, Madame de Saint-Ange, and Dolmancé the bugger, who were the enthusiastic theoreticians of these activities, implicitly confessed their failure, inasmuch as the ultimate phase of sexual pleasure, murder, was reached precisely because of the impossibility of attaining total enjoyment in the inferior stages. One ate one's neighbor's excreta because getting them out of his or her anus with one's member and one's fingers did not offer sufficient pleasure. It was preferable to suck a member because rubbing it with one's hand was immediately transformed into a mechanical act. Eugénie de Mistival's buttocks were whipped till they bled because Eugénie let it be seen that she was too eager to allow herself to be penetrated from the front and from the back, which, paradoxically, made her more impenetrable and more evasive, because once she had been penetrated from the front and from behind, one realized that no definite result had been obtained and yet there now remained nothing else to penetrate. One arrived at murder out of desperation, and above all so as to get out of the sphere of sexuality which, as the various practices proved, offered no satisfaction. It was always necessary to begin all over again, not so as to repeat a pleasure already experienced, as the theory maintained, but to see whether it was possible at last to experience it. The proof that it was not a matter of repeating a pleasure already experienced was that there had been a first time that the act had been carried out, and that that first time lacked any sort of

empirical reference. Nor, doubtless, was much pleasure to be
attained from murder, inasmuch as it was a matter of mere
substitution. Murder during the act, which might have been
said to consist of a complex form of sexuality, was in reality a
gesture of impatience: since nothing solid could be gotten
from that sweaty, gesticulating body, one did away with it.
The same arguments might have been used as a justification
for suicide. The inability to attain satisfaction was owed no
less to one's own body than to that of the other. In reality, the
Chevalier had to ponder all those problems so as to refute the
theoretical incontinence of his friends, and for that reason
alone. If it had been left up to him, nothing would have
prevented him from fornicating from time to time as God
decrees, with a young and agreeable woman willing to be the
mother of his children, without too much theorizing and
without hoping to obtain a memorable pleasure. Dolmancé
and the Chevalier's sister, however, were outright enemies of
procreation. The Chevalier should share their opinions out of
snobbery, that is to say, out of a lack of opinions of his own. In
general, there was every reason to suppose that the Chevalier
was resigned to those fantasies out of a lack of character or out
of sheer courtesy, traits that usually accompany snobbery.
That snobbery—a tragic snobbery in certain cases, to be
sure—could be his friends' motive was a possibility not to be
rejected out of hand. But in general it might be said, the
Chevalier doubtless thought, that it was a question of an
intense phobia toward sex and sexual activities. Had this not
been so, Madame de Saint-Ange would not have had the
constant conviction that she was corrupting Eugénie. The
persistence with which they corrupted each other was proof
that quite naturally they ascribed sexuality to the sphere of
evil. If that fairy of a Dolmancé, rather than playing the
pedant by citing vague historical and anthropological exam-
ples as a basis for his theories, had been conversant with the
way in which certain Taoist and Tantric sects conceived of
sexuality, it would have been easy for him, had he been

capable of disregarding for a few moments the asses of the young lads who surrounded him, to see that his sexual practices were not chosen by him, but were, rather, directed from outside by society as a whole, that same society whose principles he was endeavoring to trample underfoot. But the Chevalier would not have been able to draw that conclusion on his own. The time to see things from that point of view had not yet arrived. The phobia toward sexuality leapt to the eye by way of many details: first of all there were the digressions, which in the worst of cases were mere pretexts, of the crudest sort, to free themselves of the obligation to fornicate, and in the best of cases, the proof that fornication was nothing but a partial putting into practice of a general theory of nature. Certain perversions were obviously a way of lending a bit of color to sexual activity properly speaking: the husband of Madame de Saint-Ange, for example, so vastly bored as his spouse is sucking his member that to divert himself he has her shit in his mouth. Dolmancé's brief against procreation was also absurd from the point of view of sexuality. If it is a matter of fornicating the greatest possible number of times with the greatest possible number of individuals, it was evident that if one calculated the number of new generations of individuals who can make themselves available to a great fornicator, the claim to be putting a stop to procreation and preventing the birth of new generations of sexual objects is a theoretical way of limiting the possibilities of sexual enjoyment. The hatred of puritanism could also be interpreted from this perspective: if libertines made a martyr of Eugénie's mother, it was doubtless out of envy, since her chastity exempted her from the obligation of having to fornicate from morning to night. At that point in his reading and his reflections, Cat raises his head from the book and remains motionless, his eyes riveted on the blue canvas curtain separating the kitchen from the porch: little by little the images of his reading dissolve, and the awareness of being awake, alone, in the lighted kitchen, sitting in front of the book, alongside his glass of white wine, in the summer night, gradually comes over him, until he is wholly conscious, so conscious that it could be said that he is a little more so than he can bear, because if at first he experiences, for a few seconds, the sensation of being in the middle of things, of recognizing them one by one and of being able to palpate them, to feel their real consistency with no mediation, of having access to their true material, that situation disappears almost immediately and its place is taken by the painful impression that he is abandoned in some fragment of an infinite space and time, without the slightest idea of the journey he must have taken to get where he is nor how he must conduct himself so as to get out. During the next few seconds, it seems to him that the lighted kitchen, like a flimsy decorated plank floating in a black and limitless emptiness, is the one existent frail being set in a dark nothingness, until, all of a sudden, without transition, the white walls, the open door and the blue curtain, the blue and white checkered tablecloth on which the glass of wine, the open book, the ashtray, the cigarettes and matches, the empty chair are lying, are transformed in turn into an abyss, into a bottomless presence whose superficial serenity barely holds back the vortex unremittingly piling up against it on the other side. Bewildered, Cat's eyes slowly sweep the lighted area, as though he were expecting to see, from one moment to the next, the white walls undulate, the straight lines of the backs of the chairs and of the door turn sinuous, the entire room lose its cohesion and begin to disintegrate. A mosquito, just one, a tiny grayish little point that whines softly and begins to fly around in circles before his eyes, doubtless searching for the place on his body on which it will land, draws him out of his reverie and leads him to shake back and forth, two or three times, mechanically, at the level of his face, his hand, which then reaches down toward the glass of wine, picks it up off the blue and white checkered tablecloth, and brings it up to his mouth. The glass, however, which was almost full when his hand picked it up, returns to the table empty.

The others were external to him: it was difficult to perceive precisely their real desires, their real subjective states, in order to be able to compare them with his own, determining thereby the universal or the private nature of his own subjectivity. If what was happening inside him was also happening to the others: that was the problem that the Chevalier de Mirval must ponder. Dolmancé was setting up patterns with their bodies in different positions, and when he had finished setting up the composition, he inserted himself in it in turn, in the place that he had assigned himself, between two young lads. The bodies of others were for Dolmancé the elements of a personal construction: as a child does with his colored blocks, he placed them, one by one, in the place his fantasy chose. He kept endeavoring to order the world according to his own madness, until there came a moment in which the world was effaced and nothing existed except madness. But since the Chevalier was only one more colored block in the composition, it was a matter of indifference to him who set the forms in place, or that destiny should be confused with Dolmancé's madness. Nature, destiny, madness: everything must have become all mixed up in the head of the Chevalier, in whom desire—for which desire was a conventional name—on mounting to his skin, obliterated all limits. It was doubtless difficult for him to know whether he felt desire because its objects were worthy of desire, or whether, in view of the universal convention whereby those objects were desirable, he was left no other alternative than to desire. Why did he desire? Why did Eugénie's lower belly, moving in a regular rhythm thanks to the impetus given it by her hips, awaken desire in him? Why did that body that moved make him desire? It might be the case, for instance, that from this movement, generally considered to be obscene, the Chevalier could deduce Eugénie's subjective desire, which made him believe, as the person who saw it from the outside, in the universal existence of desire and hence in his own desire; but it was also possible that Eugénie, without desiring anything in particular at the beginning, adopted poses considered to be obscene because, taking as her point of departure the principle that desire already existed in the case of the Chevalier and that of the others as a universal tendency from which she did not wish to see herself excluded, she in turn deduced her own desire and acted as though there had been a desire that had motivated her actions. In any event, desire—a conventional name inasmuch as it was an indefinite series of impulses and images that no doubt varied with each individual but went by the name of desire—Elisa, sleeping naked next to him, suddenly sits up in bed, casting a slow, drowsy glance around her, without being completely conscious of what she is seeing, and flops back down on top of the damp sheet, dropping off to sleep immediately—desire in all probability had not gotten him very far, and even in all truth, nowhere at all, for, without question, each time that it began moving, that it increased in him the excitement that brought him to the convulsion of orgasm, the Chevalier was obliged to admit that when it was all over the only thing that remained with him was the unpleasant sensation of having made no progress at all and of finding himself in the same place that he had left from. Not an inch farther ahead. Nothing. Unlike Dolmancé or like his sister or like that little whore Eugénie, he didn't even have left the consolation of having trampled, as appeared to be to his friends' liking, on morality and religion, for the Chevalier did not give the impression of being one of those persons who had to trample on something so as to be able to feel at ease in life, or else, in view of the fact that he was a true libertine, perhaps he had already rid himself of everything that the others were endeavoring to trample underfoot. Nothing. Every time the whole thing began all over again, the desire to reach a definite point, a point that would change him forever, following which he would feel himself to be totally other, entirely different from what he had been before arriving at that point, was replaced, after orgasm, by the same familiar bodily awareness, the well-known titillations, without unfathomable abysses and without any particular elation, which accompanied him from morning to night and of which the sexual act, with all of its possible variants (which, moreover, were extremely limited), was a momentary and superficial interruption. Almost the moment the act was over, the monotonous buzzing set in again. It might be said that the Chevalier's desire was groundless, and should be lowered from the category of desire to that of a mere pretension. In any event, it was making him go round in circles, seeking a liberation whose taste he had no notion of, since he had never experienced it. He was the victim of an optical misapprehension; his perpetual beginning all over again—as though there were some proven advantage in the act of beginning over—set him on the path of seeking a goal that was unknown to him, which was rather absurd, since if he had no idea what his goal was in reality, he was not qualified to know whether he was on the right path or not. The force that caused him to begin all over again—about whose origin he knew nothing and which it was impossible for him to control—was closely related in secret to that fatal sentiment that had induced Count Ugolino to eat his children: hope. Blinded by that nameless thing that he called his desire, paddling endlessly in a monotonous dream, without making a single inch of progress, the Chevalier de Mirval must have been buried up to his neck in the soft paste of hope.

Cat closes the book and lays it down on the floor, alongside his faded espadrilles. For a few moments he remains in that dreamlike state which as he was reading has been filled with images and which is now like a colorless limbo that reflects, without being conscious of doing so, the lighted room in which the two naked bodies are lying motionless on the bed and in which nothing is heard except for the monotonous hum of the fan. Cat turns the switch and the sound, along with the movement that makes the two blades go round and round, gradually dies away, so that the blades, which were a diffuse, humming spot, regularly sending forth gusts of warm air, recover, as they slow down more and more, the form of metallic blades—two vanes that broaden out at their ends, joined in the center of the apparatus by the casing of the motor that drives them and protected by a circular frame made of thin metal ribs—until they finally stop altogether. The mosquito coil, on top of the tin holder that rests in turn on a little white plate, has burned all the way down, leaving on the little plate regular fragments of ash that preserve the flat form of the material that has burned up. Cat turns out the light. For a few seconds his retina retains the vague, violet form of the lamp that his eyes have been looking at before he turned off the light switch. The violet spot, with the vague form of a lamp, gradually splinters, becoming contaminated by the darkness that surrounds it, growing paler and paler, until it disappears completely. There is no longer any difference between having his eyes open or closed; a fluid obscurity, internal or external, that Cat experiences, to which he is sensitive and of which he is conscious, has come over everything known, without a break. Cat becomes motionless, enveloped in endless folds of darkness.

XII

In the beginning, there is nothing. Nothing. The smooth, golden river, without a single ripple, and behind, low-lying, dusty, in the nine o'clock sun, its bank descending gently, half eaten away by the water, the island.

In the evening paper from the day before, the beach attendant, who raises his head every so often to cast an absent-minded glance toward the beach, still deserted because of the early hour—it is barely nine in the morning—attentively reads the crime page: the white horse that he was accustomed to seeing from time to time when the trainer took it out for a gallop, had been found dead in the yard, covered with deep gashes and with a bullet in its head, the morning before, just as the laborer at the chicken ranch had told him.

It was a handsome horse, so white it was almost translucent. The beach attendant was used to seeing it trot nervously along the water's edge, when the trainer took it out to give it a workout. It was one of the best horses in the region: they were getting it ready to race, not at Las Flores, but doubtless at Palermo or at La Plata. The beach attendant raises his head from the newspaper and his eyes stare at the empty beach, and farther away, at the white house whose black blinds are still closed.

That handsome white horse, that he had been used to seeing pass by at a proud trot along the water's edge, ridden by the trainer, or that he had come across at other times, in town, in the morning, when he got out of the bus on his way to the beach, had been found on Friday morning, with a bullet in its head and its body covered with deep gashes all over. The beach attendant lowers his head toward the newspaper, laid out on his knees, and the white house that he had been looking at, almost without seeing it, a fraction of a second before, vanishes like a vision.

Since it is Saturday, there will be more people at the beach than usual, although February, the unreal month, has almost completely emptied the city and the number of bathers, compared with the number of those who come from November to January, is fairly small: but that white horse, the one he was accustomed to seeing with the trainer in the saddle, going through the town or along the water's edge, had been killed with a shot in the head, and then been brutally slashed, on Thursday night, just as the day laborer at the chicken ranch had told him in the afternoon of the previous day.

When he sees, in the ten o'clock sun, the first bathers—a blonde woman with a little boy six or seven years old—walking down the slope that leads from the street to the beach, the beach attendant folds his newspaper in two and places it on top of the rest of his belongings: the blue beach bag, the sandals, two comic books and his pants carefully folded between the blue beach bag and the comic books. He stands up: fat, tanned, with his white helmet on his head and the regulation whistle hanging from a thick cord around his neck, his legs relatively thin in relation to the bulk of his body. The arrival of the first bathers is like the starting signal for getting to work: his outward attitude changes slightly, taking on a certain solemnity. The scrawny tree underneath which he leaves his things is like his center of operations, his materialized magic circle, his animal territory, whose function he is not aware of, although he goes to and from it all day long, when the absence of bathers permits or when he wants to have a look at the entire beach and the bathers for whom he is responsible. At times, when he is walking along among the bathers in the middle of the beach he casts, without being aware of it, furtive and slightly anxious looks, when a bather—a youngster running after a butterfly or an adult looking for a bit of shade—comes too close to the scrawny tree or stays under its scanty shade for too long. At other times, instinctively, he slowly retraces his steps, and approaching the intruder, without saying a word to him, gives him to understand, with gestures that are neither brusque nor hostile, that that territory is his and that all the space around is full of unoccupied places, without a name, where he must go if he is in search of shade. Without ever having thought about it, the beach attendant nonetheless suspects that as space moves away from the place in which his body is located, it gradually loses its precision, and that the horizon full of clear and complete things that surrounds him, must undoubtedly transform itself, with distance, into a softer and more indistinct substance, until it finally turns into a colorless, viscous mass.

The blonde woman and the little boy six or seven years old have taken off the light garments covering them and have placed them near the water. The woman now stretches out face downward on the green towel that she has spread out on the sand and the little boy heads for the water's edge, two or three yards away. At the same time, other bathers listlessly come down the slope leading to the beach. It is two young couples; the men are bare-chested, with only their trousers on, carrying their shirts rolled up into a ball in their hand. The women, who are wearing light dresses over their two-piece swimsuits, are gently swinging their straw beach bags as they descend the slope to the beach, behind the men. The beach attendant, standing in the middle of the vacant beach, alternately watches, without paying too much attention to them, the woman and the little boy install themselves near the water and the two couples who are coming down the slope toward the yellow stretch of beach: someone, it is clear, is going out at night, up and down the river, to kill horses, shooting them in the temple and then brutally slashing them, as was done Thursday night to that handsome white horse that he had sometimes seen, with the trainer in the saddle, trotting along the water's edge. In the blue sky, without a single cloud, the sun gleams, giving off incandescent splinters of light all around it, so that it is impossible to look at it directly. The water is full of reflections and luminous patches that glitter. The two couples leave the slope behind and begin to walk along the beach, just as the little boy's feet, beneath his mother's absent gaze as she lies face downward on the green towel, with her head toward the river, touch the sparkling water.

He is carrying a little transparent plastic bag in his hand, no doubt full of little ice cubes. The beach attendant sees him descend the slope, walk off in an oblique line from the beach properly speaking, gradually approaching the green rowboat. He has already seen him go by, half an hour before, with the cubical bundles of hay. Now, having freed himself of their weight in the Garays' backyard, his movements are nonetheless almost as awkward as before: his head, protected by the straw hat with a round brim, sinks between his twisted shoulders and his body appears to be non-existent inside the shirt and trousers that are of an indefinable color and are too big for him. The beach attendant squats down alongside his beach bag, and with great care, so as not to wrinkle or get sand in his folded pair of pants or disturb the newspaper and the comic books, takes out his white beach attendant's helmet and puts it on as he stands up again, panting a bit. When he turns around, the beach attendant notes that Tilty has already climbed into the rowboat and that, once he has sat down, he begins to maneuver with the oars so as to move away from the riverbank. First he moves the boat backward a little, using the two oars, and once he is a few yards offshore, he begins to maneuver with just one so as to head the prow downstream, and once he has managed to do so he begins to row with both of them again. The splash of the oars in the water is muffled when it reaches the beach attendant's ears, despite its being closer than the din coming from the beach.

He has gradually moved away from the beach on an oblique line, against the background of the bathers scattered about on the sand in different positions, their din reaching the beach attendant's ears. As the beach attendant was squatting down to take his white helmet out of his bag, he has reached the rowboat, and sitting in the middle of it, with his back to the center of the river, he has begun to row with the two oars so as to move away from the shore, then with just one so as to head the prow downstream, and then with both again when he has attained the position he wanted. He is now rowing with a regular rhythm, following the current, down the middle of the river.

When he turns around and begins to walk, slowly, toward the beach, the attendant bears away with him, still sharp and clear, the image of the green rowboat moving off at his back, following the current, down the middle of the river, with the man rowing it bending rhythmically, backward and forward, maneuvering with the oars, with his back to the direction he is taking, as the boat gradually leaves behind it a smooth wake that grows wider and wider and on which the light of the sun, beating down almost directly from the zenith, reverberates. When, on reaching the middle of the beach, strolling about among the bathers, he sees it again, the size of the boat has been reduced considerably, and now the details can scarcely be made out. It is a very small craft, that is moving off downstream—and the fact that it is going off downstream is something that in reality he knows rather than perceives—as though it were suspended and weightless in the excessive light. The beach attendant remains motionless for a few seconds, watching it. Then, turning his gaze toward the white house, he sees Cat Garay, whose naked torso appears at the window, leaning out. In the open space in front of the house, covered with sparse grass, two boys are rolling about on the ground, fighting and shouting, all nothing but a game, because of the multi-colored ball that is now rolling toward the beach, passing alongside the beach attendant and coming to a stop at the feet of the blonde woman, in a sky-blue bikini, whom he has seen emerge from the water a few seconds before and who is drying herself off with a white towel, standing alongside her beach bags and her big green towel spread out on the ground.

In the heat of the afternoon, when the bathers don't dare to remain in the sun, the beach attendant is in the habit of taking a quick dip and then coming back underneath the tree, settling down in the shade to eat his lunch. Now that he has finished his sandwich and is screwing the combination cup and top of his thermos full of ice-cold beer back on, the beach attendant casts fleeting glances toward the vast open space in which the yellow sand, the white house, the caramel-colored river and the arid yellow light reverberate. When he has put the thermos away in the blue bag, he leans his back against the trunk of the tree and remains motionless for a few seconds. How is it possible that someone has been able to vent his fury on that handsome white horse? He has become used to seeing it come at a slow trot along the water's edge, when the trainer took him out to put him through his paces. The beach attendant opens his eyes and contemplates the vast open space that seems to float in the hard light. His tanned, sweating face has a somber expression. As though to make sure he is not mistaken, he reaches for the newspaper and opens it on his fat, naked legs, to the crime page. The pages of the paper rustle sharply in the silence of the afternoon siesta. The beach attendant focuses his eyes on the headline of the article, closes his eyes and his head, a heavy weight, falls down onto his chest.

A little boy, just one, crosses the deserted beach, above which the sky is less bright and lower. The youngster has just emerged, like an apparition, from the water, and is slowly crossing the beach in an oblique line, heading toward the tree against which the beach attendant is sitting. But the youngster is not walking: he is leaping along, his left foot forward and his right one in back leaning on the tip of his toes so as to gain momentum, his left arm bent at the level of his chest, with the fingers bent, and his right one hanging behind him in such a way that his hand keeps slapping his right buttock to goad his body into a gait that in reality is not a walk but a trot. The boy advances, still at a trot, across the deserted and silent beach, on which nothing is heard but the rhythmical sound of his palm slapping his buttock, and an intermittent farting noise, similar to that of horses, that he produces with his mouth. When he is a few yards away, the beach attendant recognizes his youngest son, who is nine years old. The boy goes on trotting, but in the same place, without moving ahead. His trot becomes more and more frantic and his oral farting more intense, so that drops of foamy saliva begin coming out from between his lips. The beach attendant, who in the beginning, despite a certain repressed anxiety he feels, has tried to see the amusing side of the whole thing, begins to demand that the boy put an end to his game. But the longer he talks to him, the more frantically the boy continues his trotting and his farting. The beach attendant says to himself: "He's such an animal he's sick."

The youngster has disappeared now. The beach attendant goes on sitting against the tree. The space in front of him has lost its yellow virulence, and is as though it were bathed in a dusky light. The house is vaguer, more distant; as for the trees, it is a matter of doubt as to whether they are there or not; the river goes on flowing, but somewhere else. That tawny light is exactly like a translucent river at the bottom of which, where no sound reaches, he has been deposited. *An instant goes by in which no instant goes by.* "That's not possible," the beach attendant says to himself. "It's impossible for nothing to go by. Something has to go by." And nonetheless he knows, he perceives that nothing is going by. He feels as though he were looking at the instant with an enormous magnifying glass, which produces an enlargement of such proportions that the point of the instant he is looking at, because it is so distant from the edges that continue to go by, remains motionless, without going by. The beach attendant doesn't want it to go by because he knows that when becoming reaches the motionless point, he will begin to slip, at the same time, and in a paradoxical way, upward and downward, forward and backward, to the right and to the left, quartered. In the two opposite directions at the same time: not in one or the other, but in both at once. The dark terror gives way, almost immediately, to wonderment: the beach attendant, at this instant, perceives that he is sinking, but—how is that possible?—at one and the same time, forward and backward, that the instant that he has been contemplating without moving and that is one, just one, flows in both directions at once, at the same time. In that dusky light that blurs the outlines of things a little—but he no longer knows for sure where he is, and the conviction that he is sitting against the tree and that he has in front of him the vast open space, with the house and the river, and some vague trees in the background, abandons him—, he has the impression, rather, at present, that he is nowhere that is known, or, purely and simply, nowhere.

All of a sudden, the beach attendant raises his head with a start and opens his eyes. The newspaper that lies open on his knees rustles sharply. For a few seconds, the drowsiness that invariably comes over him after eating has turned into a swift-moving, extremely light sleep, from which he has emerged at almost the very moment he dropped off. But in the vast open space, there is really no perceptible sign that might give him some precise notion of how long he has slept. He has no way of knowing that it has lasted no more than a few seconds; the perplexity that overcomes him changes, little by little, into a loss of interest. The white façade, in the background, reverberates in the pitiless, implacable light of February, the unreal month, that arrives in order to place, like a number standing for all of time, the evidence on the table. Despite the sweat running down his face and his neck, leaving traces of anguish, the beach attendant feels, after his sleep of an incalculable duration, in slightly better spirits than when he had finished eating, and eager to go on with the reading of his newspaper which he has had to interrupt, that morning, with the arrival of the first bathers. To begin with, the beach attendant re-reads, on the crime page, the article reporting the murder of the white horse in Rincón, on Thursday night. Yesterday the day laborer at the chicken ranch told him about it: the handsomest horse in the whole region, that was being trained for Las Flores and to top it all off, it was insured. The owner, a man rolling in dough, had been going and coming, all yesterday morning, from his house to the police station. The report in the newspaper is simpler, more circumspect: for the tenth time in recent months the horse-killer had come out the night before to strike another blow in the area along the river. Is it a madman? Is the whole thing a feigned vendetta? Is there a single murderer or several? The newspaper announces that it will publish, in its Saturday edition, that is to say tonight (the beach attendant says to himself, planning at the same time to be sure to read it), a special article by one of the writers on its editorial staff, Carlos Tomatis. The beach attendant finishes reading the crime page and then, turning the pages and making them rustle, looks for the sports page. For half an hour he reads, one by one, the various news items: the new local team is beginning to train for the coming championship series. There is an interview, with a large photograph, of the technical director; it is a matter, he says, of drumming into his players' heads that soccer is, above all else, harmony and combat. As the headline puts it, the "hippic jousts" will resume in March too. But the beach attendant's interest is attracted above all by the column on swimming; a girl from Paraná has won the fifty-meter butterfly event, junior class; her performance has not been exceptional: this was a secondary competition; a boy from Rafaela is planning to swim from Rosario to Buenos Aires. Someone from Rafaela? The beach attendant shrugs and smiles disdainfully: there's not even a river in Rafaela. Finally, the beach attendant turns the page, and takes a quick look at the comics that he has already read that morning.

The fever does not go down in the afternoon: it materializes. Until around five o'clock, it has been a yellow, arid, crystallized, incendiary envelope that has surrounded things, subjecting them to a bright-hot immobility like a diamond, in which everything is inert and sharp, spare and cruel—a presence that glitters, blindingly, and that through its own intensity reduces to nothing everything inside with its harsh, transparent edges. As the sun sets the transparency becomes turbid, a blurred halo encircles things in the ambiguous light;

on the sand that is beginning to grow white blue shadows are projected, and as the rigidity diminishes, a deceptive semi-intimacy comes to the fore. The fever is the result of that lack of reserve: in the abrupt cruelty of the siesta hours everything that was inside remained compact and opaque, whereas the fluidity that creeps in with the late afternoon creates the erroneous impression that something, after all, is possible. To top it all off, the beach has filled with bathers, installed on the riverbank, from which, every so often, they dive into the violet-colored river, raising profound aquatic sounds. For a moment, one even has the impression of belonging, of identity. All those bodies seem to have in common something other than their form, their physiology and their habits, other than the superficial and mechanical images of sociability—something, neither substance nor idea, common to all of them in a broader dimension than matter and animality, a little flame of the same fire of solidarity identical in each one. The beach attendant strolls among his bathers with a precarious happiness, of which he is not conscious, without the confused stupefaction of siesta time, but without any sort of hope either. A little boy emerges, tanned and happy, dripping water, from the lukewarm river. A group of young girls stand in a circle, chatting, in the middle of the slope leading to the beach: they will wear their hair this way or that when they go to the dance tonight. The beach attendant, his mind elsewhere, hears them with a half-smile; their long blue shadows intersect on the white sand, almost parallel to the river. Stretched out on the ground is a large towel with green and yellow vertical stripes; its owner must at present be gamboling in the water; the beach attendant contemplates the alternate parallel stripes that seem to be emitting warm, discreet radiations. In the west, in the direction of the city, the sky has a greenish tint; from the irregular horizon blocked by the stunted, almost dwarf vegetation, a sort of imperceptible vapor rises that veils and softens the light. The beach attendant continues his indolent stroll among the half-naked bodies scorched by the summer sun, without paying attention to the tumult of voices and noise that comes up from the beach and surrounds him, something safe and familiar. All of a sudden, on the pronounced slope that leads from the tree-lined street to the beach, he sees Cat Garay appear, mounted on the beige horse. He descends the slope, at a walking pace, still settling himself more comfortably in the saddle, dressed in the same outfit that the beach attendant has been seeing him in since the beginning of the summer: the pair of shorts, of a nearly unrecognizable white because of successive stains and many washings, the faded espadrilles. Between his legs, the beige horse continues down the slope, cautiously and nervously. From the whole formed by man and horse, there issues, without the beach attendant's being able to form any precise notion of it, an atmosphere of disorder. And they nonetheless continue to descend, at a walking pace, the one mounted on the other, along the slope that leads to the beach, against the dark background of bushy-topped, dusty trees. When the horse's hoofs leave the slope behind, a pull or a jerk on the reins by the horseman induces the horse—not without a good many brusque movements of confusion or unwilling·· ness—to break into a trot; for a moment it trots along parallel to the beach—at the end of it where the attendant and the bathers are—as though it intended to enter the river, until another order transmitted via the reins makes it slow its trot and turn in the opposite direction from the beach and begin trotting again, more and more quickly, in a straight line, along the water's edge, toward the setting sun. The beach attendant has the impression that the horse's trot, requiring three motions, consists of a series of discontinuous leaps that keep it suspended in the air for a fraction of a second and then bring it back to the ground to rebound into the air once more.

XIII Horse's work, Tomatis had said, consisted of *making prisoners sing.* With his hooked nose, his big, slightly round eyes, set wide apart and almost lateral, like those of a whale, his curly black hair cascading down his forehead and temples, weighing closer than ever to two hundred pounds, freshly bathed and shaved, dressed in his white moccasins, an immaculate white shirt and pants, freshly pressed—by his mother?, by his sister?, by his ex-wife?, by one of his occasional female friends?, by a Japanese in a laundry somewhere?—he had climbed out, around eleven in the morning, of a yellow Falcon belonging to *La Región*, with a just-lighted long, fine cigar between the fingers of his left hand, prudently held away from his body so as not to burn his immaculate shirt or get ashes on it. Standing on the porch, alongside his sack of provisions, in the warm shadow—after having taken his leave of the driver and the police reporter who would come by to pick him up at four—against the background, luminous and dry, flowing over the backyard at the far end of which the beige horse was peacefully grazing underneath the trees, Tomatis, tanned and clean, seemed to have that morning the immutable solidity of a calcined stone. After having gone inside to change, he had returned to the porch with his swimming shorts on, arranging his genitals comfortably without false modesty or false bashfulness. They had taken the kitchen table, the deck chairs, the straw-bottomed chairs and the provisions—red wine, meat and entrails for a barbecue—out of doors, transporting everything to the far end of the backyard, under the trees, near the beige horse. The foliage allowed luminous rays of sunlight to filter through, which imprinted themselves on Tomatis's hairy body, changing place at each movement of his body and returning to their initial position when his body stopped moving again: and, Tomatis had then said, that was his function, to make prisoners sing. They brought him, at night, people who had been illegally arrested, so that he could give them the workover. He was a professional, a technician, doubtless incapable of determining the proper weight of the evidence he obtained. Almost an artist, a *naïf*, Tomatis had said, able to extract the most inaccessible sounds from an instrument, but lacking the ability to find the right place for them in a system. It was even rumored that there was a little room in the police station, a concert hall, soundproofed and containing the latest and most advanced technical equipment. That it had already been built, or was about to be. For the moment, Tomatis had said, that modernization had had to be abandoned: that morning, the gang had pumped nine bullets into him, three of them in the noggin. He must still be there, stretched out face downward on the sidewalk. He had just seen him, almost all in one piece, except for the head, a little messed up, in a pool of blood that had overflowed from the high brick sidewalk into the drainage ditch below: that man had been brimming over with health. There was a swarm of police officers and male nurses, but the army had taken things in hand; a search-and-seize operation throughout the entire province; the townspeople, isolated from the rest of the world. Had they—Elisa and Cat—happened to see a group of individuals, dressed like Fidel Castro, with a sub-machine-gun? If they managed to catch sight of them, they were to call without fail, as soon as possible, Operational Headquarters. Tomatis had burst out laughing at his own witticism, and then had gone on. The asphalt highway was blocked off in both directions, a half-mile away from the town. Nobody could get through. That Sunday, nobody would be coming to the beach. In fact Elisa, shortly before Tomatis's arrival, had noticed, not without astonishment, that the beach was deserted. Not even the beach attendant was there, but it had not occurred to her to relate his absence to the shots she had heard that morning. And Cat had not seen a helicopter, but as he was drinking a couple of mates in the window at the front of the house, he had heard the noise of its engine and had seen its shadow, along with the clear shadow of the rotating blades, gliding along the empty beach. So, you see! Tomatis had exclaimed: they were patrolling the entire region, by car and by helicopter, but the gang hadn't left a trace. Apparently, one group had spent the night on the beach. The other had come from the north; from Leyes, perhaps. They had used walkie-talkies to give each other their respective positions. Horse, who, as a good civil servant, arrived at work on the dot every day, hadn't even had time to go inside the police station; he had gotten out of the red jeep, gone up the cement culvert that affords access to the sidewalk, but he had not had time to go inside the station. The white Falcon from the beach had driven up slowly, unhurriedly, and almost without stopping, had proceeded, as calm as you please, to mow him down. There had been a rapid exchange of fire with two of the gang—one of whom had been hit in the leg by a bullet—and then, everything had been all peace and quiet once again. The cars seemed to have disappeared from the surface of the earth. The soldiers' hypothesis, Tomatis had said, was that, like the god of Patmos, perhaps, they were close at hand but difficult to grasp. So they combed the whole region minutely: house by house, block by block, street by street. At that precise moment, they had heard the noise of engines and had seen a jeep and an army truck full of soldiers arrive. The vehicles, enveloped in a cloud of white dust, had stopped in the middle of the cambered street and the soldiers had started to climb out, following the orders shouted out by an officer. The soldiers, sub-machine-guns in hand, had looked suspiciously at the black car parked along the shoulder. Then they had divided into two groups, one of which had disappeared down the cambered street in the direction of the beach and the other, headed by the officer, had approached the green entry door. On seeing them arrive,

Tomatis had stood up and gone out to meet them; he apparently knew the officer and after two or three minutes of jovial conversation had talked him out of searching the house. To all appearances the officer too hadn't been all fired up with enthusiasm at the prospect of a detailed search; doubtless he had his own theory concerning the cars that they were searching for; or perhaps he was very warm, as was justifiable, since there he was, dressed in fatigues, holding his sub-machine-gun, with the sun mounting to its zenith, blinking his drowsy eyes in Tomatis's direction, while the latter, on the inside of the green entry, quite to the contrary, seemed cool and comfortable in his short white bathing trunks that revealed his hairy, tanned body. The officer seemed small and frail, despite his sub-machine-gun and his contingent of armed soldiers, compared to the heavy-set, half-naked civilian who stood there smoking his cigar with a self-satisfied, off-handed air. For a few minutes, until the patrol returned from the beach, the voices of Tomatis and the officer continued to reach the point where he, Cat, and Elisa were standing alongside the deck chairs and ready to come join the officer the moment they were summoned, underneath the trees, near the beige horse that appeared indifferent—or was that a thought that had just occurred to him?—in the presence of the army troops, with neither he nor Elisa clearly perceiving the meaning of the words or even the overall meaning of the conversation. Finally the officer had decided to take off, and even gave a brief, cordial salute in the direction of the trees at the back of the yard. Tomatis had waited in the sun, near the entry, for the soldiers to climb back into the truck and the jeep, in which the officer had installed himself, in the front seat, next to the driver, and for the vehicles to start up, backing up slowly and raising a cloud of white dust—he had been able to see them, moving off in reverse, through the privet hedge separating the rear of the yard from the side-walk. Tomatis had returned at the same disarticulated pace at which he had headed for the front entry; since he was barefoot, he leaned his weight on each foot cautiously, so as not to hurt himself on the thorns, the bits of branches and the little pieces of brick that were strewn all over the ground; if by chance the sole of his foot came down on a sharp shard of the detritus, his entire body began to go into contortions, and once he even had to stop altogether, grimacing in pain and writhing more than ever and crossing his right calf over his left knee, he had pulled out a little thorn stuck in his heel. After that he had come the rest of the way on tiptoe, and sitting down in his deck chair again, had gone on inspecting the sole of his right foot so as to remove all foreign bodies from it. Then he had grabbed the mate gourd that Cat held out to him and begun sucking at the sipper: that officer kept coming to the newspaper to ask for favors because he was a member of a rowing club and liked publicity. He had met him a short while before in the police station and the officer, calling him aside, six feet away from Horse's body, had reproached him for the fact that in *La Región* many more news items about a rival club were published than about his own, and that the following week he would be coming to see him so that Tomatis would see to it that two or three articles on the activities of his club came out in the paper. Tomatis, on handing back the mate gourd, had made a gesture of immeasurable disdain: it wouldn't surprise me if they shot into the crowd, after that, he had said. He had begun almost immediately to explain the reasons for his presence in the town. The publisher of the paper had called him at eight-thirty in the morning—"At eight-thirty, can you imagine?" Tomatis had repeated, turning his index finger around and around at his left temple—to tell him that the first piece he'd written was marvelous; and just at that moment, on the other telephone, the publisher had been informed of the bumping off of the chief of police. The publisher had then asked him to come to the city with the police reporter to see what was going on. He had agreed without a moment's hesitation, since he'd seen a chance to kill two birds with one stone; on the one hand, the

piece about the execution; on the other, a little barbecue at
Cat's. He had gone to get the meat in María Selva, at a little
market in the Calle Pedro Centeno, which could be relied on.
Horse hadn't died in vain—Tomatis had accompanied this
last statement with a quick little laugh and a rhythmical,
repeated furrowing of his tanned brow. Unfortunately, there
also existed the negative side of things; at four o'clock they
would come by to get him to take him back to the newspaper
office, since he had to lock up the Sunday literary page. When
they had finished drinking their mate the three of them had
gone out to the sidewalk, going past the black car parked on
the shoulder heading almost directly into the ditch, covered
with white dust, just as the trees protecting it from the sun
were; they had gone down the slope leading to the beach,
crossed the yellow expanse, and stopped for a moment at the
water's edge. For several minutes, on the deserted beach
turning to ashes in the luminous oven of midday, the cries, the
laughter, and the compact aquatic sounds of plunges into the
river and arm strokes had resounded. When they came out of
the water, they had sat for a while on the riverbank to dry off
and have a cigarette. There wasn't the slightest breeze blowing, nothing. There had been that dead-still, hot air at midday
that now, lying in bed, he remembers with near-panic.
Tomatis and Elisa, sitting opposite, on the sand, stood out
against that mineral air, and the smoke of their cigarettes
mounted, slow and terrible, toward the sun whose light, arid,
burning-hot and metallic, filled the entire sky. Once dry,
shaking the sand off their swimsuits, they had slowly returned
to the backyard. Tomatis had spread the raw meat out on the
papers it had been wrapped in, on the cleared table, and had
begun sprinkling salt on the entrails, the ribs, the fat. At a
certain moment he had lifted up in the air a kidney cut in two,
and had started declaiming, slowly and satirically, as though
he were improvising, though it was really the parodic verse
that had been his favorite for several months now: *Ever and
always, without pause/let us sing the praises of Captain Fontana/*

who turned this world into a slaughterhouse/defending it for the vegetarian cause. Every so often two or three enormous green flies alighted on the pieces of raw meat, indifferent to the rapid and violent waves of Tomatis's hand to chase them away. He had lighted the fire, in the strip of yard that had been cleared, between the trees at the very back beneath which the beige horse grazed ceaselessly, and the dry weeds that extended almost to the edge of the porch and amid which there lay, in the beaming sun, the batteries and the worn-out tires, half-buried and stained with dried mud, and the two rusted oil drums of corrugated tin, one vertical and the other lying on its side. He had gone to get wood at the far end of the yard, behind the trees, from the pile heaped up against the wire mesh, hidden from sight and bent over by the weight of the honeysuckle vine, which marked the border of the property. He is thinking now about honeysuckle, about the scent of honeysuckle that comes back to him, and that his memory pictures so clearly that it is as though he were smelling it, despite the fact that he is lying in bed, in the greenish semi-darkness that the five o'clock sun is casting its light into as it filters through the trees along the sidewalk. For a few seconds, the strength and the distinctness of the scent are so great that he wonders whether by some chance Elisa hasn't placed a branch of honeysuckle in the room, and he checks by casting a quick glance all around, until, absorbed and well-nigh amazed by the presence, in his senses, of that consequence without a cause, he fails to realize that he is smelling so intently that all of him is disappearing or is, rather, being transformed into the scent. Then that passes and he lets himself be carried away, once more, by the primary rhythm of memory. The images he forms in his mind are of a relative and varying clarity; they impress themselves upon him without cohesion, in fragments: Tomatis, dressed in white, takes his leave of them with a wave of his hand and installs himself in the front seat of the yellow car, next to the driver who begins to turn the car around so that it faces in the opposite direction from the beach, in order to head back along the highway to the city. He is now sitting opposite him, on the other side of the table; the three or four glasses of wine that he has drunk since he began barbecuing the meat have made him sweaty and excited. He chews the first mouthfuls of fat meat as fast as he can, bringing them to his mouth one after the other, going on talking without stopping: it is perhaps at this time that he tells him that on Monday night there is going to be a clandestine game of baccarat and that, if he likes, he can go with him. He replies that he'll decide the next day—that he'll doubtless go, if it's not as hot and if he goes with Elisa to the city. Tomatis's dry solidity has been spoiled by fatigue, the wine, the closeness of the fire; the hair on his chest is completely stuck to his skin between his protruding nipples, just as his black hair is plastered to his temples, because of the sweat pouring forth from his forehead, his upper lip, his neck and sliding down his tanned skin, leaving dark traces. Now, with his fingers stained by the black grease of the grill, he grabs a bone and begins to tug at it with his teeth to remove from it the last fibers of meat, of singed and crackling tissues, of grease and of cartilage. When he leaves the glass empty on the table, his fingerprints are visible on the transparent surface. Now Cat observes, opposite him, beyond the foot of the bed, the upper part of the wall facing him, whose whiteness is attenuated by the greenish semi-darkness that the trees along the sidewalk allow to filter through. He is lying face up, naked, sweaty, amid a silence so excessive that he moves a little in the bed to do away with it but the creakings of the box mattress echo briefly and clearly and immediately disappear, swallowed up by that intense, homogeneous silence. The creaking of the bedsprings resounds again, as Cat leans over the edge of the bed and picks up off the red tiles the newspaper of the evening before that Tomatis has given him that morning; the paper, folded in four, has a four-column article—the first of a series of three—devoted to the horse killings. In this first piece, Tomatis talks about Ajax and the Atrides; reading

it, Cat smiles and shakes his head: Tomatis—that smile,
tender and knowing, and those shakings of Cat's head appear
to signify—must have told himself that the mixture of artistic
prose and erudition would impress the paper's publisher and
induce in him a state of mind favorable to the granting of a
double bonus or a raise in salary, or would reinforce in him his
devout dependence on Tomatis's Olympian facility for
journalistic rhetoric: from the Atrides, Tomatis proceeds to
the rites of the scapegoat: the usual proportion of aggressive-
ness—Cat interrupts his reading here to light a cigarette,
taking it out of a half-empty package that he puts back down
on the night table, an operation that he repeats with the box of
matches—is gotten rid of by foisting it off onto an individual,
or a species, or a group or a race that takes the blame for what
is negative in everyone and thereby contributes to lessening
social tension; another explanation, Tomatis's article goes on
to say, might be that of ritual crime; some sect or other had
decided from one day to the next to adopt the horse as its
sacrificial animal; in other eras and other places, other animals
had fulfilled that function: bulls, lambs, stags, and so on.
There was no reason to be surprised that this time it fell to the
lot of horses: in other countries, consideration for horses was
non-existent; in France, for instance, there were special
butcher shops where the one thing sold was horse meat—in
France, the country of Descartes and Voltaire! At this point in
his reading, Cat's smile turns into a quiet, intermittent,
abstracted laugh, which soon crystallizes into an astonished
grin: according to Tomatis, certain nihilistic tribes of Oceania
begin killing, at certain times of the year, an unspecified
number of animals of the same species, standing symbolically
for the general extermination of all living species; an English
ethnologist, Leopold Bloom, according to the very last part
of the article, has given this ceremony the name of 'ritual
synecdoche.' The fixed grin of amazement on Cat's face turns
into a loud guffaw, the newspaper folded in four falls alongside the grayish pair of shorts lying on the red tiles, next to the

bed, as Cat's naked body is convulsed with laughter on the
damp sheet and his chortles resound in the room darkened by
the half-shadow of a greenish color that the trees along the
sidewalk allow to filter through. For at least a minute, Cat's
guffaws resound in the empty bedroom until, gradually, the
convulsions of his naked body grow farther and farther apart,
less intense, and finally cease to begin all over again. The room
is plunged once more into complete silence, for several
seconds, when Elisa, who has come in from some other room
without a sound, as though not even her naked feet have
alighted on the red tiles, appears in the rectangle of the open
doorway. All she has on is her bikini and a multi-colored scarf
tied tightly around her head, holding back and hiding her
black hair. Her washed face, without makeup, is oval, full,
just a bit soft, and the color of her skin all over her body has
more than ever the texture and the gleam of reddish-yellow
bronze, against which there stands out the stretch fabric of her
bikini, of a bright orange color with oblique black stripes.
Elisa's questioning look shows that she has heard Cat's guffaws and has come to the bedroom to determine the cause of
them. Cat explains before Elisa opens her mouth: "Tomatis,"
he says. "Didn't you read his article?" Yes, she has read it; and
didn't she see that it was full of absurd details that he'd made
up? Well, maybe; yes . . . well, maybe. In the final analysis, no;
she wasn't sure. And was that what had seemed so funny to
him? Elisa in turn shakes her head and smiles. She walks across
the room enveloped in greenish semi-darkness, and sits down
on the edge of the bed, almost at Cat's feet. Ceasing to smile
and shake his head, Cat looks at her: the words that she has just
uttered, her movements and her breathing, are the only signs
forthcoming, fleetingly, from that body curled up on the
edge of the bed; her dark eyes too appear to emit a gleam,
something indefinable, omnipresent and immaterial, to
which it is impossible to assign a precise meaning and which is
also, like her words or her movement, a sign of life. Chaste
and solid, as she now looks at him, the bronze flesh seems to be

supported by that indefinable emanation floating at the level of her eyes. To test her reality, Cat moves his foot and touches, with toes clumsy for touching, her thigh flattened against the sheet; his toes, his toenails, run over the skin that affords a hint of the tension of her muscles, the conglomerate of nerves, veins, arteries, tissues, looped around the impassive bone. On her knee can be seen the scattered crusts, like a dark archipelago, the dried scars of a healed scrape; his big toe caresses them and the toenail of it, deliberately, lightly scratches at it. But the bronze flesh remains motionless; now that Elisa has lowered her eyes so as to follow the movements of the foot that is grazing it, her eyelids, lowering in turn, intercept the humid emanation, full of bright intermittent sparkles, and her body appears to close in upon itself, solid, external and definite, to the point that Cat, withdrawing his foot, also closes his eyes and stops moving.

XIV

As on a deserted planet, as on a desert, not a sound is heard. The beach is empty. For some unknown reason, the Sunday bathers have not turned up. Nobody has stretched out on colored towels to get some sun, nobody is strolling along the beach, nobody is wetting his or her feet at the water's edge, nobody, nothing. Not even the beach attendant, who is always there at his post from nine in the morning, and even earlier on Sundays, seems to have turned up today. On the opposite bank, the low-lying dusty island, with its slope gently descending toward the water, turns ashen in the sun of ten in the morning, the one, terrible sun of February, that strips everything naked with its harsh, arid, motionless, fathomless light like a yellow maelstrom. Before me, beyond the open space of the beach, of the river, which appears to be motionless, is the low-lying, dusty island—it is the low-lying, dusty island turning to ashes in the February sun, against a cloudless, smooth sky, the only blue part of which is near the horizon, because the rest seems to be split apart to infinity by those hard, scintillating splinters. It is that low-lying, dusty island in the silence of what I call morning.

The aluminum kettle is sitting on the windowsill, the inside half of the wall which the black frame divides in two. I pick it up and slowly fill the warm mate gourd that I am holding in the hollow palm of the other hand. When the green, iridescent foam reaches the opening on top of the gourd, I place the kettle back on the windowsill, put the sipper between my lips and begin to suck. The bitter taste of the mate fills my mouth, and the hot liquid, that makes me sweat and seems as though it is sweeping away the remains of sleep, goes down my throat, until the very last sips, which bring less and less liquid to my mouth through the sipper each time, finally produce, in the bottom of the mate gourd, a hoarse, muffled gurgle.

Before me, beyond the open space of the beach, of the river, which appears to be motionless, is the low-lying, dusty island, turning to ashes in the February sun, against a cloudless, smooth sky, the only blue part of which is near the horizon, because the rest seems to be split apart to infinity by those hard, scintillating splinters. It is that low-lying, dusty island in the silence of what I call morning.

A helicopter engine, nearly inaudible at first, then clear, and coming closer and closer, begins to be heard in the empty morning. The aluminum kettle that I have just put back on the windowsill, holding it by the handle, remains suspended in the air, with the spout inclined toward the opening of the mate gourd, which I am holding in the hollow palm of the other hand, but no water comes out of the spout since I halt midway in my gesture of pouring, standing

motionless so as to hear better and discern the exact direction
from which the sound of the helicopter is coming. I finally
manage to make it out: it is coming from the west, from the
city, and must already be flying over the town. From the
increasingly loud noise, I realize that it is coming closer and
closer and that it must be flying very low, very nearly on a
level with the rooftops and the treetops. All of a sudden, I
realize that it is almost directly above my head, since the
noise, which already is a din, breaks down into a complex
series of mechanical sounds. I lean out the window and raise
my head to watch it go by, but there is no helicopter in the
incandescent sky. Like a mute sign, the only thing I see go
by, on the yellow sand, gliding along parallel to the river,
is its black shadow, which keeps changing slightly because
of the gentle unevennesses of the terrain, so clear that from
the window I can even see the whirling shadow of the
blades, whose movement is visible because of a rhythmic
change in the shade of blackness of the shape it traces on the
ground.

Before me, beyond the open space of the beach, of the
river, which appears to be motionless, is the low-lying, dusty
island, turning to ashes in the February sun, against a
cloudless, smooth sky, the only blue part of which is near the
horizon, because the rest seems to be split apart to infinity by
those hard, scintillating splinters. It is that low-lying, dusty
island in the silence of what I call morning.

The aluminum kettle is sitting on the windowsill, the
inside half of the wall which the black frame divides in two. I
pick it up and slowly fill the warm mate gourd that I am
holding in the hollow palm of the other hand. When the
green, iridescent foam reaches the opening on top of the
gourd, I place the kettle back on the windowsill, put the
sipper between my lips, and begin to suck. The bitter taste of
the mate fills my mouth, and the hot liquid, that makes me

sweat and seems as though it is sweeping away the remains of sleep, goes down my throat, until the very last sips, which bring less and less liquid to my mouth through the sipper each time, finally produce, in the bottom of the mate gourd, a hoarse, muffled gurgle.

The ones in the light-colored car who have spent the night on the beach—Tomatis doesn't know this—have carried out the criminal attack. Did the others perhaps direct the operation by walkie-talkie, did they inform the killers of Horse's movements, did they go on ahead so as to guide the light-colored car as it made its getaway? Hard to say. Was there perhaps just one car, the one that the police officers saw and on whose occupants they opened fire? Several witnesses saw two light-colored cars, the one following closely behind the other, on the asphalt highway, heading in the direction of the city. But the thesis upheld by the army was that the car or cars couldn't have gone too far, since, like the god of Patmos, Tomatis says, they are close at hand but difficult to grasp. Horse, Tomatis has said a moment before, had had time to go up the culvert to the high brick sidewalk, but not time enough to go inside the police station. He's there now, he has said, lying face down, soaked in his own blood, on the bricks.

Standing at the edge of the water, Elisa and Tomatis, their backs to the house, are clearly outlined against the low-lying, dusty island and the ashen blue of the sky. They look at the warm water, golden or caramel-colored, flowing past, almost imperceptibly, toward the south. Behind is the semi-circle of the beach, with the white house that is dazzlingly bright in the sun and that no longer projects, on the expanse of sparse grass preceding the beach properly speaking, even a narrow stretch of shade. The air, at certain times, seems to be clouded by an ash-colored haze, and the contrast between the blue of the sky and the yellow light creates a sort of greenish transparency. As we crossed the yellow expanse of beach, the sand burned the soles of our feet. We were obliged to walk as though we were bouncing up and down, so as to lessen the pressure of our feet on the hot surface. Elisa and Tomatis, their backs turned to me as I place the cigars, the cigarettes and the matches on the ground, stand out against the low-lying, dusty island and the ashen blue of the sky, criss-crossed with greenish reflections. All of a sudden, Tomatis squats down and begins looking at the strip of soft, damp sand that separates the beach from the water. "Look," he says. "Tracks." We squat down next to him: on the smooth, damp strip a little bird has left, sharp and clear, repeated several times in an irregular line, the imprint of its feet: an acute angle divided by a bisector, a fragile miniature skeleton of a fan, a sign. Tomatis gives a laugh, slow and brief, engrossed, staring intently—panting a bit because of the uncomfortable position of his body—at the tiny track.

Upstream, on the edge of the ford, a fair portion of the ground is torn up by horses' hoofprints; dry, superimposed pools, like earth trampled on deliberately, and constantly, by innumerable hoofs, form a surface tormented by a script less clear and subtle than that of the birds on the beach, a desperate, archaic idiom that stammers out panic and confusion.

From the edge of the ford, upriver, I see Elisa and Tomatis slowly go into the water. Tomatis precedes her, taking more and more laborious steps as the water's depth increases its resistance.

We come out dripping water, panting and laughing. The great empty, calcined space is filled with the sound of our voices and of the aquatic din that our legs make, a din that becomes less and less profound and noisy as we gradually approach the riverbank. When we emerge from the water, our bare feet walk quickly across the sand, barely touching it, and our bathing suits, stiff and heavy because of the water, make a harsh rustling sound as we sit down, in a circle, to smoke.

The shade of the farthest eucalyptuses, at the very back of the plot of ground, has protected the honeysuckle from the sun; the wire mesh that separates the plot of land from the vacant lot next door has half toppled over and disappears amid its leaves. This whole area of the yard smells of honeysuckle. The little flowers, yellow and white, languishing, dot the dusty foliage. Along with the wood that I have gathered, as I walk away from the back of the yard, making the dry eucalyptus leaves crackle, heading for the spot where we have set up the table and the chairs, I bring with me the scent of honeysuckle, either in my nose or in my memory, I can't tell which, the one feeble coolness in the gleaming midday that surrounds, to infinity, the narrow patch of shade where we have installed ourselves and our equipment.

The motor of the pump labors in the sun. The water overflows the red plastic pail, whose outer surface allows mobile veins of light reflected by the translucent water to show through. The overflow constantly washes over the outer surface of the pail, intercepting the luminous veinings and making them undulate. Without turning off the motor or the faucet, allowing the powerful white stream of water to splash on the ground, filling the air with drops that rebound and produce fleeting iridescent reflections, I head toward the beige horse that begins to move, in an impatient but dignified manner, its front legs and its head. The smell of the meat being barbecued on the grill, around which Tomatis moves back and forth, with a knife and a fork in his hand, appears not to penetrate the horse's warm aura in which even the heat of February becomes bearable and changes. After passing through the column of smoke that rises, obliquely, from the grill and gradually disappears among the trees, Tomatis, continually blinking his teary eyes and rubbing his forehead with the back of his hand so as not to get himself greasy, stops for a moment and looks at us: "If Elisa doesn't bring you," he says, "you can always come on horseback tomorrow night." Without even waiting for me to react to his joke, he bends over the grill again, piercing a piece of meat with the fork. When I set the red pail down on the ground, the yellowish-white horse bends its long neck and begins, noisily, to empty it, burying its nose in the cool water.

With his fingers stained with black grease from the grill, Tomatis takes a cigar out of its box, slowly lights it and throws the match, after shaking it a number of times to put it out, onto his plate full of bones picked clean, bits of fat and salad. Then he picks up the bottle of red wine, with the long, thin, smoking cigar between his lips, and fills their glasses. Then he leans once more against the back of the chair and smokes, not saying a word. His tanned face now lacks its Olympian solidity of that morning. Around his eyes, too wide open, the skin is full of wrinkles and the sweat, dripping continuously from his forehead, runs down his face and his neck, leaving dirty trails. His breathing has grown noisier, and his belly has swelled a little, because of the wine and the food. It is evident that behind his forehead thoughts are passing, swift, unexpected, incomprehensible, like stampeding animals. He keeps constantly unconsciously sucking and nibbling on the end of his cigar, till it falls to pieces altogether, turning aside every so often to spit out the bits of tobacco adhering to his lips or his tongue. The patches of light that filter through the foliage return, obstinately, to their place on his skin each time that, after a nervous and purposeless movement, his hairy, scorched body leans against the back of the chair once more.

They have already, doubtless, carried him away. They must have already lifted him up off the sidewalk. Later on, when everyone has left, a policeman will no doubt wash down the uneven bricks. The flies, greedy as they are, must have had a real Sunday feast.

Daytime is disillusionment and delirium. Colored shadows, with their own volume, pulsations, texture. They are compact; a fist cannot punch through them, as it can smoke; each one of them, sharp and clear, occupies a place. There is transparency between them. A light that changes—it is called the sun—illuminates them, shifting, imperceptibly, second by second. That is daytime. At night, the light goes out. The night is black, uniform, but it is nothing but the day still proceeding on its way, the same light that turns black precisely by virtue of its continuity. Here, of course, everything is deserted, but there is no such thing as deserted places. Nobody has ever seen an empty place. When someone looks at it, it is no longer empty—that someone who is looking, the look, the place are one and the same thing. If there isn't anyone, there is no look and no place either. The day begins again, slowly, or rather, continues, with the light that emerges, again, from the shadows that preserve, ever-constant, their color, volume, pulsations, texture. There is transparency once more, distance, between them. No bigger than the eye of a needle, that is to say, incommensurable. Elisa interrupts him; Tomatis abruptly turns his head and looks at her, waiting. Day before yesterday, in the afternoon heat, Elisa begins, without going on, just day before yesterday, as she was about to cross the street at the corner of the central market. . .but, no, no, what's the use, it's not worth the telling, she says, falling silent, moving her shoulders and her head, stroking, distractedly, deeply engrossed in her own thoughts, with the fingertips of her left hand, her right shoulder whose skin gleams, smooth and tanned. Her memories, impenetrable, pull her inward, like a dead weight, causing her to fall motionless and her brow to furrow, just as the furrows in Tomatis's brow force his head to sway back and forth, to open his mouth, stare into empty space, shred to pieces with cruel, distracted fingers his cigar that has gone out.

There are, between us, forms, volumes, colors, movement and light, transparency and wasteland.

The yellow car accelerates as it heads for the city, its rear wheels raising a cloud of white dust. I hear the sound of the engine and see it drive off, fragmentarily, through the holes in the gray and dusty privet hedge that separates the yard from the sidewalk. Now that I have turned around, more or less halfway, before me are the dark-colored, sun-singed weeds, the old batteries, the half-rotted and half-buried tires, stained with dried mud, the rusty corrugated tin oil drums, one vertical, the other lying on its side, in the unreal sunlight of four in the afternoon that lengthens my bluish shadow—and farther on, having become nothing more than its sheer heartbeat and attention, entrenched in its warm aura consisting of chewed grass, of excrement, of life, the beige horse, which, now almost a member of the family, though without condescension or disdain, leaving off chewing for a moment, with its mouth half-open, the lower jaw slightly misaligned in relation to the upper one, slowly, discreetly, looks at me.

"I'm dropping by first to see my mother," I say, "and then we'll meet to have dinner together. In the bar in the arcade, okay? In any case, according to Tomatis, the game doesn't begin till eleven o'clock."

"All right," Elisa says.

The rain makes the sandy street hard, and Elisa drives carefully, trying not to get too close to the roadside ditch. The windshield wiper clears, with a regular rhythm, the water falling in torrents on the windshield. We make a turn in the direction of the main square. We pass by the police station. There is no visible sign of yesterday's killing; there is nobody in sight, the big doors are open, and there is an army van parked alongside the culvert that leads to the high brick sidewalk, but lately army vehicles have frequently been seen on the street. The town is deserted. In the main square, the rain is lashing out at the red, yellow and white flowers of the *palos borrachos*, breaking many of them loose and scattering them on the ground. We drive slowly, in second gear, down the main street, between the oleanders that the rain is finally washing, meticulously, after so many months. In the rain, in the gray light, things seem closer or more porous.

"Are you sure that Simone is going to give you an advance?" Elisa asks. The end of the main street joins the asphalt highway at a perpendicular angle. The car skids slightly on the embankment, makes its way with difficulty up the incline and reaches the paved highway. Elisa accelerates.

XV There is, in the beginning, nothing. Nothing. In the light of the storm, in the imminence of the downpour—the first one, after several months—, things take on reality, a relative reality doubtless, which belongs more to the one who describes or contemplates them than to things properly speaking: the white house, with the enormous trees that bury its side

wall in shadow, the open space of the beach, the sparse trees downriver, the grills, the slope that goes up to the sidewalk, the low-lying island whose slope descends gently, its edges all eaten away, toward the water, the smooth river, without a single wrinkle, polished and steel-colored like a motionless sheet of metal that reflects the steely sky.

Everything is in its proper place within the kindly transparency which abruptly ends at the low, black sky, and which turns livid and greenish, for a brief moment, with every flash of lightning. There is a vegetable excitement, discreet but definite, in view of the imminent rain. One senses a general state of alertness in the grass, in the bushes, in the trees, in the rustlings of leaves, the slow straightening out of fibers, the revival of roots and branches.

At the back of the yard, underneath the trees, the beige horse, motionless, alongside the red plastic pail turned over between its front legs, is waiting for the next flash of lightning and clap of thunder, long and multiple, that will follow it. When the flash comes, suddenly and close at hand, making the air turn pale and at the same time giving it a fleeting greenish tonality, the horse makes a number of rigid movements with its head as though inspecting, without being overbold, the surroundings. And when the thunder begins to roll, far-distant at first, more and more intense as it comes closer, the solitary animal begins to move its legs, pawing the ground, without changing place, making his stamping more rapid and forceful as the thunder approaches, until the sound vanishes and its movements grow calmer, tending, gradually, to recover their previous state of tense expectation and immobility.

Standing on the riverbank, the beach attendant sees the rowboat slowly approaching, on the luminous, polished surface of the river: a wake, whose width is greater the farther behind the stern it is, follows along after it or looks, rather, like a substance secreted by the boat as it proceeds, like the trail of a slug across a mirror.

Then the green rowboat touches the riverbank and stops, the trace of the wake that is growing wider and wider is still visible in the distance, downriver. Tilty, with his back to the shore, stands up, laboriously, and, taking his time, picks up the two cubical bundles of fodder that make him sway from side to side in the beginning, and that balance each other when he leaps down from the prow, not without being obliged first to bend his legs so as not to trip. When he straightens up—if that body like a big knotty root can really straighten up—Tilty begins walking, crossing the empty space at a diagonal, toward the white house.

A flash of lightning makes the air, darkened by the imminence of the downpour, but still transparent nonetheless, turn pale. After a few seconds' silence, a clap of thunder follows it. At first it is a distant point of sound, overhead, among the low clouds, steely and dark, and as it comes closer it gradually grows wider and more violent, spreading out, becoming more remorseless and resounding with such force that things, insecurely attached to the earth's crust, begin, in unison, to vibrate.

Elisa is of the opinion that, despite the approaching storm, it still has not cooled off enough, and yet she already has a certain feeling of well-being. The cup of coffee, still steaming, that she is holding in her hand, brings to her nose a heavy, real odor, mixed with the whitish vapor that rises to her face and that nonetheless seems less visible. Her clean hair, damp and hence darker, pulled back, circles her head, emphasizing, in the gray light, her tanned face, her broad forehead, her thick, compressed lips, her eyes made to look larger by skillfully-applied makeup, her ears barely separated from her head, her neck that reveals two vertical hollows between the tendons standing out because of the erect and slightly rigid position of her head. The stiffness of her expression, which appears to be the result of a distracted self-satisfaction, is prolonged by the immaculate stiffness of her white dress that leaves her arms bare from the shoulders down and her legs from the lower half of her thighs. The straps of her sandals cross several times on her calves, forming triangles and rhombuses and keeping in a state of tension, above her insteps, the bronze rings from which in turn two short, firm, tightly-stretched straps lead, to be lost from sight between her toes. Her fear of getting her feet dirty in the dusty yard and a vague apprehension with regard to the flashes of lightning prompt her, heedlessly, to remain standing on the porch, with the steaming cup of coffee in her hand, her eyes not focused anywhere, not even noticing the intermittent starts of the beige horse that begin all over again with each clap of thunder and seem to calm down with the transitory silence that follows it.

He moves, slow, regular, exterior, in the darkened air, his entire silhouette enhaloed in a gray scintillation against the low, smoke-colored sky. A flash of lightning, for a fraction of a second, makes the dark air pale. From somewhere, two birds, chasing each other with irregular thrusts of energy, always at the same distance from each other as though they were the fixed parts of an immutable whole and were moving from place to place thanks to a single mechanism, cross the sky within the view of Tilty, who follows their trajectory as they dive into the trees that bend over the side wall of the white house, disappearing among the leaves. As he walks forward, Tilty's body leaves behind, empty and more and more vast, the space that separates his body from the green rowboat, an empty space full of a heavy, uniform light of a watery transparency. The space that separates his body from the rowboat gradually stretches out: exterior to the calm exteriority of the whole, opaque and rough, forming part of the rough and opaque bulks—trees, the beach attendant, grills, the boat, the white house—scattered as though at random and with no order between the low, smoke-colored sky and the yellowish earth; in the transparent air, as though by some miracle, Tilty's body, at each movement, does not remain imprinted on that air, multiplying itself to infinity in an infinitude of motionless poses, all along his trajectory. Now the sparse grass, standing slightly erect because of the imminence of the downpour, crackles beneath his tattered espadrilles, and the expanse that separates Tilty from the house is of a pale green that contrasts with the ashen yellow of the beach. A clap of thunder, the echo of the flash of pale light that has illuminated the darkened air a few seconds before, makes the whole space tremble for an instant; a slight tremor causes Tilty's pupils to vibrate for a fraction of a second, and he resolutely picks up his pace: beneath the trees, the black car, parked along the shoulder at an oblique angle, points almost directly toward the ditch because of the tilt of the cambered street. The peal of thunder increases little by little in volume, discontinuously, as Tilty approaches the house. The espadrilles slap against the hard sidewalk now and Tilty, beneath the enormous treetops that darken the air, goes past the two black windows in the side wall of the house. A flash of lightning, for the fraction of a second, turns the air pale. Tilty goes past the black car and leaves it behind him: when he comes out, rigid, exterior, at a regular pace, at the entry, a clap of thunder begins, far in the distance, to descend.

Cat's face, carefully shaved, is reflected in the bathroom mirror, and Cat contemplates, touching them, his tanned cheeks, the skin underneath his chin, in the electric light that he has had to turn on so as to bathe and shave himself, since the morning brightness that comes in through the high window, traversing first a dark, stormy, lowering sky, would not be enough to light the bathroom. Cat turns out the light and leaves the bathroom. In the living room, folded over the back of a chair, at the feet of which are his highly polished brown moccasins, are his white pants, of coarse cotton cloth, washed and ironed, and his navy blue polo shirt. Cat puts his arms and his head through the sleeves and the neck of the polo shirt, and raising a little his white undershorts that reach halfway down his thighs, he puts his pants on over them. Cat tucks the bottom of his navy blue polo shirt under the belt of his pants. Standing up and thinking of something else, Cat puts his brown moccasins on his clean sockless feet; his attention is attracted, for a fleeting moment, by the telephone book opened to the first pages, lying on the table, and by the two piles of envelopes on either side of the phone book. To the left, the pile of blank envelopes; to the right, the envelopes on which, the night before, he has written, until almost two in the morning, in alphabetical order, the names and addresses of several hundred strangers. The flash of a ray of lightning, greenish and livid, comes, through the windows and the open doors, into the living room. After a few seconds' silence, a thunderclap begins, far in the distance, to descend. It sounds like a jagged boulder rolling down a set of inclined planks. When the din reaches its paroxysm, and its point of maximum proximity, furniture, windowpanes, glasses and chairs begin to vibrate, until all is silent once more and the vibrations stop. Picking up the cigarettes and the matches off the table, he puts them in the pocket of his pants and, leaving the living room, crosses through the open black door frame and enters the kitchen. The smell of coffee, wafting all through the house—which he has been perceiving without realizing it—is so strong and so peculiar in the kitchen that Cat, for the sheer pleasure of smelling it, stops alongside the table on which the coffee pot, full of boiling-hot coffee, resting on a little white plate so as not to burn the blue and white checkered tablecloth, gives off, through the S-shaped spout, a little column of whitish, frayed vapor.

The day before, he had found himself obliged to go back the way he had come, at a distance of a mile or two from the town. The entrance to the town was blocked off. A few minutes before, just outside La Guardia, he had already seen, from the window of the bus, a number of army cars and trucks go past at top speed. Without even stopping at the highway checkpoint, the convoy had split up: part of it had gone on, due north, in the direction of the town, along the road following the riverbank, and the other had taken the turnoff to Colastiné Sur and Paraná. As they approached the town, in the bus that had found itself obliged to turn around right there and then, the beach attendant had recognized the trucks that were blocking the road, filled with troops armed with sub-machine-guns, as being some of the same vehicles that had speeded past the bus near La Guardia. They had been forced to go back to the city with no explanation: he had tried to explain to them that he had to get to his job at the beach, that if an accident happened to any of the bathers, he would be the one who was responsible, but the soldiers, brusquely, almost threateningly, had ordered him to get back into the bus. The only ones they let through were people who lived in the town, searching them for weapons first and making them sit down to wait on the narrow wooden bench, near the olive green trucks parked across the highway to block it off. The beach attendant had understood the reason for the deployment when he heard the news report at noon over the radio: a group of guerrilla-fighters had killed Horse Leyva that morning. The same news, with more details, has been broadcast over local television on the eight o'clock news; they showed the corpse, lying face down, in a pool of blood, on the high brick sidewalk outside the police station. And, before going to sleep, the beach attendant had read the news in *La Región*, which had also carried a rather fuzzy photo of Horse's body. That morning, the beach attendant remembers seeing Tilty leap out of the rowboat, stumbling a little, with two cubical bundles of fodder, holding one in each hand by the place where the wire crossed; as he came in the bus that morning he had wondered if they would let him through, but as it neared the town, at the point where it had had to turn around and go back the day before, he had noted that the trucks were no longer blocking the highway, and after getting out of the bus at the main square, which was fairly deserted, to tell the truth, on going past the police station, by way of the sidewalk on the opposite side of the street, just in case, he hadn't noticed anything out of the ordinary, except perhaps for the olive green army van parked alongside the gutter. A flash of lightning, with its sudden, greenish light, encircles the silhouette of Tilty who is walking, slowly and steadily, across the empty expanse of beach, in perfect balance because of the cubes of hay, identical in weight, that he is carrying, one in each hand, grasping them by the intersection of the wire around them. At a certain point in his trajectory, Tilty makes a gesture with his head, as a sign of greeting, which he answers by raising his hand to shoulder height, with his fingers held apart and the palm facing outward, and waving it three or four times. Tilty slowly walks on, toward the white house and the pronounced incline that leads to the sidewalk. The beach attendant watches him move away, clearly outlined, solitary, into the empty space, amid the flashes of lightning and the ear-splitting claps of thunder, an irrefutable and self-contained presence in the light of the storm, and when there is already a dozen yards between them, the beach attendant, mechanically, begins to walk behind him, at precisely the same pace, so that the distance that separates them in the empty expanse neither increases nor decreases a single inch. Tilty goes on walking without noticing that he is following along behind him, which is not surprising, since not even the beach attendant himself is conscious of the fact that he is following the same itinerary that Tilty is tracing out a few yards in front of him, and that the speed at which he is walking is identical to that of the other person, as though the two of them were obeying an inaudible rhythm. Tilty leaves the beach behind him and begins to go up the embankment that leads to the sidewalk; when he reaches the top, he appears to halt, not moving, for a fraction of a second and then goes on, disappearing on the sidewalk darkened by the shadow of the trees. The beach attendant goes on walking, without changing pace, and his bare feet feel the sparse, rather rough grass that grows in the strip of ground that separates the embankment from the beach proper. In a few seconds he has crossed it and begins to climb, laboriously, up the embankment, in the fleeting light of the flashes of lightning that are becoming more and more intense and less far apart, causing a chain reaction of thunderclaps that ring out from one end to the other of the low, blackish sky, and whose endless sound reaches even the tops of the trees, making them tremble. Two birds that he has seen fly into the branches, a few seconds before, emerge again, excited, after having warbled and fluttered, invisible, amid the foliage, and passing above his head, one alongside the other, head almost in a zigzag, like ballerinas or ice skaters, toward the river. The beach attendant reaches the top of the embankment, where the sidewalk begins; the lateral façade of the house, with its black windows that overlook the sidewalk, gleams slightly in the dense shadow of the trees. Beyond the tunnel of shadow, in the gray light that follows and continues down the whole length of the block—one might even say the whole street—to the center of town, Tilty, having reached the back entry, has just set the bundles on the ground, one on each side of his body, and is straightening up again, facing the yard. At the same moment that he spies Tilty, the beach attendant feels the first drop of rain spatter against his cheek.

With the palm of her free hand, Elisa touches the cup and immediately withdraws her hand; the coffee is still too hot. Cat follows her out of the kitchen onto the porch. Elisa casts a rapid glance at him over her shoulder, just to see the blue canvas curtain move, rigidly, behind Cat, who walks past

Elisa, in silence, and goes to stand at the end of the porch, with his hands in his pockets, looking at the low sky that resounds with a deafening noise. With his well-polished brown moccasins, his white pants of coarse cotton cloth, his navy blue polo shirt, freshly bathed and shaved, Cat, in Elisa's eyes, has the calm, vacant air of someone who is unaware of his own elegance and even of his own body, but who is too absent-minded to be aware of his well-being. It is merely forgetfulness, self-abandonment, Elisa thinks, that is not at all like words, to which the rain that is just about to fall and the escape to the city that he is planning for this afternoon are doubtless not unrelated. Elisa in turn forgets Cat, touches the cup with the palm of her free hand, and since the heat of the smooth surface is now a little more tolerable, leaves her hand resting against it, though without deciding nonetheless to take the first swallow of coffee whose smell, almost more visible and denser than the vapor, and no doubt more present and more intense, mounts to her nostrils.

The beige horse, at the back of the yard, underneath the trees, gives a start at each clap of thunder, moving its legs and turning its front quarters in a semi-circle, shaking its head that falls motionless in expectation, in the interval, now shorter and shorter, that separates one clap of thunder and the next.

Beyond the dried-up bushes, the rusted corrugated tin oil drums, one vertical, the other lying on its side, the old batteries half-buried and the old rotted tires stained with dry mud, Cat sees, from the edge of the porch where he is standing, with his hands in his pockets, the beige horse that shivers all over with each clap of thunder, pawing the ground where it is standing, shaking its head, waiting, anxious and confused, with each silence, for the next clap of thunder. Cat steps down into the yard and begins to cross it; so as not to get his pants dirty, he proceeds in a roundabout way, avoiding the dry, dusty weeds, and, passing by the stretch of hard

ground with not a single clump of grass left after he and
Tomatis cleaned it up some time ago, without much of a
coherent plan in mind, he gradually approaches the horse,
unhurriedly, as it looks at him. When he enters its aura—he
has known, before he went out there, that he would enter it,
would enter the aura of animal heat, of excrement, of chewed
grass, of sweat, of dense life—the horse, on the alert, falls
motionless, and when Cat, feeling the animal's warm, damp
coat under his hand, begins to stroke its neck, something in
the tension of the muscles, of the organs, of the skin and of the
mind, archaic and somber, yields to his hand, tiny in relation
to the size of the neck, that runs over the yellowish-white
coat.

Elisa, on the porch, raises the cup to her lips and takes the
first sip of coffee, savoring it. The first drops of rain are
beginning to traverse, giving off a dim, fleeting gleam, the
gray transparency of the air, ending up spattering on the
ground, which immediately absorbs them. The taste of the
coffee, unique and corporeal though indescribable, lingers in
her mouth, warm and sweet, as Elisa looks at Cat and the
horse, in the rear of the yard, close to each other, Cat stroking
the yellowish neck that yields a little, with its head tilted to the
side opposite Cat, so as to leave plenty of space for the soft
hand running over it. Cat feels, at the same time, a shuddering
of skin, nerves and muscles, of hair and sweat, at the tip of his
fingers and in the sensitive protuberances of his palm. Tilty,
observed, without his being aware of it, from the end of the
sidewalk by the beach attendant who through sheer idleness
has followed him this far, has just set the cubical bundles of
hay down on the ground, on either side of his body, and is
slowly straightening up, raising his hands at the same time so
as to clap them together and in this way attract the attention of
the occupants of the house. His hands, however, hesitate for a
moment and remain suspended in the air; one of them, the left
one, feels a drop of rain on it, the first, on the index finger

which protects his other fingers owing to the vertical position
of his hand, facing the right one, which reproduces, in
reverse, the same position; in this attitude, above the green
stripes of the wooden entry door, Tilty sees how Cat, standing next to the beige horse, strokes, gently, the long neck of
the animal which leans its head toward the other side, with a
delicate stiffness in which the last traces of mistrust are concentrated. A flash of lightning illuminates, with its livid,
greenish light, the outlines of the trees, of bodies, of things.
Drops of rain streak the gray transparency of the air. For an
incalculable lapse of time no measure could approximate,
everything remains, subsists, isolated and simultaneous, the
soft, sweaty coat, the hand, the confidence, the relief, the
look, the taste of the coffee, the coffee, the gray transparency
of the air that envelops, almost in splendor despite the low
dark sky, the bodies that palpitate monotonously and the
emptiness that separates them, streaked by the intermittent,
oblique drops, more and more numerous, that end up splat-
tering against the ground. When the hands finally hit each
other, resounding, the beach attendant turns around and
begins to descend toward the beach, Cat raises his head,
looking toward the entry door, the second swallow of coffee
sticks to the first one in Elisa's throat, the beige horse begins to
shake its head beneath the downpour, and the incalculable
lapse, *as wide as the whole of time is long*, that would have
appeared to want, in its own way, to persist, sinks, at the same
time, paradoxically, into the past and into the future, and
founders, like the rest, or dragging it along with it, inexpres-
sible, into the universal nothingness.